The War of Independence
1920-22

Dan's Diary

PATRICIA MURPHY

Published 2016
by Poolbeg Press Ltd
123 Grange Hill, Baldoyle
Dublin 13, Ireland
E-mail: poolbeg@poolbeg.com

1

A catalogue record for this book is available from the British Library.

ISBN 978-1-78199-841-0

Typeset by Poolbeg Press Ltd

Cover illustrated by Derry Dillon

Printed and bound by CPI Group (UK) Ltd, Croydon, CR0 4YY

www.poolbeg.com

About the Author

Patricia Murphy is the author of *The Easter Rising 1916 – Molly's Diary*, published by Poolbeg, and the prize-winning *The Chingles* trilogy of children's Celtic fantasy novels. She is also an award-winning Producer/Director of documentaries, including *Children of Helen House*, the BBC series on a children's hospice, and *Born to Be Different*, Channel 4's flagship series following children born with disabilities. Many of her groundbreaking programmes are about children's rights and topics such as growing up in care, crime and the criminal justice system. She has also made a number of history programmes, including *Worst Jobs in History* with Tony Robinson for Channel 4, and has produced and directed films for the Open University.

She grew up in Dublin and is a graduate in English and history from Trinity College Dublin. She has a post-graduate diploma in journalism from Dublin City University and a master's in film studies from Leeds Metropolitan University. She now lives in Oxford with her husband and young daughter.

Dedication

For my football-mad nephews and nieces – Daniel, William, Patrick, Alex, Cian, Senan, Aoife, Isabella and Conor – and in memory of my grandparents, Dan and Bridie.

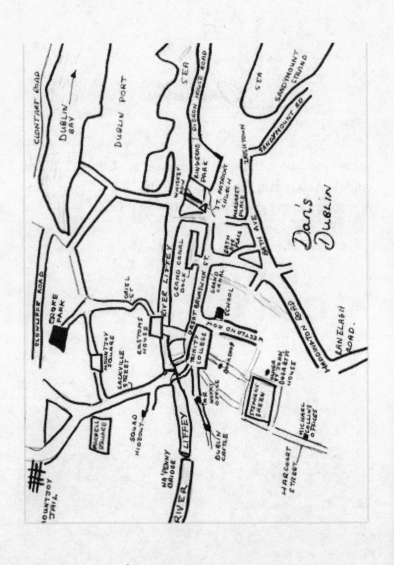

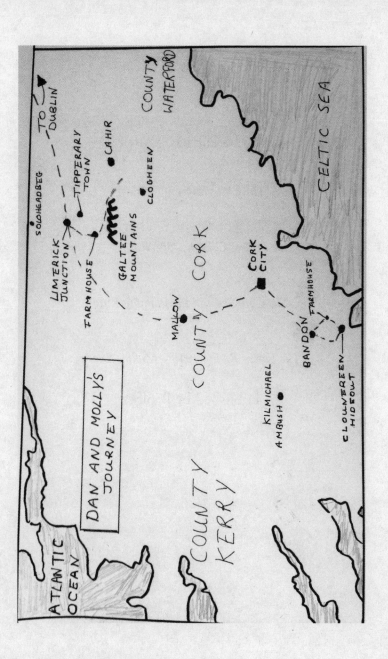

Also by Patricia Murphy

The Chingles from the East

The Chingles Go West

The Chingles and the Vampire King

The Easter Rising 1916 – Molly's Diary

Published by Poolbeg

It's 1920 and Ireland is in a state of near-anarchy. A group of nationalists are fighting a bloody guerilla war in a bid to win independence from the British Empire.

One young boy is caught up in events that will decide Ireland's destiny and his own. This is his diary.

Here are ten true facts about me.

1. My name is Dan O'Donovan and I am twelve.
2. I can keep a ball up in the air without touching the ground for longer than anyone else.
3. I love my country but I love football more. Gaelic, soccer, rugby. Once it has a ball, I chase it.
4. There is a guerilla war in Ireland – that's Spanish for "little war" – nothing to do with gorillas in the jungle.
5. Michael Collins, the "Big Fellow", is our leader. He's the Scarlet Pimpernel. They can't catch him. He leads an invisible army.
6. Our enemy is the British Empire. But on the streets it's the special forces called the "Black and

1

Tans" and the "Auxies". They are mean devils brought over from England because the Irish police don't like being shot at.

7. I am kind of in the Fianna Boy Scouts. We are boy soldiers for the Republic. That means we want Ireland to be free and don't want a king.

8. If my mam or dad find out they'll kill me. Except me da won't because he's on a long sea voyage.

9. Yesterday morning, fourteen British spies were hit by Collins' elite hitmen "The Squad". I saw some of it. I didn't like it. In the afternoon twelve people were killed at a match in Croke Park. I was there. I didn't like that either.

10. The truth is I'm only writing this diary because my cousin Molly told me to. She said: "Writing will help you forget." But how remembering will help me forget, I don't understand. Molly, who is nearly seventeen and saved my life during the 1916 Rising, is ace so I'll do what she says, even if she's a girl.

So I'm going to start. Even if my hand is trembling.

Chapter 1

The Man on the Bicycle
November 1920

A few weeks ago, I was coming up Westland Row after school. I was last out as usual. Brother Grace had held me in detention for writing with my left hand instead of my right. I hate Disgrace, as we call him. He gave me ten leathers in his office and said I wasn't to use "the devil's hand".

Outside, I immediately began a game of "keepy-uppy". You have to keep juggling the ball in the air without letting it hit the ground. You can use any part of your body except arms and hands. Simple to say. Hard to do.

I counted quietly. One, two, three kicks on my left foot, fourth kick to my knee, straight to my chest. I'm a lefty to my toes and luckily for me Disgrace doesn't care what foot I score goals with. Then a sweet little bounce to my right foot. Back to left and so on. I had my school satchel strapped across my chest with the bag behind my back so I didn't try anything too fancy. But I kept moving towards the train station with the ball.

I reached for a topspin and bounced the ball on my head a few times. Then I saw out of the corners of my eyes that there were road-blocks on both ends of the street. It was dead quiet, with no sign of the usual bustle into Westland Row Railway Station.

A group of British Tommies, regular soldiers, were up near the railway bridge. They were stopping and searching a few stragglers from the station. They all waved their guns around, and grenades hung off their webbing. The Black and Tans, the ones with the mixed uniform of khaki and green, manned the other barricade down the street behind me.

The Tommies held up a respectable-looking man on a bicycle. He was courteous with them and then pointed over in my direction. They all craned their necks.

"Not bad for a Fenian!" a Tommy called out to me good-naturedly.

"Bet you a half crown he won't keep it up for a fresh count of a hundred," snarled a mean-faced Black and Tan. He had snuck up from the other barricade and was scouting around like a ferret.

"You're on!" shouted the Tommie back.

I felt a prickle of sweat on my collar, as all their eyes turned to me.

Then he began to count: "One, two three . . ."

4

It was like I was on a stage. So I pretended to myself I was just in my own backyard. Someone else picked up the count at ten. Eleven, twelve, thirteen . . .

I cheekily lobbed the ball onto my head. Then dinged it a few times on my forehead and dropped it on the top of my knee.

"Twenty!" I got in ten quick headers and moved forward. Thirty.

Then another twenty easy left-to-right-foot chips. Followed by some chest and thigh bounces. It wasn't long before I was at seventy.

As I was about halfway between the two barricades, I felt a prickle on my skin like I do when a defender makes a move. A young fellow dropped from a high wall by Trinity College, at the back of a gap between two houses. His gabardine coat flapped behind him. I saw the black of a gun and the red trickle of his blood from a head wound.

He froze at the mouth of the passageway when he saw me. He was still hidden from the road but the Tans and the soldiers would see him for sure if he ran out. That split second lasted forever. I flicked my eyes and shouted out "Soldiers! Louder with the count!", hoping he'd realise that he was trapped.

"Seventy-two . . . seventy-three . . ." a couple of soldiers chorused.

The gunman stayed still as a statue as they continued.

"Seventy-four . . ."

I needed to buy him time. So I attempted a fancy move,

5

curving the ball behind me. It hung suspended against the blue heavens when I turned, before dropping like a stone. It was a miracle that I caught it neatly on my left ankle, tilting it for a cheeky topspin on my toes before curling it to my head.

"Seventy-five!" I called out.

I danced around a fair bit, attempting risky moves to keep their attention on the ball. It worked. They watched me like their eyes would fall out, for the next twenty kicks. The gunman didn't move.

"Ninety-six! Ninety-seven!" someone called out.

Then all hell broke loose! Whistles, shouts and catcalls at me.

"Stop, you little blighter!"

"Stop it now!"

"Blimey O'Reilly!"

The mean-faced Tan moved forward and cocked a gun in my direction. "You with the ball! Stop, you little Fenian brat, or I'll shoot!"

He advanced towards me, his eyes flaming down the barrel of the gun. I thought I was going to wet myself with fear.

On impulse, I skied the ball straight up to heaven. It soared higher than the rooftops. Everyone tilted their heads. From the corner of my eye I glimpsed the young rebel making a run for it towards Saint Andrew's church on the opposite side of the road.

"*POW!*" a shot rang out.

I prayed it wasn't the rebel. But the lifeless thud of my

ball was almost as bad. The Tan had shot my dearest possession. But they hadn't even seen the gunman!

"You owe me half a crown, Hamilton, and the kid a new ball!" a red-haired solider called to the Tan.

Laughter erupted. Two Tommies ran towards me, the ginger one and a really young-looking one. They hoisted me on their shoulders. I hammed it up a bit, raising my arms in victory to annoy Hamilton the Tan. He spat in annoyance. But I was just relieved to see that the gunman had disappeared inside the church.

"Champion!" the younger soldier said.

They let me down then and, patting me on the back, the ginger one handed me my sad punctured ball.

They waved me on through the barricade and then the man on the bicycle for good measure.

I ran off up Brunswick Street, then crumpled on a step. I gripped the deflated ball tight, the sound of my heart thumping in my ears.

A shadow loomed over me.

"I saw what you did, lad."

I looked up. It was the businessman with the bicycle from the checkpoint. He had a lilting country accent, soft as butter.

"Would you like to play for a free Ireland?" He smiled from ear to ear. "What's your name, son?"

"My mammy said I wasn't to talk to strangers," I mumbled.

"Do you know who I am?" he asked.

I looked at him and my heart skipped a beat. I knew exactly who he was. Michael Collins, the most wanted man in Ireland. But at that moment, even God coming down from heaven wouldn't have stopped me feeling sore about that ball.

"You should play Gaelic Football." He wagged his finger. "Soccer is a British game."

I scuffed the toe of my shoe on the ground. "It's just a game, sir," I said quietly. Sometimes I have the devil in me and I won't give in. Stubborn, my mother says. It's why I get extra lashes from the Brothers who teach us.

Michael Collins just threw back his head and roared with laughter. "You don't waste words and you stand your ground. If only we had more like you!"

Over his shoulder, I saw an armoured vehicle come around the corner. He must have seen the alarm in my eyes. Without a word, he was back up on the bicycle and out of sight as if he had wings.

I walked home with lead boots. That ball was my pride and joy.

That evening I worked extra hard at my algebra so Mam wouldn't notice I didn't have my football. She'd skivvied in Sandymount for a month, to buy me that ball. Scrubbing the floors of rich people from five in the morning until eight.

I didn't sleep a wink that night, worrying how I was going to explain it. I tried saying the rosary. But the feel of the beads kept reminding me of little footballs. My beautiful

8

bouncing ball that flew through the air! Not like the bundle of rags weighted down with a stone the other kids in the park played with.

"Dan, I'm glad you're leaving that ball behind," my mam said as I left for school the next morning. She patted my cow's lick down and kissed me on the forehead. I loved when she did that. But this time I put my head down and walked out.

I resolved to own up to her when I came home.

But I didn't have to.

As I rounded the corner into Westland Row, a woman fell into step with me. She handed me a round bundle.

"Open it," she said.

I ripped off the paper. It was a beautiful new leather ball. Brown as a conker with stitched seams. I could have kissed it.

It was Susan Killeen, the smiley woman who worked in O'Hegarty's Bookshop on Dawson Street. That's where my cousin Molly buys her medical books.

"From the man on the bicycle, Dan," she said.

I was surprised that she knew my name.

I gripped the ball like a magnet, the leather smooth in my hands. I couldn't resist trying a little header.

But my parents had drummed into me never to accept gifts from strangers.

"I can't take it."

My arms felt like lead, handing it back to her. Like the ball was my heart and I'd ripped it out of my chest.

"M-maybe I could earn it," I stammered.

She didn't take the ball. "Just enjoy it," she said, patting me on the arm.

Then right between us, dead rude, another lad cycled up on a messenger bike. He was older than me with terrible spots on his face like he had leprosy or something.

Susan whispered something to him. Pus-Face listened with a frown. Then, before I could give her back the ball she was gone!

The lad on the bike looked at me as if I was dirt on his shoe. I knew him to see. He lived in Ringsend somewhere near Nanny O'Brien's shop. I didn't like the look of him. He had mean eyes. He cycled alongside me as I rounded the corner, hemming me in.

"Hey, Big Ears, are you in the Fianna?" he asked.

The mean so-and-so! I wanted to call him Pus-Face. But my mam said never to say bad names back. I said nothing.

"Cos if you are, you can go on a job."

A job! I nodded, trying not to look too excited. I wasn't really in the Fianna. I just used to march about a bit with the other boys down in Ringsend Park until I got tired of the boys call me bad names. McIlroy, the leader, thinks he's "it" and he's a bad bully. Mammy prefers me not to play with them anyway. We keep ourselves to ourselves. So others think we're stuck up. That's maybe why they pick on me. But I resolved to join there and then.

"Susan should know I'm getting too old to be a lookout. It's a job for a little gurrier like you." He smiled at me now but not in a nice way, showing me his big greenish teeth. He

10

leaned into me and made to grab the ball.

I wanted to walk on. But he'd blocked me in against the wall with the bike.

"Just kidding, you eejit! Go on, it's a chance for you to be 'in it'."

I raised my arms to jostle him aside but he pinned me in tighter, his breath foul.

"I get it – you're yellow."

"I am not!" I roared. I wanted to tell him why I got the ball. But that would be going down to his level as my mam said.

"It couldn't be easier." He leaned in close to whisper to me. "Meet a tall fellow named Todd at ten to nine in the morning at Charlemont Street Bridge. Have a kickabout with the ball and keep your wits about you. You'll be the lookout. Shout 'goal' if any Tans or Auxies come along."

I hesitated but I felt excitement bubble in my tummy. I would be "in it". Part of the action. I would be able to lord it over them goms in the park. They couldn't call me "shoneen" or "Castle Catholic" any more. Or shout "*Dan, Dan, you'll never be a man*" after me. Just because we're a bit different. My mam was born a Presbyterian and my grandfather – my father's father – was in the British army in India, though he'd been a surgeon fixing people up. Now I would have a secret. That would make me just as special.

"What are you going to do?" I asked him.

He tapped the side of his nose. "Special operation down the country," he said.

A Crossley Tender sped around the corner in the

opposite direction. They're those ugly trucks the Tans drive around in, with benches inside for about ten men. Before I could even say yes, Pus-Face had jumped back on his bicycle and was gone.

Chapter 2

Bloody Sunday
21 November 1920

All night I'd tossed and turned, worrying if I should go or stay. But when I heard the morning church bells at eight, I made up my mind. I had to go or they would have no lookout. Pus-Face might have been full of it and flakey. But I wasn't. I felt grateful for the ball.

I got out of bed and headed out the door, cramming my mouth with a cut of bread. I told Mam I was going to get some milk from Julia O'Donovan's creamery in Rathmines for Josephine. My little sister is always sick – she doesn't eat much but she loves the cream off the milk.

The sky was steel grey but the day was mild. There were a few people heading into Mass in Ringsend Church. Tommy Whelan, a nice country fellow, gave me a big wave. He works on the railways and sometimes even joins our kickabouts. Then I realised where I knew Pus-Face from.

They lodged in the same house.

"Where's your flat-mate?" I called out.

"He's gone to see his granny in Drogheda!" he called back.

So much for Pus-Face being on a special operation! I glanced up at the church clock. It was almost a quarter to nine. I'd have to run like the clappers to get to the bridge on time.

At the canal on Charlemont Street Bridge, I met up with the big lanky fellow named Todd and told him I was the lookout. He's a keen soccer player, handy with the ball. I'd watched him play for University College Dublin. I liked him because he has sticky-out ears like me. He looked at his watch and said it was ten to nine.

Three other fellows turned up. I didn't know their names. The older man, Coughlan, seemed to be the boss. He took a closer look at me.

"You're a young skelp for a big job," he said. "I can't afford any messing."

"Susan said to meet here." I wasn't telling a lie exactly. She had told Pus-Face.

But it seemed to satisfy Coughlan and he nodded. "What's your name, kid?"

"Dan."

"Have you got your 'dogs' on you?" he asked the others.

One of them smiled and patted his breast. Another took out a gun.

I shrank back. The "dogs" were their guns.

"He goes by the name of Captain Noble," said Coughlan. "He's staying in a boarding house in Ranelagh.

Our orders are to shoot him on sight. But only him."

I felt a cold shiver run down my spine. The others were pumped up, excited. What had I got myself into? I would have run but at that moment Todd tackled the ball off me.

"Imagine a little chiseler like you having a proper ball," he said with a grin. "We only ever had a shammier, just an old tennis ball. Did you rob it?"

I shook my head and he gave me a friendly shove.

We kicked the ball as we set off for Ranelagh Road, a street with redbrick terraced houses.

"Do you support Shelbourne or Bohemians?" Todd asked me, breathless.

"Shelbourne." It's the local Southside soccer team nearest our home. In truth I supported neither. Or both maybe. I just love looking at any game.

"Bohemians all the way!" said Todd. "We have Laverty, McConnell and Irons. Not like your gang of gougers."

"You should only play Gaelic football," said Coughlan. "Soccer is a British game."

"Get away out of that!" laughed Todd. "Gaelic's a bogman's scrap. You only need three skills – field the ball, kick it high and hard toward the goal, and give your opponent a box around the ears. That's why all the clodhopper farmers' sons love it."

"You'll see when our Tipperary men tan your hides at Croke Park," said one of the other fellows.

Tipperary was playing Dublin later that day.

"I'm hoping to see that match," I said. "The brother

15

Willie and me are meeting up in Mountjoy Square. We're going to try sneaking into Croke Park, like."

We dribbled the ball along, dodging, passing, shouldering as we went. To take my mind off things, I did a few of the moves I'd been practising.

"You've got a talent, young fella," Coughlan said. "Some day you'll play for Ireland."

"It'll have to be Gaelic," said the Tipperary man.

"Patriots play soccer too. Look at me!" Todd said.

We rounded the corner to our destination. It was Number 7, Ranelagh Road, a redbrick Georgian house with steps up to the front door, an upstairs and a basement.

"Danny, just stay close to the house," Coughlan said to me. "Shout 'goal' if you see any Auxies or Tans."

Auxies wore these slouchy black caps that they call "bonnets". They're supposed to be officers to keep the Tans in line, but they are even more cruel.

We stopped at the front steps of Number 7 and the men cocked their revolvers. Tense like cats stalking a mouse.

"Remember," said Coughlan. "Our orders are to shoot him alone."

One of the lads went round to the back garden to block any attempted escape.

Coughlan was about to walk up the steps when, as if out of nowhere, two other fellows in trench coats turned up. I knew by the cut of them they were important.

"Are you from the Squad?" I heard Todd ask.

They nodded at him, their faces sharp. I didn't get a

good look at them but they were hard men all right. They looked like they meant business.

Coughlan banged on the front door with his stick. A girl of about fifteen years opened it. He pushed the stick in to stop her slamming the door in his face.

I concentrated on my ball, kicking it against the kerb right in front of the house. A few minutes later, a woman's scream rent the air. I panicked and crouched down by the garden wall, clutching my ball. *"Hail Mary, full of grace,"* I prayed aloud, terrified.

More shouting and screaming came from the house. There was a sharp smell, a crackling sound.

I glanced up. Smoke was billowing against the upstairs windows! One flew open, smoke escaping into the street. I saw something or someone emerging from the smoke like a twisting demon and teeter on the window ledge. He jumped into the garden below, landing like a cat. Snakes and weird creatures like dragons and birds writhed all over him like in a nightmare. He paused for a moment, dusted himself off and swore in an English accent. He was naked from the waist up, his torso covered in tattoos like some of the sailors in Ringsend had on their arms.

He ran full pelt down the path. I cowered behind the wall. He glanced at me, his face contorted, ferocious like a ghoul. For one split second, we locked eyes. I cowered, then I blinked and he was gone.

My heart slammed in my chest. Did I really see someone? Or was I having an attack of the heebie-jeebies?

Sometimes I get those nightmares bleeding into the day. They give me the creeps.

The fellow guarding the back came round and took hold of my arm, giving me a jolt. "They need our help!"

We ran through the open door.

"Form a chain! The upstairs is on fire!" I heard Todd shout.

"There's a tap in the basement!" a man called out.

Todd grabbed me and we ran down the steps to the large dark basement. We filled buckets with water and passed them in a chain of men up the stairs to the top floor.

"We bungled it," Todd told me as he passed me a bucket slopping with water. "Noble wasn't there. While they were searching for his papers, somehow the room went on fire – I don't know how."

I passed the heavy bucket on to the next man in the chain.

"I nearly shot the lodger who tipped us off," gabbled Todd. "The fellow was shaving. His safety razor froze in mid-air, he was that petrified with fear. But he's all right now."

We hefted more buckets. My arms ached.

"Those two hard men who turned up were from Collins' 'Twelve Apostles', otherwise known as the Squad," Todd said in a whisper.

"That's a big deal," I said in awe.

"We're only one little part of a big operation," he said. "They've targeted the British spies who they brought from the Middle East – you know, the Cairo Gang. There were at least twenty targets. Different units were all supposed to strike at nine o'clock. You know, shoot them."

Fear twisted my stomach. Collins' Squad was famous, like cowboys. But Andrews wasn't impressed.

"They were worse than Tans. Overturning furniture, pushing people around. Noble's girlfriend was there and one of the Squad slapped her. Little children were in the house too. Coughlan got the poor kids to safety. The Squad men left as soon as the fire started. Coughlan's fit to be tied with anger at them. Disgracing the cause."

"Was there another spy? Covered in tattoos?" I asked.

He shook his head and repeated the question up the line. The word came back. No one had seen such a man. I must have been seeing things.

Smoke billowed down the stairs, making me cough. It took at least half an hour to quell the flames.

I heard the rat-at-at of gunfire somewhere close by as we all left the house at last.

Outside, a taxi was waiting. The men, except for Coughlan who was still in the house, threw their guns through the window of it. The taxi sped off with only the guns inside.

I stood gawping for a minute, not knowing what was going on.

"The taxi is taking the guns to one of our arms dumps," Todd explained. "It's less suspicious if we all leg it separately."

Two of the fellows slid off in separate directions.

"Dan, you should lie low," Todd said to me as he sidled off, beads of sweat on his forehead. "I'm going to Mass in Terenure. Some of the lads are heading to Confession. I don't know whether to feel glad or sorry we missed our man."

It was only ten o'clock.

Coughlan came out and clamped his hand on my shoulder. "You better head home." He was holding a letter in his hand in a buff-coloured envelope, the edges singed from the fire.

"I'm supposed to go to Julia O'Donovan's for some milk, in Rathgar Road," I said, feeling like a gom after I'd said it.

His face lit up. "Take the letter there. They'll know where to send you. Say it's for Mr. Field."

Then he handed me two tickets for the Dublin-Tipperary game! I was thrilled. One for me and one for Willie – he'd never believe it. I'd never been to Croke Park before. I'd be meeting him after I'd got the milk and taken it home.

I took a few backstreets to get to the dairy, which was only about five minutes away.

There was now a strange silence in the air.

A paperboy I knew called out as I cut across the corner near Rathgar Road.

"Watch out, Dan, there's a job on! Collins' Apostles have taken out the British spies!"

"Is it in the paper?" I called back.

"Nah," he said, spitting into the street. "Too early yet.

20

But us paperboys are always the first with the news. We see everything."

Most times I love going to Julia's dairy, with its big churns of milk and the hustle and bustle. But it was quiet as I walked up to the door. A dairymaid dashed out as if she was waiting for me. She told me to take the letter to Julia's house, not far away on Airfield Road. I forgot to ask for the milk.

There was a man at the end of Julia's street fixing his bicycle.

"Where are you off to, son?"

I saw the telltale bulge under his jacket. A gun. He was a lookout.

When I told him I had a letter for Mr. Field, he nodded me through.

When I reached the house, it was an age before anyone came to the door.

"Who is it?" a girl's voice asked through the letterbox.

"Letter for Mr. Field," I said.

The door opened and Eibhlin, Julia's daughter, who's a bit older than me, peeked out. She pulled me inside and led me to the basement. We're distant cousins on my dad's side. Cork people like Collins.

"The Big Fellow's downstairs," she said in an excited whisper. "I hope it's not another consignment of 'butter' and I have to strap up our old pony. Last week it was heavy bomb casings and the poor old pony nearly died for Ireland!"

I was dumbstruck.

21

"You best not say too much to you know who," continued Eibhlinn. She meant Collins. "He has a hard job keeping track of it all – code words, troop movements, the lot. His spies are everywhere – some say even in the Castle, right in the heart of British rule itself." She poked me in the ribs. "You're not a double agent, are you? You're in the heart of operations now. The big time."

"Would you give over," I said. "I'm only an errand boy."

The Big Fellow had his feet up on a desk, working through a stack of mail. His face was grim in the flickering gaslight of the basement. He glanced up. Then, seeing the letter in my hand, he gave me a big grin.

"Aha! Valuable papers. Been through the wars by the looks of it!" He tore open the fire-singed envelope and read the contents in a second. He gave me a piercing look.

"You liked the football well enough, you young skelp?"

I nodded, smiling. He remembered me.

"Do you know who Sherlock Holmes is, boy?"

"The detective in London, written by Arthur Conan Doyle," I answered. Willie and me had read them all.

"Well, Holmes had his Baker Street Irregulars, his street urchins who were his eyes and ears. And I have mine." He gave me a big wink.

My heart swelled with pride. I'm in, I thought.

"I have twenty-five thousand pounds on my head. If you hurry now, you could be rich!"

"Nnn-never, sir," I stuttered.

"I'm supposed to ride around on a white horse like the

22

Scarlet Pimpernel. '*They seek him here, they seek him there . . . is he in heaven or is he in hell . . .*'"

He shook his head and went back to reading the letter.

"Is there a stop press out yet?" he asked then. He meant had they managed to print a special headline in the newspaper with the latest big news.

"No, sir. Though the newsboys know there was a job on. I was in Ranelagh Road. The target wasn't there." I felt important saying that.

"We bungled a few all right. But we got a few undesirables who've made the lives of ordinary citizens miserable. The very air is sweeter."

He put the letter on a pile. Then he paced up and down, jumped on me and caught me in a headlock.

"For myself, my conscience is clear. There is no crime in detecting and destroying – in wartime – the spy and the informer." It was like he was practising a speech. "They have destroyed without trial. I have paid them back in their own coin." He mimed chopping off my head.

I tried to shake myself free but he was strong as an ox. I gave up on wriggling and became a dead weight. Then I reared up and gave him a dead arm. He dropped me like a sack of potatoes, enjoying the sport.

"Bedad, we have a live one here! You were the same when you were a kid. Do you remember me from Craig Gardiners Solicitors?"

As I picked myself up off the floor it dawned on me where I'd met him before. When I was seven, I ran a few messages for a solicitors' firm. He was a young clerk there. My dad stopped me doing it because they were all republicans like Collins.

There was a knock on the door. A slight man with a thin face and jerky, nervous movements came in, breathless.

"Joe O'Reilly, me right-hand man! Any news on McKee, Clancy and Clune?" Collins asked. His mood had changed, anxious now.

"They're at the Castle since their arrest last night," said Joe. "The Auxies will torture them for sure."

Collins raked his hair and swore. "McKee is my trusted lieutenant. And Clancy is a volunteer. But Clune was just in the wrong place at the wrong time. We target known spies and criminals. To them, anyone Irish is the enemy. Remember that, Dan."

I thought about the children in Number 7 who almost went on fire, but said nothing.

"Julia doesn't know about the arrests," Joe O'Reilly said. "She's laid McKee's place for lunch as usual."

Collins face darkened. "This is the brutal mathematics of war. They are too strong to beat our invisible army. Do you get me, boy? We are using their own power against them. But they will kill the innocent as well as the guilty."

He returned to his papers and dismissed me with a wave. "Keep your counsel, Dan. And never let one side of your mind know what the other is doing."

"What about the match? Should we not cancel it?" Joe O'Reilly asked.

The heavy door slammed shut and I didn't hear the rest.

As I went out the front door, Julia's daughter ran after me with a different letter in another buff-coloured envelope. There was no address on it.

"Hey, Mister Errand Boy, you're to drop this to 15 Clonliffe Road. I've got another job to do and Collins said you were to do this instead. The third brick at the bottom on the left-hand side of the door hides a drop-box. Flick it out and push the letter through the slit."

I ran out, letter in one hand, my ball under my arm, and hid behind a wall. A sudden trembling came over me. My hands shook so badly I could barely hold the letter. I made myself do the one hundred times tables in my head. It calmed me down. Then, with a bit of broken glass, I unpicked a small gap in the lining of my coat, folded up the letter and pushed it inside.

I heard a distant clock strike. I was due to meet Willy at Mountjoy Square in half an hour. At least I knew the way. Croke Park was near Clonliffe Road. We used to live on the North Side docks in Oriel Street, so I knew that part of Dublin quite well. I could kill two birds with one stone: meet the brother and deliver the letter.

Willie was thrilled. "Janey Mac, Dan – tickets for Dublin against Tipperary! They're like gold dust! It'll be the match of the century. This was worth getting out of school for. Who did you kill to get these?"

I laughed too loud at his joke and he gave me a funny look. He was nearer the mark than he thought.

I was glad he was happy. Willie is ace. Not mean like a lot of older brothers. He doesn't give me dead legs or anything. He's a scholarship boy at Blackrock College. They used to beat him up all the time. Until he became the best goal-kicker in the last twenty years. De Valera, the President of Sinn Féin, was a scholarship boy there too.

We went around by the old Georgian houses of Mountjoy Square. As we got closer to Croke Park, the streets were milling with people. I felt safer with all the crowds. I could feel the heat coming off all the warm bodies even though it was cold and drizzling. Concentrating on the game would take my mind off the panic of the morning.

We neared the ground between the canal and the railway embankment in Jones Road. Rumours were buzzing around the crowd.

"Collins got all those spies brought over from Egypt," a woman said.

"On a Sunday!" said an older man, shocked.

"It's that crowd up from Tipperary that did the shooting!"

"That's wrong," said another man, lowering his voice. "It was the Squad."

"They shot one man in front of his pregnant wife."

"Another was a war hero with one leg."

I told Willie what I knew without saying I'd been on a job.

"Maybe we should go home," said Willy. "They might cancel the match."

I insisted on going on to Croke Park. No way was I going to miss this match – if it was played, that is. Besides, the letter from Collins burned like a brand in the lining of my coat. The crowds were too thick now to forge my way through to Clonliffe Road. As we were swept through the turnstile, I reasoned I'd do the drop on the way home.

"If anything is going to happen, we're safer in a big crowd," I said.

"True enough," said Willy.

"They were all shot in their beds," I heard a woman say.

I plunged my hands in my pockets as we milled along a brick tunnel into the grounds.

"I saw a stop press," said a man. "Shootings in seven different houses, mostly south of the Liffey. Except for the Gresham Hotel on Sackville Street."

"Merciful hour, my sister is a chambermaid there!" said a woman.

"They waited until the clocks struck nine o'clock," continued the man. "They were posh houses so housemaids opened doors to find themselves staring into the cold eyes of gunmen."

The woman was nearly in tears. "Did they kill the maids?"

"Not that I heard. The hits were on the 'Cairo Gang' – all suspected British agents. Fourteen are dead. Another five were wounded. There were a couple of running gun battles. Only one gunman has been captured."

I wanted to say it wasn't all like that. But I kept my

27

mouth shut like I'd been told.

There was a crackle in the air and a heavy stone of worry in my stomach from the morning. But I was still excited to be inside Croke Park for the first time. Along the Jones Road side were two wooden terraces for spectators. On the north was Hill 60. It got called that after a battle in Turkey in the Great War where loads of Dublin Fusiliers died.

"Does your mother know you're here, you scallywag?" rang out a familiar voice.

"Molly!" I cried, delighted to see my cousin. Then I looked a bit shamefaced because she was too near the mark. "I got free tickets," I mumbled.

She cuffed me on the ear for a joke. Her wild red hair was pushed into her Saint John's Ambulance cap. She shook her head at me. But then she turned all serious.

"I walked over from Phoenix Park and saw quite a few Crossley Tenders heading over this way. Maybe you should go home."

"Only if you will," I said. I shrank back a bit. Molly had a way of looking into my soul.

"The match is a fundraiser for the wives and children of prisoners. I owe it to Jack to stay," said Molly.

Her brother Jack risked his life in the Rising gathering funds for the families of those who fought. He's in America, in the circus, now. Molly loves him to bits and had risked her own neck to help him.

She held up her First Aid kit with the Red Cross on it. "Besides, the players usually beat the living daylights out of each other, so I'd better be on hand."

She gave me a little wave and walked over towards a First Aid station, which was near the dressing room.

Molly is sixteen and a bit, but already studying medicine at Trinity College. They let her in especially as she's so clever. Professor Mahaffey the provost arranged it.

As we headed up to Hill 60 we saw an old friend of ours from Oriel Street. Jetty, who used to mind us. She was now about seventeen. I called out her name, thrilled. Her real name was Brigid but I couldn't say it when I was young and the nickname stuck.

Jetty threw her arms around me. "I can't believe you're so skinny now," she said, pinching my cheek. "You used to be a little round butterball."

I felt myself go scarlet right to the tips of my ears. I just muttered hello but I was delighted to see her. Still the same old big-hearted Jetty who used to give us sherbet and penny apples. She hadn't lost her cheeky grin and rosy cheeks.

She introduced her friend Cassie. I remembered Cassie as the coalman's daughter. I saw Willie's eyes light up when he saw her. She had grown up to be quite pretty, I suppose.

"Stonewall Jack on the Dublin team is my sweetheart – most of the Dublin team are from O'Toole's club," said Jetty, naming the club near our old flat. "He said not to come after all them shootin's this mornin' – there's going to be trouble. But I wouldn't miss the match for the world."

Cassie the coalman's daughter glanced shyly at Willie.

"Come and sit with us," said Jetty. "We go at the sideline where there's a few seats for the players' families."

We surged through the crowd. There were lots of people wearing scarves with the green, white and gold of the Tipperary team. Dublin supporters wore blue ribbons and sashes. The slashes of colours livened up the sea of men, women, children, old and young, in their Sunday best.

We got great seats with a view of the pitch.

"Loads of the Tipperary men are freedom fighters," whispered Jetty. "They might shoot the Dubs if they don't win!"

"How do you know who's scored?" Cassie asked, batting her eyelids at Willie.

"It's like a cross between rugby and soccer," said Willie. I could tell he liked her by the way he leaned in closer. "There are fifteen men on the team but the ball is round, smaller than a soccer ball. You can slap the ball out of an opponent's hand or fist it."

"You score one point for getting it over the bar and three for kicking it into the goal, you gawney eejit," said Jetty to Cassie impatiently. "I explained all this to you this morning. You're only pretending not to understand." She gave me a wink like we were on the same team.

I liked her for her cheekiness.

The crowd murmured at the delay in starting the match. A man with a towel over his shoulder passed by – Charlie Harris, the coach. He's a legend. He coaches both soccer teams, Bohemians and Shelbourne, and every so often he comes to see my mam and asks about signing me. He even says I could play for an English team that he scouts for. But Mam isn't keen.

"Good to see you here, Dan," he said, shaking my hand as if I was a man.

"I didn't know you trained Gaelic footballers as well," I said.

"It's all the one to me, and I'm glad you think the same," he said.

Tommy Whelan, who I'd seen on his way into Mass at Ringsend, stopped for a chat. He knew Jetty and her boyfriend. "Your fella has his work cut out today. Thomas Ryan, their fullback, could flatten a mountain. And Hogan is a streak of lightning."

"It would take the Tans and the Auxies together to flatten my Jack. He's not called Stonewall for nothing!" laughed Jetty.

Tommy held up his hands. "I'm strictly neutral. I'm a Galway man meself!"

Cassie went all googly-eyed looking at Tommy. She dug Jetty in the ribs when he moved on and said, "He's a beaut. He should be in the filums. What's his name?"

"That's Tommy Whelan," said Jetty and, when Cassie turned to bat her eyelids at Willie again, she whispered to me, "Yer one Cassie likes anything in a pair of trousers!"

There was a roar to lift the roof off the world when the thirty strapping players came out. They lined up for their photograph.

At about quarter past three the referee threw in the ball. Above the cheers of the crowd, there was a strange low hum. I looked up to see a two-seater airplane. It circled the ground twice and shot a red flare from its cockpit. Strange.

Ryan, the walking mountain from Tipperary, was about to take a free kick. The ball fell into play. Hogan from Tipperary and Burke, a Dublin player, tackled each other for the ball. A ripple ran through the crowd.

Something was wrong. Ryan, who had a shock of dark curly hair, threw himself on the ground. From nowhere, shots like the crack of a whip rang out. Merciful Hour! There were troops at the four corners of the pitch! Then another burst of machine-gun fire.

"Mother of God, we'll be murdered!" Jetty cried.

Rat-at–at-at went the guns. I froze. Confusion and terror gripped the stadium.

People were screaming and the crowd began to stampede like cattle. Most of the players ran off the pitch.

"Stonewall, my sweetheart!!" cried Jetty.

Willie tried to pull her to leave but she wouldn't move.

"Run!" Harris the coach passed near us as the crowd heaved and lurched.

"Stonewall!" cried Jetty.

"Stonewall and some of the players made it into the dressing room," we heard Harris shout before he was carried off in the opposite direction.

Sparks flew off the railway-embankment wall at the further end of the pitch. People were trying to climb over it.

Others lay on the ground – shot.

Willie pulled my arm, but I was stuck to the spot.

Cassie was in hysterics, screaming. But Jetty had come to her senses and linked arms with her. People milled about, terrified. As they stampeded around I saw terrible things on the pitch, like snatches from nightmares.

Two of the Tipperary players, who had lain flat when the bullets started, got up from the ground. They made a run towards the wooden paling of Hill 60.

Hogan surged forward but he fell down, shot. Ryan, the big farmer, went to him and tried to lift him but the wound in his back was spurting blood.

"Jesus, Mary and Joseph! I am done for!" Hogan called out. His jersey was covered in blood.

Some man from the crowd knelt beside him and whispered into his ear – maybe a prayer. A woman ran forward and threw a coat over Hogan. Then the kneeling man got shot too.

"Dan, for God's sake!" Willie pulled my arm.

It was only the sight of so much blood that roused me to my senses.

Shots were roaring out now at intervals. People surged around us and I got separated from Willie. Things became a blur of bodies swirling, noise and panic – like cows in an abattoir.

British soldiers and Tans were on the field.

I passed by another Tipperary player who was lying out flat on the ground just a few feet from the sideline. All at once British soldiers surrounded him and kicked him in the arms and legs.

"You're one of those murdering hitmen," they accused him.

The player pulled up his shirtsleeve. "The last gun I fired was on the Continent of Europe. That's my regiment tattoo."

They pulled him up then bundled him towards the dressing room. I didn't see what happened to him.

I scanned the area, alert now. It was all one big crush of bodies like a monster, with the Tans yelling.

"Halt!"

"Hands up above your heads!"

"Get into groups!"

They pushed people together at random, searching them, while firing in all directions.

An RIC officer ran across the pitch, *"Search everyone!"* he screamed.

My blood pumped in my veins. What if they discovered the letter!

I made a run for the paling. As I reached it, I saw an Auxie loading a round into the breech of his rifle. He was looking in my direction. Ryan the Tipperary player was alongside me – he was the target. Both of us dropped to the ground at the same time, but a boy nearby fell wounded.

Ryan helped me to my feet and over the paling. Then he joined me and held onto me so I kept my footing. We were swept out of the grounds with the crowd. I glanced back, desperate to see Willy. Around part of the pitch were iron railings. One man had become impaled on the spikes between the road and the wall. The spike had gone through his thigh. Others were using his body as if he was a step. I went to go back to help him but Ryan pulled me with him, as two big men came to the poor man's aid.

We made our way somewhere outside the grounds. Ryan was ahead of me now, his jersey covered in Hogan's blood. I noticed the tricolour on the sleeve and on his stockings and shorts. The little green, white and orange flag would be a red rag to a bull for the Auxies and Tans. It was like he was wearing a sign saying: "I'm a nationalist – kill me."

Behind us, people were still jumping from the wall out of Croke Park like in a mad human steeplechase.

Where was Willie?

We ran up Clonliffe Road.

Ryan turned his head to me, beads of sweat on his forehead. "Lad, I don't know Dublin. I'm on the wanted list. I need to get out of here."

We saw an open door in one of the houses. We ran inside and slammed it shut. It was a lodging house. A nervous blur of faces hung over the bannisters on the landing.

We were still catching our breath when a woman holding a baby in the hallway called out. "They're coming, God help us!"

We heard the roar of vehicles, shouted commands.

"*It's the Black and Tans!*" a voice screamed from outside

and the message was relayed by others like an echo. *"The Blacks and Tans! The Black and Tans!"*

"I have a letter . . ." I said to the woman with the baby. I took it out, hoping to push it down a floorboard. But my arm was quaking so much I could barely hold it.

"Give it to me here," said the woman, grabbing it from my hand. She put it down her blouse, clasping her tiny baby tight to her breast. Then she retreated to a doorway.

"Open up!" someone roared from outside.

We all froze like statues.

Then a fearful knocking. *Boom! Boom!* Like a canon. An old man rushed forward just as the front door came crashing in. A horde of Tans and Auxies pushed through, a swirl of khaki and snarling, blackened faces.

"Show some respect in my home," said the old man in a quaking voice. "My lodgers are all women and children or old people."

A skinny Tan with a scar on his face knocked him down with a blow from the butt of a revolver.

One of them saw big Ryan and pointed to the tricolour on his jersey. "There's one of those Tipperary assassins!"

"Take him out and shoot him!" roared another one of them.

My legs began to buckle under me. Two of the Tans had bayonets drawn, the cold steel glinting in the light from the door. They knocked Ryan down and ripped the socks and jersey bearing the tricolour off him. His arms were flailing as they raised their rifle butts ready to strike.

"Stop that at once!" an English voice rang out. It was an

officer. "Take that player back to Croke Park to face his punishment with the rest of the team!"

The brutes dragged Ryan out the door, half naked, and marched him down the road, back towards the Park.

In a daze, I made to follow, but the woman with the baby restrained me with a protective arm as if she was my mother. We watched them retreat through the door that was half hanging on its hinges.

Two other women came out to help the old man up. He had deflected the blow of the revolver butt by crumpling before it hit him. But he was shaken.

The woman led me upstairs to her rooms. "My husband works for Collins," she whispered, placing my letter inside a biscuit tin. "I'll see it gets to the right place." I told her the address and she nodded. She lay the baby down in its cot. Her rooms hadn't much furniture but were comfortable and spotlessly clean. She gave me a drink of hot sweet tea. Then she watched what was happening through field glasses from a window that overlooked the grounds. The baby started to fuss and she went to attend to him.

I took up her position with the field glasses, trying to follow what was happening to Ryan. It was getting late now but the clouds parted and there was a flash of brightness before dark. Down the lens I saw a jumble of things happening, all jumpy and swirling as if I was watching it through a kaleidoscope.

The arrest posse cut through the crowds like sharks in high seas. Ryan, wearing only his shorts, stood out in his near-nakedness. Near the stadium, a man with his hands up took off his coat and threw it to Ryan. His thanks was a blow from the butt end of a rifle from one of the Auxiliaries.

The people in the grounds holding their hands up were collapsing from the strain.

I saw someone I'm sure was Molly attend to someone on a stretcher as it left the grounds. It was all mixed up like a nightmare: blood, shouting, guns, screams. A man holding his head, a woman lying on the ground, soldiers searching the crowd like vultures. All the time I had one thought: where is my brother?

Over at the railway embankment, a horrible sight. Tans lined up a group of players by the railway wall inside Croke Park, their hands in the air. One of them had a white jersey. No. It was his white chest. My heart skittered. Ryan! He was at least still alive. But a firing party of Auxies had their guns cocked at the ready.

A senior officer ran up. I thought he was going to give the order to fire and I said a quick Hail Mary. But he roared at the soldiers and pointed at the players. Time stood still for that instant. My breath stopped and I wanted to look away but couldn't. But they dropped their guns and the players went inside the dressing rooms. Alive for now. I gulped for breath, heaving the air into me.

The baby was screaming. The woman looked tired and flustered. I thought with a quick pang of my mother and Josephine. I hadn't even got the milk. It was time for me to go. So I thanked the kind woman and took my leave.

I ran again, my feet beating the ground like a drum, not stopping until I reached Oriel Street. I was jangling with worry about my brother. I staggered to a doorway, feeling sick in my stomach.

Some instinct had brought me to my old home and I collapsed on the steps. People scurried about as lorryloads of Auxies combed the streets.

"Go home, you blighters!" shouted an Auxie from a lorry.

"But it's too early for curfew. It's not even five o'clock!" someone called out.

But the Auxies fired shots over people's heads. No one was going to argue.

I knocked on the door of the house but no-one answered.

I don't know how long I stayed there. It was dark by then. The cold settled in my bones. I must have fallen asleep. A hand shook me awake and I cried out in horror but it was Jetty. She threw her arms around me.

"Dan, thank God you're safe! I told Willie you'd be fine."

"Is he here?" I said, panicky.

"Me da put him on a tram. He had to get back to the college. We said we'd make sure you were fine, and here you are as if an angel delivered you." She put out her hand and hauled me up, then linked arms with me. "The Auxies are looking for trouble. Stay the night. A lot of the Tipperary Players are staying with the Dublin players who got away."

"Me mam will be out of her mind with worry," I said.

"She'll lose her mind altogether if a Tan shoots you in the dark," Jetty said.

Before I knew it, I was in the house of a player called Stephen Sinnott, somewhere off Seville Place.

There were a couple of big fellows there. One of them was Thomas Ryan! It was like a miracle after I'd seen him lined up.

"That officer saved our lives," he said. "He called it a 'bally disgraceful show'."

They gave me a mug of hot sweet tea and a slice of bread and butter. I was ravenous and rammed the whole slice into my mouth, slurping the tea down. We didn't talk much at first. When we did it was in whispers.

"I'll have to go on the run now. Won't be seeing much of my little farm," Ryan told me. "Maybe time to join the new Flying Column."

"How does that work?" I asked.

"It's a new way of fighting," he said. "There's about twenty of us. All wanted men. We live in the hills and then we strike in an ambush. There's loads of columns setting up down the country. Have you heard of Dan Breen? He's going to set ours up."

Had I heard of Dan Breen of Tipperary? He was famous like a cowboy. He'd been in loads of shootouts and was a wanted man.

We stayed quiet and tried to sleep. All the houses were dark. The only light in the room came from the street lamp poking a finger of brightness through the curtain and the tongues of flame in the grate.

I dozed but awoke to the sound of heavy lorries driving

into the road. I crouched by the window.

Auxies jumped out and snapped on bayonets, combing the street, searching several houses at once.

We looked at each other with frightened eyes.

"What'll we do?" asked Ryan.

Someone cried out, then a shot. Without discussion we crawled past the window and headed to the back door into the yard.

By the light of the moon, I saw a big pile of manure. Two of the men ran into the middle of the heap and covered themselves. Ryan followed them. There wasn't enough room for me.

I scaled the wall into the back alley that ran between the houses. I knew it like the back of my hand. Kicked ball in every square inch of it. Something snagged my feet. I'd tripped over a small bundle. I picked it up. It was wrapped in rags, but I could feel the unmistakable shape of a gun inside. If the Auxies found it, they'd know there were Volunteers nearby. I thrust it, still in its rags, inside my coat and tightened the belt so the gun wouldn't fall down.

I made my way, crouching, to a dry ditch covered in rough bushes that ran across the bottom of the alley. I crawled in and stayed there. I didn't know what else to do.

I must have slept because I awoke to drizzle falling on my face. The streets were quiet, the sky so dingy and grey I didn't know if it was dawn or dusk. But then all the happenings of yesterday came flooding in. I guessed it was about eight o'clock when I heard the early morning chapel

41

bells. I was filthy and stiff and smelly but still alive.

I crossed the Liffey by ferry. The ferryman knew me but didn't say a word. As I went up by Windmill Lane, I ran into a roadblock manned by Tans. I saw murder in their eyes. Cold sweat ran down my spine. The gun in its rags inside my jacket felt like a ticking bomb. How could I have forgotten it!

"Out killing us, were you, Fenian brat?" the Tan said, pushing the cold steel of the bayonet attached to his rifle against my chest.

To my shame, I started to snivel. He was about to strike me with the butt of the rifle but when he fixed on my face he burst out laughing.

"Why, if it isn't the ace left-footer! Not so cocky now, you little blighter!" It was Hamilton, the mean Tan who'd shot my ball when he'd lost the bet. He enjoyed lording it over me. "Get home and stay there. You lot are in a whole heap of trouble."

I ran like blazes all the way back to the Pigeon House Cottages right by the sea, relieved to feel the cold cutting breeze.

My mother was dozing in the chair when I slipped in the back door. I thought she would be mad at me, but she embraced me silently. I was too scared to hug her tight in case she felt the gun. I began to shiver.

Without talking, she led me to my bedroom. Luckily she didn't try to take my coat off. I had to hide the gun before she saw it. I asked for a drink of water and she went to get it. Then I hid the gun under the floorboards where I kept my secret things. Special stuff like my football cards, and the Maharajah ball invitation to my grandfather in India. When my mother came back she helped me undress and put my pyjamas on like I was a little kid.

I fell into a deep sleep, but awoke in a fever. I tossed and turned in the bed and cried out, half aware of my mother in the room and her hand holding mine. I dreamt of blood and bullets and monstrous shadowy beasts in black caps. I thought the gun under the floorboards was shooting fire not bullets and I was roasted by the flames of hell. The blanket on my bed pricked as if needles were piercing my skin. At one stage, I thought Molly and my mother were talking at the bottom of the bed but I might have been dreaming because I also saw my father and Mick Collins. Sometime in the soupy night my mother rubbed some terrible concoction into my chest. The smell of it made me gag.

This feverous half-life went on for what felt like days.

I awoke one night and my mother was sitting by my bedside, her face stained with tears. She was praying, under her breath. "Please God, spare my son, keep him safe."

"Mam, have they come for me? The gun!" I called out in a weak voice. I thought soldiers were knocking at the door.

She held me close. "There's nobody there, child. There's no gun. You are safe with me."

I fell back asleep in her arms.

When I awoke, the terrible weight on my chest had lifted. I had survived my illness.

I lay in the bed another while and enjoyed being

coddled, enjoying the cool touch of my mother's hand as she smoothed my brow. Towards evening of the following day I was well enough to get up for tea.

I knew I was getting better myself because that night I started to worry about the gun. It was like the cold steel of it was prodding me. When I awoke with a start from a dream, I went and lifted the floorboard as careful as a mouse. There was a gleaming full moon. As I rooted the gun out, my fingers brushed the tin box containing the old Indian ball invitation that belonged to my grandfather. The envelope had a stamp with an upside-down head of the King on it that always gave me a great laugh. I had promised to show it to Nanny's niece, Bridie, the little girl who worked in the huckster shop in Ringsend. I eased open the tin and took out the letter. I put it in my coat pocket and stuck the gun in its rags under my mattress.

The next morning I got up and dressed for school. I pulled off the filthy rags and threw them under the floorboards. Then without looking at it too closely, I covered the gun with a handkerchief and put it between my trouser waistband and my skin. I pulled my belt in an extra notch so it wouldn't slip. Then I put on my coat, all tattered from Bloody Sunday and buttoned it up.

I went downstairs and made a great show of being well.

"Are you sure you're able for school?" my mother asked, her face creasing into anxious lines.

"Never better!" I puffed out my chest and she had to laugh at me.

"That coat is only fit for the rag-and-bone man now," she said, looking at the big rips in the back.

I tied the coat belt hard, nervous about the gun.

"Alright, you can wear it today but tomorrow change into Willie's old coat."

I rushed out. As I had my hand on the door, my mother called me back. I trembled, fearing she had seen the bulge of the gun. But Josephine had started coughing and my mother was busy attending to her.

"Can you call into Nanny's shop and ask her to make me up some more ointment for Josephine?" she said. "We used a lot of it when you had your fever."

I nodded my head in relief.

The fever had passed and I knew what I had to do.

Chapter 3

The Tattooed Stranger

I walked with heavy boots down by the Pigeon House Road, a sea breeze slicing into me. My breath was still rattling in my throat and my schoolbag bounced on my back. But what weighed me down was the gun tucked into my trousers under my coat. Even though it was covered in the handkerchief and was made of cold metal, I could almost feel it burn my skin.

I decided to bury it in Ringsend Park. But as I got to the gate at the bottom of the cottages, I heard someone call out my name.

"Dannser, hey, come and have a game!"

It was Christy McIllroy. He's a terrible bully and one of the big cheeses at our local Fianna branch. It's why I don't go much. He and his cronies, ugly-looking curs they were, started chanting.

"Dan, Dan,
You'll never be a man,
Hit his head with a frying pan!"

Ha blinking ha. I pretended I didn't hear them and dashed off by Brendan's Cottages at the far end. But then I saw he and his gang were straggling out of the park and I didn't want to run into them. So I ducked through the green half-door into Nanny's shop in Whiskey Row. It's one of the little whitewashed cottages in a row by St Patrick's Church.

Bridie was sitting up on the counter reading the newspaper they use to wrap the fish in, aloud to herself – she doesn't have much else to read. Even though she's only eight and a girl, she's dead clever so she is and I really like her. That doesn't mean I want to marry her or anything. Just that she's nice for a girl. Her mother is a fishmonger who everyone calls "Mother O'Brien". She helped us get away from Oriel Street during all the trouble during the Rising.

"Is it yourself, Dan?" Bridie's voice was soft and lilting. Imagine how freshly fallen snow would sound if it talked, or wispy clouds on a summer day.

I immediately felt better. The small little huckster shop was cosy on a wintry morning with a kettle boiling on the fire at the back. There were bags of potatoes and coal down by the counter and a box of broken biscuits. I could smell the baskets of smoked fish on a shelf beside the weighing scales. Glass jars filled with penny sweets, bulls-eyes and aniseed balls gleamed on a high-up shelf out of temptation. The lower ones were lined with various packets of things like soap powder and tins of fruit.

"I've just come in to order that ointment that your Aunt Nanny makes for Josephine," I said.

"Just as well you don't want your fortune told," she said. "Nanny has a customer. He's been in there for ages." She nodded out back.

I glimpsed Nanny through the doorway reading a man's hand.

"I see a big ship – oh, there's travel to you," I heard Nanny say. "And a tall dark stranger."

Bridie and I had a fit of the giggles.

"The maid from the Shelbourne, the coalman, and the big lanky schoolteacher are all travelling and seeing dark strangers," Bridie said.

"It's true for the coalman when looking at himself in the mirror!" I joked.

"Will my business with this stranger go well?" the man demanded.

"At first," said Nanny. "But there's trouble ahead."

The kettle over the fire hissed, coming to the boil.

"What's that under your coat?" Bridie misses nothing.

I pretended not to hear her but she kept jabbing her finger at me. I knew what would distract her.

"You know I told you about that stamp with the King's head upside down? Do you want to see it?" I slipped it out of my pocket and handed it to her.

Her eyes widened with astonishment. The stamp was pink and white with "India Postage and Revenue" on the top and a price of "ONE ANNA". There were two columns on either side and little curling elephants in the corners. Right in the middle, King George V was wearing a fancy crown – his head upside down!

"They made a mistake on the Indian stamps," I said. "But the governor had already sent some out for a Maharajah ball, so a few slipped out like this one to my granddad. My father took it to a dealer once but he said it was a forgery."

"Or maybe he really was standing on his head!" Bridie codded.

I showed her the faint stamp mark. "Patia," it said.

"That's a place in India," I explained. "We have a ceremonial sword too that Mammy keeps in a strongbox. It's shiny and grand."

Bridie looked impressed.

The paraffin lamp on the mantelpiece flickered. I glanced up to see Nanny's customer filling the doorframe. He had crept up soft as a panther. It was impossible to know how long he'd been standing there. But when I looked at him, he did a double take. I thrust the letter into my pocket.

He was a lean man with bulging muscles, like a boxer. His shirtsleeves were rolled up. A black snake tattoo with red colouring curled from the third finger of his right hand. He flashed me a smile and I saw he had a gold tooth like a pirate. He gave me the shivers. I almost expected to see a snake tongue flash out between his teeth.

"Do you really have a stamp with the King's head upside down?" His accent was peculiar. Like someone English who had lived somewhere foreign for a long time. His mouth was fixed in a grin but his eyes were hard and glinting.

Bridie and I exchanged a look. She wouldn't talk about what we'd been doing if I didn't.

"No, I was just telling Bridie that my granddad saw one in India."

"The King collects stamps. Did you know that? Paid over a thousand pounds a few years ago for a stamp from Mauritius with the wrong colours. Fancy that."

"Who cares what the King does?" I answered back and then regretted it.

"Have we a young rebel here?"

I saw his gold pirate's tooth flash in his fake grin.

It felt as if the gun had worked free and was about to drop out at any moment. I could have kicked myself. What if he was a spy?

"Bridie, would you attend to the kettle?" Nanny called out.

"Don't you have school, young 'uns?" said the man. "Strange time to be hanging about in a shop, listening to men's fortunes."

"I'll make your cup of tea for reading the tea leaves," Bridie cut in.

She jumped down from the counter. She was nervous. Her dark curls shook as she wittered on about whether he wanted milk and sugar. All the while he stood there, getting the measure of us like we were horses he was going to buy at the market.

"Nanny, me mam wants some more ointment for Josephine," I called out in a nervous voice.

Bridie made a big racket, clanking a chipped china cup on the counter. She rattled around with the big blackened teapot that never seemed to be empty.

"Make sure it's the good china so I can see the leaves!" Nanny called.

I turned to go. "I'll be back later," I said to Bridie.

"Young fellow, has somebody sent you?" Nanny's customer asked in an aggressive tone just as I had my hand on the knob.

I turned beetroot and was about to make a run for it when there was a big clatter. I nearly jumped out of my skin! The noise reminded me of Croke Park. Drops of tea scattered all around, hitting the wall and dribbling down like blood. The tattooed man yelped and held up his hands to wipe some scalding tea off his cheek. The black-and-red snake bared its jaws and thrust its forked tongue most of the way down his third finger. Its body extended and fattened on the back of his hand, then curled round his wrist and all the way up his arm.

"Oh, mister!" Bridie exclaimed. "I'm such a mawsey eejit! I'll get some ointment for you!" She must have flung the cup, pretending to trip, and had spilt the tea everywhere.

51

"What's all this racket?" Nanny said.

She took one look at the customer and fetched a cloth. She dipped it in a bucket of cold water and dabbed his face. The customer flinched at her touch.

Then he bent to pick up the broken crockery. There was something about the way he bent down, agile as a cat, which reminded me of something, giving me a chill. But I was so scared I couldn't think what. I couldn't fix him. He seemed to be able to change shape before my eyes. Making himself big or small at will.

Bridie caught my eye and made a frantic shooing motion with her hands.

I slipped out and ran like the clappers, back into Ringsend Park. I scrabbled into a remote part by the sea wall with thorny bushes and straggly trees beaten crooked by the wind. Someone had dumped old furniture and clothes there a long time ago. I found a spot I'd be able to find again, near a stout old tree.

I unwound the handkerchief. The gun felt cold and sleek in my hand. It was an Mk IV .455 Webley. British army issue – a prized weapon known as "The Boer War" model. I'd seen it in a magazine but never saw one in real life before. It had automatic extraction – when you opened the barrel to reload, the spent cartridges came out automatically. You didn't even have to cock the hammer to shoot. Good for shoot-ups! I couldn't resist aiming it, pretending I was shooting at the horrible tattooed man.

My finger, as if by instinct, pulled the trigger. The force

of the recoil knocked me off my feet as the bullet ricocheted off the park wall and lodged in a tree. I looked around, terrified the deafening bang would bring a lorryload of Tans to arrest me. But all I could hear was the rush of the sea beyond the wall. Then the high thrill of a blackbird settling in the branches.

I fumbled the gun back into the handkerchief. I worried then that it might get destroyed. So I decided to wrap it in my coat – it was due for the rag-and-bone man anyway. I'd just tell Mam I'd thrown it on his cart on the way home from school. With my bare hands I tore at the earth. But that wasn't good so I found a rusty old pot and used it as a shovel. I used a plank to heave out more. I hit a large slab of rock a good two feet down and placed the gun bundled in the coat on it. Then I threw some old sacking that was lying about over it and a couple of rusty tin lids to keep the rain off. When I was satisfied with my makeshift coffin, I pushed the earth back over it and covered it with decayed braches and leaves. I walked three paces and carved a big X into the tree, lodging a stone at its heart. A chill ran down my spine. I wondered if a shot from the gun had ever killed a person.

It was only when I turned to leave I remembered I'd left my grandfather's invitation with the upside-down stamp in my coat pocket. I heard the church bells and decided to leave it with the gun for the moment.

I tore out of the park and over Ringsend Bridge so fast I didn't look right or left. I didn't see the man come out by Shelbourne Park. We hit each other bang slap and both of us fell to the ground. The man got to his feet first and put out his hand to help me up. I nearly died when I saw the snake as he pulled me up.

We both caught our breaths. The contents of my schoolbag had spilled all over the road but I was too winded to pick them up. He gathered my belongings and riffled through my bag. There was nothing there but books, copies and a pencil case. I grabbed the bag off him and made to go.

"Thanks, mister," I said.

But he grabbed my arm.

"That stamp. I don't think I was seeing things," he said, leaning in. He reeked of cologne and stale tobacco. "Lost your coat, boy? You were wearing it earlier."

"I . . . gave it to the rag-and-bone man," I stammered. "My mam told me to."

"Not in your trouser pockets, is it, the stamp?"

I stepped away and pulled out my empty pockets to show him. I didn't want him to smell the earth and the shot of the gun off me.

He gave me a look of contempt and raised his arm. I flinched. I thought he was going to hit me. But instead he reached into his breast pocket and took out a card. He handed to me.

"If you ever have anything to tell me. About stamps or anything, you can find me here."

I took the card without even glancing at it and ran. I didn't look back.

I pelted into school. By some miracle Brother Disgrace hadn't locked the front door yet and I got in just before the bell for the next class. It was the first time ever I was glad to go in.

At lunchtime I looked at the card. "*S Jameson, Commercial Traveller*" it said and there was a Post Office Box address. S for "snaky", I thought, and decided to put him out of my mind. But that tattooed snake kept slithering into my thoughts. I drew it on the back of my copybook.

But something else jabbed into my brain. The tattooed man I'd thought I'd imagined jumping from the burning house in Ranelagh Road on Bloody Sunday. He'd landed like a cat. Surely a coincidence?

Chapter 4

All at Sea

When the bell rang for home, I shot out of school like a cannonball. I was freezing cold without my coat. I whizzed up Brunswick Street across Ringsend Bridge. I kept an eye out for Snaky Jameson. Lucky for me the coast was clear. As I passed Whiskey Row, I remembered I was supposed to collect the ointment from Nanny O'Brien for Josephine's chest. I was half afraid to go in but the shop was crowded. Bridie was at the counter again, reading out bits from the newspaper to some "aul ones" and "aul fellas". Like loads of people in Ringsend, they all had weird nicknames like Bungo and Seven Asses. She gave me a smile and glanced back down at the paper.

"It says here that the fellows arrested before Bloody Sunday were shot trying to escape," she explained for my benefit. "They had something to do with the killing of all those British spies."

My blood ran cold. Poor McKee, Clancy and Clune. If the Tans knew what I was doing, they'd shoot me dead too.

"Terrible business. We'll never know if they were guilty or innocent,' said one of the shawlies.

"Dem Tans and Auxies are no better than murderers themselves," said another.

One of them wanted Bridie to read a letter from the council. Even though she's only eight, she reads and writes as well as a grown-up. I hung back, waiting to get a chance to speak to her.

She hopped over to me when the old women started chatting.

"That snake man was a quare one this morning," she said, fear in her eyes.

A woman burst into the shop.

"They've arrested Tommy Whelan from Barrow Street! Saw it with my own eyes. Said he shot a Captain Baggallay on Bloody Sunday!"

"No way!" cried Nanny, running out. "Sure wasn't he sitting beside Dinah Deegan at nine o'clock Mass! She told me about it in every detail. Good-looking fellow with a shock of black hair. Rides a motorbike and works at the train depot. All the girls are in love with him, just like Dinah."

"Is it that Galway lad?" said a young fellow from Tunney's public house who'd come in after getting his paper in the newsagent's next door. "I saw him coming out of Mass. He'd have to be the Holy Ghost himself to be in two places at once."

"Them that did it are on the run, not waiting for the Tans to come and get them," said an old man, scratching his head under his cap.

I remembered seeing Tommy going to Mass myself and later at Croke Park, looking like he hadn't a care in the world. There was no way he was on a job.

Nanny saw me at the back of the shop. "Young Dan, will you run along to Michael Noyk on Dame Street? He's the Volunteers' solicitor. Tell him there's witnesses. Tell him I sent you."

"Dinah won't want her new fella to know she's still pining after Tommy," said another neighbour.

"We'll twist her arm," said Nanny.

She scribbled down the name and address and gave me sixpence. I was glad of the job. If I was on the move, I couldn't think.

There was an unfamiliar hush in Dublin. People no longer chatted at street corners, as lorryloads of Tans raked through the streets in posses. They had blood in their eyes. Spoiling for a fight. I hugged close to the buildings.

Noyk's Solicitors office was just up from Trinity College in a big grey building.

A smart young fellow, of about seventeen, showed me in. He wore a yellow waistcoat and carried himself as if he owned the world.

"I'm Seán MacBride," he said.

I knew the name. His father was a hero – executed in 1916. Molly had met him in Jacob's Garrison. She'd told me that his mother was a famous beauty, Maud Gonne, who poets wrote about.

Seán had a strange accent. He told me he'd been raised in France. That explained the way he pronounced his "r"s. He listened to me like a hawk.

"Tommy has loads of witnesses," I said, not mentioning I'd seen him myself.

"The British executed my father. Then locked my mother up in Holloway Prison without trial. I do not trust their justice," he said.

MacBride went in with a sheaf of papers to talk to the solicitor. I was alone in the waiting room. I saw a football in the corner in a wastepaper bin and couldn't resist it. I rolled the ball, easy like, along my foot, then practised spinning it on the toe of my shoe.

MacBride returned with Mr. Noyk, a small, intense man with a wide smile.

"No, don't stop!" he said. "Flick it to me."

I gave him a straight pass and he deflected it with a deft touch to MacBride who stumbled flat-footed.

The three of us kicked ball for a few minutes.

Mr. Noyk stopped breathless and heaved his chest in laughter. "That's the best fun I've had in ages. Did you know I'm the solicitor for Shamrock Rovers? I'll tell them to snap you up, lad."

"Shelbourne's my local team," I said.

"Who's your favourite player?"

"Louis Bookman. He's another left-footer. He's brilliant. He won us the League and the Leinster Cup last year. I'm sorry he's gone to Luton."

Mr. Noyk beamed at me. "He's Jewish like me. The first Jew to play for Ireland. I used to play for Adelaide. But he's a genius. Luton paid nearly a thousand pounds for him even though he's over thirty. I negotiated his contract. I'll do the same for you, lad, if you ever go professional."

I turned beetroot. "What about Whelan?" I asked.

"Sounds like the accused has a cast-iron alibi. Good work, son."

Mr. Noyk insisted I take another sixpence, with the hope that someday I'd be capped for Ireland too.

He chipped the ball back into the wastepaper basket. "I keep that there in case I ever get the chance for a kickabout. Drop by if you fancy some practice." Then he added as he waved me out the door, "And you could even do some messenger work."

As Seán MacBride walked me out I summoned up the courage to ask him about what was playing on my mind, a worry like a rat gnawing in my skull. "Can you be arrested for hiding guns? Or being a lookout?"

He slapped me on the back good-naturedly. "Not if you keep your mouth shut." He paused. "So you'd be able to get your hands on a gun if the need arose?"

"I'm saying nothing," I said.

MacBride smiled. "You're a quick learner. A nod's as

good as a wink to a blind man. I might need to ask you a favour someday."

My feelings were all jumbled up. I felt better for confiding in MacBride and ten feet tall after meeting Mr. Noyk. I could tell he was a man likely to keep his word and I might get a bit of work off him. It made my heart sing after my encounter with Snaky Jameson. But the idea that MacBride might want the gun worried me. I tried to kick the worries out of my head by thinking of ball moves.

Back in Whisky Row, all the oul' ones said I was a grand lad. But my delight faded when I saw Nanny's customer emerge from the back room.

Snaky Jameson was back again! He gripped the doorway, and it looked like the snake was trying to break it down. All the old fellows and women took one look at him and scooted off.

"It's all go at Nanny's shop," he said in a phony voice when it went quiet. He leaned on the counter as if he owned the place. "You must know all the secrets here, Nanny. About the innocent and the guilty."

Something in his tone annoyed Nanny who had followed him out. She faced him and gave him a hard look. He stood up straight then. She had a face like an Eskimo woman that I saw in a book, piercing eyes with long thin lips and high cheekbones. You didn't mess with Nanny.

"I might even know yours, Mr. Jameson. If that's your real name," she said. The air went cold as if someone had let in a draught.

61

"Any secret worth knowing, you pass on to me." He dropped a florin on the counter, where it spun and landed on the King's head.

"Then it wouldn't be a secret," she snapped.

"I'll see it goes right to the Big Man himself."

"The Big Man himself is God, and I can talk to him myself," Nanny said.

"Do you serve king or country, missus?" he asked.

"I serve fish and potatoes. Do you want some?"

He laughed and then thrust out his right hand, the one with the snake, palm up.

"You were holding something back at the last reading. I want to know if I have good fortune."

"Them that live by the sword die by it."

He laughed again, his gold tooth glinting. "I'll take my chances," he said. "Where's your pretty little niece with the curly hair? You'd want to mind a sweet girl like that. Wouldn't like to lose her."

I clenched my fists at his threatening manner. Nanny took his right hand in hers and gazed at his palm with narrowed eyes. For a minute she went into a trance. Then her eyes flew open – a look of horror on her face.

"What have you seen?" he pressed her.

"You . . . should go and live a good life," she said, her voice faltering.

"You've seen something, you old witch," said Jameson, his voice cruel.

Nanny shook her head.

"Tell me. I could make you." He loomed over her and put his horrible snaky hand on her upper arm, giving it a hard squeeze like bullies do, all sneaky like.

Nanny winced and he dropped his hand.

"You have a short lifeline," she said. "Even shorter if you threaten me or mine." She thrust the coin back at him.

He shrugged and laughed like a devil. He gave me the creeps.

"I'll let myself out the back way," he said.

I watched him go through the back room and out into the back yard that ran along by the Dodder River.

I set off home with the ointment for Josephine. But I'd only cut up by Ringsend Park when I felt the hairs on the back of my neck prickle.

A shadow loomed over me.

"Boy, can I have a word?" Snaky Jameson fell into step with me. "That stamp you were on about? It's worthless but I'd like to see it out of curiosity."

"I told you already," I said, panic making my voice unsteady.

He flattened me up against the wall. I thought he was going to strike me. But to my surprise he tousled my hair. His gold tooth glinted.

"Slowly, slowly, catchee monkey," he said and strode off.

I got home to find Mam staring blankly out the window.

I thought she would be glad of the money I'd earned. But she was stern with me.

"Daniel, I don't want you to get mixed up in anything.

63

Promise me you'll stay out of trouble."

I muttered something and I saw her wipe away a tear. "Your father's ship should have been home last week. I'll have to go down to the office to see what's happened. Will you come with me tomorrow after school?"

I nodded. She gave me a note to ask for me to be let off early.

Next day, Mother met me outside the school, wearing her best clothes. I was wearing Willie's old coat instead of my raggy one so I felt quite respectable too. Mother preferred not to come into the school for me. See, she's not comfortable around Catholic priests and Brothers. She was raised as a Presbyterian by her grandfather. He's a minister out in Kingstown. She only became a Catholic to marry my father. Then both of them got kicked out of their families. Though during the Rising her grandfather gave us shelter in the manse and has tried to keep in touch.

We walked to the shipping office on Bachelor's Walk to save the tram fare. It was a tense journey. Troops drove through streets at a more rapid rate than usual. We had to take more than one detour as Tans were putting up roadblocks and raiding shops in broad daylight. When one poor shopkeeper protested, they hit him with the butt end of a rifle. My mother rushed to help him but was pushed back by the Tans.

The shipping office was all polished wood and leather-bound ledgers. A line of clocks told the time in different parts of the world. Dublin, London, New York, Sydney, Rio de Janeiro. The names were like stories, other worlds. I wanted to ask about them but I was too nervous.

The clerk there shook his head when we asked about my father. My mother went pale. I just felt blank. Like my heart stopped beating for a few seconds.

"Is he dead, Mammy?" I could hardly say the words.

"Now don't you be worrying, Dan." She put her hand on my arm for reassurance. But her own hand was trembling.

The clerk rustled around in a big ledger and pointed to an entry. "'*Able Seaman Edward O'Donovan transferred onto the Moore/McCormack Line in New York.*' They are to begin sailing transatlantic liners to Irish ports soon. I cannot help you." Then in a quieter voice he continued, "There's a lot of Shinners – you know, Nationalists – working on that line. The British think they're smuggling arms. I heard they've asked the Yanks to investigate and there have been some arrests. You could telegraph their New York office." He wrote down an address in New York.

My mother held herself together. "My husband is not mixed up in anything," she said.

The clerk nodded in agreement but I could tell he didn't believe her by the way he averted his eyes. I kept my head down, fearing he'd see I was up to my neck in it.

We went up Sackville Street, past where they were still rebuilding the GPO. It was shelled to smithereens by the British in the Rising.

The temporary post office was by the Rotunda Hospital.

Mam sent a telegram to the New York shipping office. It read **"Any news Able Seaman Edward O'Donovan?"** She also sent one to Uncle Daniel, Molly's father, who I'm called after. As Chief Technical Officer of the GPO, he's on a special trip to America. He's checking out the latest telegraph systems from the famous inventor Thomas Edison.

When we got outside, my mother brushed away a tear with the back of her hand. "It might be just bad weather that's delayed them. But how are we going to pay the rent and feed us all?"

"I'll leave school and work as a messenger boy," I said.

She turned all serious. "You most certainly will not. The only thing that keeps me going is knowing my boys are getting an education. I'll go down on my hands and knees skivvying before I'll see you leave school."

As we walked along the quays, I thought I saw a man like Jameson dart into the doorway of a pub. My eyes were playing tricks now. I'd have to keep my wits about me.

When we got home, Molly was there, showing Josephine how to put bandages on her dolly. She made my mother a cup of tea and sat down for a long chat while I went outside to kick ball.

I was practising a simple move that I call "Around the World". You kick the ball up with one foot and circle it with the other before it lands back down on the kicking foot. It looks amazing but is quite easy. I started doing this stuff because I'm football mad and only could ever play in small yards at the back of the houses we've lived in. I saw a fellow do ball-juggling like that in a circus once. Maybe one day I'll go and join my cousin Jack the Cat in the circus in America. That would be a grand life away from all the troubles.

Molly came out to watch me. "You're more like Jack every day. Nimble as anything." Reading my thoughts as usual.

I balanced the ball on the top of my head, then slid it down to my left knee and then my left foot. Jack was in the Fianna too. Thought it was a great thing to fight for Ireland. I avoided looking at Molly. She goes to Quaker meetings. They are a different religion. They don't believe in having priests or anything. They just sit in a room and say prayers. Molly says they don't quake! They don't believe in war or violence of any kind. Molly's mother is a Quaker but Molly was brought up as a Catholic. She likes the Quakers more. She hates fighting.

"Remember when I found you on Easter Monday? There you were, hanging around Stephen's Green in the middle of the Rebellion!"

"And I spied Countess Markievicz's feathered hat through the railings, like a strange bird had landed on her head."

Molly's face darkened. "We saw that poor man shot by the rebels for trying to take his truck off the barricades. He was a nationalist too."

I dropped the ball. I tried never to think of that, the first dead body I'd ever seen. But sometimes it came back in nightmares. The man's blood, the girl's keening. Lately it had been in my dreams of Bloody Sunday.

"You and me have seen some terrible things – it's not surprising you have nightmares," she said, reading my thoughts again. "That's why I'm so determined to be a surgeon. I think if I can save a life for all the ones lost, then there's a reason I survived."

"Do you have to cut up dead bodies when you're training?"

Her mood changed like lightning and she laughed. "I will soon. But it's mostly boring lectures about anatomy and blood circulation."

"I don't think I could cut a body – dead or alive," I said. "I don't even like the smell from the butcher's."

"I hope that means you have no interest in firing guns," she said, turning serious again. "I want Ireland free as much as the next person. But I don't believe in doing it down the barrel of a gun."

She was getting a bit preachy so I practised the "Super Seven". I bounced the ball from my head to my left shoulder. Then my left knee, left foot, right foot, right knee, right shoulder. She snatched the ball and held it out of my reach.

"The British declared war on us. They won't let us have our own government. It's self-defense," I said.

"War is a deadly game, Dan. It's like this awful game of chicken. Tit for tat until we're all dead." She shook her deep-red curls, like flames from a fire.

"So what are we supposed to do? Stand by while the

Tans and Auxies kill us all?"

Molly bit her lip. "I don't know the answers, Dan. The British government pushed all the moderates into the arms of the gunman. But that doesn't make it right to kill."

"Dan! Molly! Your tea!" Our mother cut short our argument.

I tossed and turned again that night, awoken abruptly by a vicious knocking at the door. I cowered under the covers.

"Open up, missus. Your rent is overdue!" It was Mr. Hunt, the rent collector.

My mother crept into the room, carrying Josephine, and whispered, "Quiet – he'll go away in a minute." She sat hugging us on the bed.

"We'll be back same time next week with the bailiff if you don't pay up!"

After an almighty shove against the door, he was gone.

"Don't worry," she said. "I'll get the money."

I noticed her hair had grey in it and her eyes were red.

That afternoon, when I came out of school, MacBride fell into step with me. He handed me an envelope. "Special job. Delivery from the Big Fellow himself. There's a shilling for your trouble."

I didn't hesitate. I was going to make sure that rent collector never battered down our door again.

Chapter 5

Messages

"All your goodness will come back to you!" Mam said as she stood in our new rooms in Margaret Place, a cul-de-sac off Bath Avenue. We had the whole first floor with four airy rooms, much pleasanter than the pokey cottage. She was speaking to Mother O'Brien, not me, who was helping us move our few possessions. It was she who helped me find the place when I told her about the horrible rent collector terrorising us. I'd earned all the money to pay off the old demon by running messages like billio for a few days. But I was happier with Mam thinking that Mother O'Brien was our saviour.

Mother O'Brien just nodded and gave me a hard look. When I'd asked for her help, all she'd said to me was, "I don't know what you're up to. But stay safe. If the lads get their republic I hope they remember you."

She might well have figured out my secret. She could rival Collins' intelligence network.

"Dan," my mam had said to me one morning as I left, pretending to go to school, "you should use your brain and not just your feet."

I had just headed the ball out the door and tried not to catch her eye. I didn't miss every day in school so the Brothers didn't get too suspicious.

"Hey, Dannser!" McIlroy called to me as I went past him and his gang having a kickabout on the road.

I didn't want to mess around because I had a job to do for the Big Fellow. But I jumped in and scored a goal before they knew. Showing off, like. Sometimes I just couldn't help it.

Cousin Molly would have been angry if she knew what I was getting up to. But I didn't ask too many questions. I was doing it for Ireland. And for Collins.

Since Bloody Sunday, things were even more hairy. MacBride had told me they were inundated with cases. Five hundred arrests of rebel suspects had been made inside a week. Including the acting Sinn Féin President Arthur Griffith. He was supposed to be in charge while de Valera was in the States trying to get money and support. But we all knew it was Collins who was boss. We might have crippled their spy network but they were fighting back. Tans and Auxies were everywhere, spoiling for a fight.

But we were getting round them. Dublin was full of Collins 'irregulars'. Young lads running messages, dropping ammunition, passing guns. Girls and women too. No one

71

noticed us, scurrying about like mice. The only thing that stuck out about me was my ears.

But I went one further. I was the kid with the ball. And that opened doors. British Army doors, Auxie and Black and Tan doors. They let down their guard when I messed about with my ball. Too busy looking at my latest tricks. It's a rare man who can resist the kick of a ball.

I called into Noyk's Solicitors first. Seán MacBride gave me some documents and told me to pick up a book at O'Hegarty's bookshop on Dawson Street. I ran all the way, thankful that there were no roadblocks.

The shop assistant Susan Killeen, who gave me the ball, was one of Collins' most trusted couriers.

When I went up to the counter, she was in conversation with a tall man with a moustache.

I was so desperate to get rid of my package, I just blurted out, "I'm here for my aunt's delivery."

She gave me a searching look then glanced at her customer. "Can't you see I'm helping this gentleman here?" She smiled at the man. He was all swagger with his gold-tipped cane and white gloves. His shoes gleamed and he had a long nose and a smart look about him. A military look.

"These young guttersnipes have no manners," he said. He had a plummy English accent and a sneery, silken voice.

I took in his pile of books and felt itchy under my collar. There was a lot of poetry – like Yeats and Lady Gregory – and a big book about stamps.

"Dan is a nice respectable boy, one of our messengers,"

said Susan. "Doesn't the King collect stamps as well? Have you ever met him?"

"I have the pleasure of being a member of the same philately club. A word derived from the Greek, meaning love of stamp collecting."

"Amazing!" said Susan. "It must be funny for him, as they are all pictures of himself!"

The man gave a faint, superior smile. "He loves to collect stamps from his Empire, especially rare ones."

I kept my head down. Funny, both him and Jameson keen on stamps.

"Now, you wanted a book on Greek Mythology." Susan said. "Oh no! I must have left it over there in the history section. Do you speak Greek?"

"Yes," he said, smiling.

"I bet you're awful clever. What does *al salaam* mean? Is that 'I love you' in Greek?"

"That's Arabic, I think." A look passed over his face, as if he'd said something he shouldn't have.

"I'd love to go to all those foreign countries," she said, looking wistful.

The Englishman's face went dark, mistrustful.

But Susan just grinned. "I better not say *al salami* or whatever it is to any Indians I meet!"

"India isn't an Arab country." I spoke before thinking. "My father was born in India."

"Well, I don't need to worry as I'll never go far from this shop! Now let me get you the book," said Susan.

"I can fetch it if you like," he said gallantly.

I felt his keen eyes beam into me.

She smiled at him. "It would be so kind of you. The history section is over there around the back of that stack of shelves."

As soon as he was out of sight, I slipped the documents to Susan and she passed me a packet of books tied up in string.

"Watch him," she muttered. "Just new in town. He might be another intelligence officer shipped over from the colonies."

She'd just been pretending to be stupid so she could sniff him out. All that "*al salaami*" nonsense was to see if he spoke Arabic. The British got a lot of their spies from Arab countries, like the Cairo Gang from Egypt.

She turned round the name on his order form. "*Captain George Lees.*" Another snippet to pass on to Collins.

She glanced up, checking that Lees was still out of sight. Then she tapped the spine of the middle book in the pile. I nodded to show that I understood.

She leaned in closer and said, almost too softly for me to hear, "The goose has laid the golden egg." That was the code.

I went round to a back alley and crouched in a doorway to have a peek. The middle book, Macaulay's *History of England*, had a false cover to conceal letters and documents. That was a little joke between her and Collins.

There in Susan's tiny handwriting was an address in

Middle Abbey Street and a list of groceries – butter, eggs, bread and milk. There was also a one-pound note folded up tiny. I was mystified until I put two and two together. I reasoned the list wasn't a code for bomb parts or ammunition but real food!

Nassau Street was crawling with Auxies. Some were in ordinary clothes, but they had a way of walking in twos and threes that gave them away. And they always had polished shoes – couldn't shake off their military training – so I always looked at their feet.

I nipped into Findlaters grocery shop, and bought what I needed. Then, just in case anyone was following me, I took a roundabout route. I skirted round via Crown Alley, then doubled back through Westmoreland Street. I cut down by Burgh Quay to cross over the Ha'penny Bridge. I thought about ball moves in my head but tried to walk steady as I was carrying eggs.

"George Moreland Cabinet Makers" was my destination in Middle Abbey Street. Inside, a stout woman with a big hat was speaking to a spruce, thin-faced carpenter.

"I need the wardrobe and the kitchen dresser for when we move next month," she said.

He went into a small office with a rough desk behind a glass partition, and consulted a calendar. Carpenters in white aprons scurried about.

"We can't start before Christmas," he said when he came back out.

"Ah, that might be too late," she said and left.

Two of the younger fellows winked at each other as if this was a joke.

The head carpenter spotted me just as I was about to leave, thinking I'd made a mistake.

"Young fellow, do you want something or are you just standing in out of the rain?"

I held up the groceries and told them the goose had laid the golden egg. They let out a shout of delight like I was Father Christmas or something. Then, putting up a closed sign, they led me out back into the builders' yard.

"Give us some bread," one of them said, attacking the bag. "I'm starving!"

I took a closer look at the carpenters. They were all trim and alert and had pockets in their aprons for tools. But I guessed they were hiding guns. They were a bit like those fellows who had turned up at Ranelagh Road on Bloody Sunday. I put two and two together. It was a hideout for Volunteers!

After they'd polished off the food most of the carpenters drifted back into the shop. But the two younger ones stayed to talk to me. Their names were Vinnie and Charlie. Vinnie was a real Dub, cool as anything. Charlie was more like a student. They weren't much older than me but had this air of authority. They impressed and frightened me as they looked me up and down.

Charlie in particular stared at me hard. He had a slight graze on his upper forehead. Then he stood and shook my hand.

"You're the young fellow with the ball who saved my life on Westland Row," he said.

I smiled in joy. I hadn't recognised him. "How's your head?"

He nodded. "Still on my neck."

Vinnie patted me on the back. They both relaxed. It was like I had passed some test.

"The cabinetmaking is just a front," Vinnie said, tapping the side of his large nose. "Though meself and one or two others are proper carpenters. But now we're making coffins for the British." He smiled at his own grim joke.

There was a newspaper around the bread and Charlie raked through it. "It says the British are rebuilding their intelligence network. There's going to be another crackdown."

"Charlie's one of our top intelligence men," said Vinnie to me.

"What if you're raided?" I asked.

"We'll have an answer for them. If we can get the bullets," said Vinnie.

He was tough and wiry, a real fighter. He looked like he knew how to shoot straight.

"Anything strange?" he asked me.

Before I could think, I told them about Lees the British Officer I'd met in O'Hegarty's Bookshop. A look passed between them.

"The government is bringing in a whole new brace of spies since Bloody Sunday," said Charlie. "I met a fellow in

77

a pub off the quays. Said he supported revolution and could get arms for us from the Russians. Strange man, had a tattoo on his right arm."

I dropped the cup.

"Spit it out," said Vinnie. "No piece of information is too small."

I told them how Snaky Jameson had been asking questions when Whelan was arrested. How he was boasting he knew "the Big Man" whoever he was. I still had his card and I gave it to them. I also told them it might have been the same fellow covered in tattoos I saw jump from the burning house in Ranelagh Road. They exchanged more looks.

"Could be useful," said Charlie. "I also heard talk they've shipped in some fellow from the East who is a master of disguise. So keep your wits about you."

I was in awe of them. They looked much like ordinary fellows, but had the wariness of stalking cats.

"We don't answer to anyone except the Big Fellow – Collins," said Vinnie. He took up the paper and took out a scissors, cutting out the report about the British re-grouping. "For my scrapbook," he grinned.

He wrote me out a note.

"Take this to Harcourt Street."

When I got outside I had to pinch myself. They weren't just ordinary Volunteers. I'd been with the top men, the Squad, Collins' "Twelve Apostles". I was "in it" all right. I didn't know if I felt better or worse for telling them about Jameson and Lees.

I hurried up Grafton Street, nerves on end, watching out for patrol cars. I cut through an alleyway and skirted round the back streets to get to Harcourt Street.

As I came near Number 76 there was only the paper seller on the corner. I was as jumpy as a rasher on a hot skillet. I knocked on the door. When I said I had a message for Mr. Field, a smartly dressed older woman with bobbed hair and glasses let me in. Her hand on the bannisters was ink-stained.

"You're Molly's cousin," she said, introducing herself as Addy Killykelly. She had a kind smile. "I made her first diary for her when I was a stationery worker. Clever as anything, is Molly!"

She accompanied me to the top of the building. On the first floor, I saw one man sifting through a mailbag while at another desk a woman went down a long column of figures. On the second floor, through a doorway, I glimpsed another woman reading through a letter. She was underlining words with a pencil.

"She's decoding. We're all doing intelligence work," said Addy. "We also copy out a lot of documents in case they raid our offices. That's why we're all so inky with carbon paper!"

I wondered if they'd handled the letter I'd given to the mother in Clonliffe Road on Bloody Sunday. It made me think of Ryan, the Tipperary player. I didn't know if he was safe or lying dead in a ditch.

"What do you do if you get raided?" I asked.

Addy gave me a wink. "We have special cupboards and hidey-holes built in all over the place. It's like a magician's cave, this house!"

In an attic room at the back of the building, with his feet on a desk, Michael Collins was scrutinizing a document, a revolver at his elbow.

"So here is Mr. Field!" said Addy and with another wink left.

I gave Collins the letter. He read it in a flash. Then he pushed it down the join between the desk top and the leg. On closer inspection it looked thicker than normal. Another concealed hiding place.

In another corner of the room, O'Reilly, his assistant, was date-stamping papers and pinning them to envelopes.

I passed Addy in the doorway as she came back in with what looked like a bunch of typed letters in her hand. I hung back in the little corridor outside the door.

I peeped in and saw her lay the letters in front of Collins. He began to sign them.

"If you decide to meet Archbishop Clune, it might be a trap to capture you," I heard her say.

My ears pricked up. Archbishop Clune was the uncle of one of the men arrested and killed in the Castle the night before Bloody Sunday. He wasn't even a rebel – he'd been killed in revenge for Collins taking out the Cairo Gang.

"We've paralyzed the British intelligence system," Collins said. "My guess is they'll soon declare martial law. If Archbishop Clune wants to broker a truce, there's no harm in talking." He took a letter out of a drawer and, signing it, handed it to O'Reilly who popped it in a white envelope.

Collins watched O'Reilly as he left the room with the letter. Addy also left with another bundle of papers. When he saw me hovering in the doorway he balled up a newspaper and tossed it towards me, trying to catch me off guard. I caught it in my left hand and hurled it back at him.

He laughed. "A *citóg*, are you? A left-hander! We'll make a Gaelic footballer of you yet!"

His eyes fell on another slip of paper on the desk and his face took on a worried frown. He took a large banknote from a drawer. He folded it up in the paper and passed them to me.

"This money and message needs to go to de Valera's family in Greystones right away. His children can't eat fresh air while he's flitting about America. Run down and give them to Addy for that lazy galoot O'Reilly when he comes back. He's always missing when you need him. Anyone would think there was a war on!" He laughed at his own joke.

I put the folded paper in my pocket.

Suddenly I heard Addy shouting: "But we're just an office here!"

"Quick, Michael!" The woman who'd been underlining the documents rushed in. "There's RIC detectives downstairs."

With one bound, Michael Collins jumped up on his chair and disappeared through the skylight. It was like he'd been plucked by a hand from the sky.

The woman immediately ran down the stairs to join Addy.

O'Reilly rushed back in and slid back a false wall. We piled in as many papers as we could then crouched down and crammed ourselves in too.

O'Reilly slipped the false wall back in place. We were squashed in like rats in a hole, him in one corner and me in the other with the mass of papers between us. Through a spyhole I saw a Castle detective scan the room but he only glanced at the papers.

"This one's empty," he called down.

Then he did something strange. He closed the skylight! He must have been one of the detectives on our side.

There was the sound of heavy boots on the stairs.

"Seize all the papers," an officer with a British accent commanded.

"You can't," said Addy from the stairwell. "This is all legal business."

"Do as you're told or we'll arrest you too." The cruel posh voice gave me a cold shiver in the pit of my stomach. He sounded like that Captain Lees who had been at the bookshop. Could it be him?

"Let me help you do it properly," said Addy, speaking very loudly. "Otherwise when they come back they'll be all out of order." She was on the floor below, trying to delay them for as long as possible.

"There's only an old attic up here!" shouted the first detective.

They must have believed him for no one else came up.

I was too nervous to move, nor did O'Reilly, but after a while Addy knocked on the false wall and called, "The coast is clear! They took some unimportant papers but they're all in code and we have the duplicates. "

I burst out of my hiding place like a cornered animal released. But O'Reilly had vanished! I looked around, bewildered, shaking the pins and needles out of my legs.

"He's gone down to the basement." She pointed to a narrow, barely visible trapdoor in the floor of the cupboard. "There's a concealed narrow chute between every floor that leads to the basement. Then there's a tunnel out to the street from there. It's too tight a fit for Mick!"

O'Reilly must have been Houdini the master magician to slip through the tiny space. It would have been a squeeze for me.

"It was lucky that detective didn't search too closely," I said.

"He's one of ours – MacNamara," Addy whispered. "Don't accidentally put him in danger if you meet again."

"I won't. But, Addy, Mr. Collins gave me a message and banknote you're to give to O'Reilly to take to de Valera's family." I pulled the message out of my pocket and handed it to her. "He said it was urgent."

Addy held the papers in her hand, thinking. "O'Reilly is already hiding somewhere else. I can't go because they'll be looking out for me outside."

"I'll take it!" I volunteered.

She looked at me, dubious.

"I'll say she's my aunt and the money's from our uncle. What can they do, Addy? I'm a kid. "

She took the folded message and, opening it up, read it. "There's going to be a raid on the house tonight! We need to warn his wife. The note is in code – they'll never decipher it. Promise you'll be careful."

Addy told me to take the tram to Westland Row train station and gave me a few shillings. "Keep your eyes open, Dan. They watch de Valera's house all the time." She told me de Valera's address and sketched a rough map of the route from the station in Greystones.

I put the money in my sock and the note in my handkerchief. I left my ball for safekeeping.

I eased out of the skylight and clambered down the ladder, dropping onto the metal fire escape that ran down the back of the building. I was excited to be following in the Big Fellow's footsteps!

I felt a bit like my cousin Jack the Cat though he had done much more daring things than this in Easter Week 1916, and under fire. I cut through the Standard Hotel next door. None of the staff batted an eyelid at the sight of a schoolboy using their lobby as a shortcut.

But, outside in the street, my legs turned to jelly. It was sheer force of will that got me to the tram stop on the Green to Westland Row Station. More people were about now. I pulled up the collar of Willie's coat against the cold November wind and kept my head down.

I sat near the door at the front of the tram, behind the driver. We had only gone a couple of stops when the tram slowed near Merrion Square. Up ahead a group of Tommies in tin hats were coming towards the tram.

I glanced around and, to my horror, saw Captain Lees in uniform sitting at the back of the crowded tram. It put the heart crossways in me. Now I had two enemies on my trail.

I huddled in my seat, paralysed.

An old woman opposite noticed my plight. "Are you all right, son?" she asked me.

I flicked my eyes towards where Lees was sitting. She glanced back and nodded. She stood up, and then fell to the floor in a dead faint.

"Quick, open the tram door!" somebody shouted.

The driver obliged. I leaped through the door as passengers helped the old woman to her feet, blocking the aisle. I caught my breath and, looking back, saw Lees trying to barge his way through. Then the door snapped shut. The last thing I saw was his angry snarling face as he banged on the door with a white-gloved hand.

All my blood pumped to my legs and I vaulted over the railings of Merrion Square. I ran like blazes through the park up towards the Pepperpot church.

I was nearly run over by a bicycle. But luckily for me it was Anto, a messenger boy for Findlaters and an old friend of Jack the Cat's. He lost his big toe in the Rising.

I explained I was going to Westland Row to catch the train to Greystones. He leapt off his bicycle and threw it over to me. He grinned at me. "Leave it there. Findlaters are used to donating their bicycles to the cause." He hobbled off with his packages without a backward glance.

I pedalled so furiously I made it to Westland Row Station in record time. With luck, there were no army cordons or Brothers from the school about to wonder what I was doing there in the late afternoon.

I was quite excited to be on the train, and looked out the window as the scenery unfurled like a ribbon. I was panting so much an old lady gave me a hardboiled sweet to suck, telling me it would be good for my asthma!

When I got to Greystones there were several distracted mothers with young children getting off. I tagged along behind them, hoping the stationmaster wouldn't notice me.

The sea air was a tonic. I wondered if my father was still smelling the same briny tang on some ocean far away. I followed Addy's hastily drawn map, going south away from the sea, and found my destination in about five minutes.

The house was a grand villa behind white pillars surrounded by a leafy garden. It reminded me of my great-grandfather's rectory in Kingstown where we stayed for a few weeks after the Rising – that great big stuffy house that was like being in a tomb.

The road was lonely with few houses. A wind whipped up, combing blades of grass and bashing branches. I pulled Willie's coat tight and cursed my short trousers. I felt more exposed here than on the crowded, dangerous Dublin streets.

Through the gates I could see a young boy my own age playing ball in the garden, pretending he was passing a defender like I often did. It was like looking into a mirror of my own loneliness when I used to play keepy-uppy in back yards.

A soulful-looking woman like a Celtic queen opened the door. It was Mrs. de Valera. She took me straight to the kitchen. She offered me some dry bread, with an apology that she'd just run out of butter.

I gave her the note and money. Her face changed as she read.

"I'll go straight to my parents," she said. "Can you tell Vivion to come in from the garden and get ready?"

I tackled the ball from Vivion much to his delight. Just before we came inside, I showed him one of my new moves.

His mother watched us from the back door, wiping her face with the back of her hand, like my mother does. Hiding her tears.

"It's fairy tales you should be reading not running errands," she said, a catch in her voice.

She asked me a few questions about myself and nodded when I told her I went to Pearse's old school in Westland Row. He was the leader of the Rising that got executed. Everyone thought now he was some kind of saint. Except the British of course. But she was impressed that my brother Willie was at Blackrock College and their star goal-kicker.

"A scholarship boy just like my husband!" she exclaimed. "Dev's happiest days were at Blackrock. I'll let you in on a secret. Dev loves rugby, though he can't let on, it being one of the banned garrison games. I always have to keep him up to date with Blackrock's scores!"

A baby cried somewhere in the house and Mrs. de Valera rushed off. I heard a clock chime the half hour.

I waited a while to see if she would come back. But, when she didn't, I slipped out, not wanting to miss the train back.

Just as I reached the gate, Vivion ran up to me and gave me a parcel in brown paper.

"Mother said this is for you and your brother."

I thanked him and left. I felt his eyes follow me for a long time.

In the station I peeled back a bit of the paper. I knew by the shape of it. A deflated oval rugby ball. Good leather if a bit scuffed, a nice rough, nobbly grain to give you a good grip.

Raindrops slashed the darkening windows and Dublin's southern suburbs went by in a blur. I was so bone-tired I nodded off. I was glad of Anto's bike for the cycle back home to Margaret Place. It wasn't yet seven o'clock but people were scuttling into houses. Curfew must have been brought forward. As I rounded the corner into Brunswick Street I heard a stop press.

"Raid in West Cork. Seventeen Auxiliaries Dead."

Seventeen! A fear gripped my stomach. The balance sheet of war. That could only mean there would be more reprisals on ordinary people. I pedalled furiously up

Haddington Road. But some unease like a hum in the air made me pull up after I started down Bath Avenue. Our house in Margaret Place was just off the avenue – in a dead end.

I propped the bike against a building and crept cautiously towards the corner of our road where I hid behind a low half-built wall that skirted the corner building.

Brilliant white flares from Verey lights lit into the darkness. There was a sleek black car pulled up in the road. A dozen Tans poured out of the back of a Crossley Tender. Their shouts and catcalls echoed down the street.

They banged on our door first.

Soldiers shouted commands.

"Don't move!"

"Open up, missus!"

The back door of the car opened and, caught by a flare, there was the glint of a gold-tipped swagger stick. Then the gleaming boots and long legs of Captain Lees.

They were about to raid our house.

Chapter 6

On the Run
December 1920

"What's all this hullaballoo?"

My mother stood at the door with Josephine on her hip. I hunched behind the low wall and watched them through a small gap.

"We have orders to search your house!" a rough-looking Tan yelled in her face.

"I wish to speak to a superior officer."

Something about the firm way she spoke stopped the soldier in his tracks. Catching sight of Captain Lees, she addressed him. "My husband is an able seaman on a long voyage and I am of the Presbyterian faith. What is the nature of your business?"

"We have received a tip-off. Stand aside!" snarled the Tan.

A tip-off! Jameson must have told Lees.

But my mother held her ground.

"Where are your sons?" demanded Lees.

"One is at boarding school. The other is visiting his great-grandfather at the Rectory in Kingstown."

"Oh yeah?" said the Tan.

"My boys come from a respectable home. They hope to follow their cousin to Trinity College," my mother said, her voice quivering now. It was like she wanted them to think we were "the quality".

"Strange place to live for such a fine lady," said Lees with a sneer.

My mother looked him in the eye. "All the more reason for you not to smash up my few possessions. Where I come from, we don't judge people by what they own but what is in their hearts."

My mother held her ground in the doorway and Captain Lees moved closer in a way I didn't like.

"Perhaps we could be of use to one another," he said in a pretend-nice voice, all smarmy.

I clenched my fists in anger. The back of my eyes prickled as they do before tears.

"I will pray for you all and your mothers. I warrant they raised you to show respect, no matter what your orders."

The soldiers who were about to jostle her aside stopped in their tracks.

Captain Lees ordered them to back away from the house. "Consider it a warning. Next time we won't knock."

Under the lamplight I saw his ungloved hand, the snake

curling up his arm. Like Jameson in Nanny's shop! He put his hand on my mother's arm and leaned in close. I didn't hear what he said but my mother flinched and ran inside. She returned with the tattered old photo album. Under the light of the lamp Lees raked through it like a hungry savage. In a flash, I knew what he was after. That stupid letter with the stamp from India with the King's head upside down! The same one that Snaky Jameson was on about. That was now buried with the gun. He stopped cold at the page where I'd torn it out long ago, threw the album down in a rage and stormed off.

My blood ran cold. Surely two men couldn't have the same tattoo! But they looked so different. Sounded so opposite – one rough, one smooth. Different heights even. Or were they different? Dalton had warned that a policeman who was a master of disguise had come from the East. Could it be more than a coincidence that Lees wanted that stamp too for some reason? Maybe they were in the same gang and their mark was a tattoo. Perhaps the stamp was valuable after all. But at any rate it was well hidden with the gun.

I shrank into myself. I knew I should make a run for it but my legs wouldn't budge.

Like a bloodhound, Lees seemed to catch my scent. "Comb the area. Make a thorough search!" he bellowed.

Something trundled around the corner.

"*Oi, hands up, everyone!*" a soldier shouted out.

I was cornered. I was about to get up, hands raised, when an almighty clatter erupted. There was a fishy smell.

A slithery wet thing landed on my head, putting the fear of god in me. It was . . . a fish.

"Be japers, you told me to put me hands up! That's why me fish barrow took off by itself!" It was, of all people, Mother O'Brien. She must have nearly launched the old cart into space the way the fish had showered all over the road.

"Get that blinking cart out of here!" shouted Lees. A large gleaming piece of ray like a bony fan had landed on his shoulder and he took it off in disgust.

"I'm terrible sorry, sir. I'll be out of your hair in no time."

Some of the soldiers swore at her. Others laughed. They righted the barrow and turned it around. Mother O'Brien fussed around, putting the tarpaulin back over it. Then she tidied the little apron of check cloth that hung down beside the wheels to trick it out as a fish stall. She picked up scaly fish and put them back in their baskets. She glanced though the gap in the wall and arched her head towards the barrow. As the soldiers thundered on our neighbour's door, I slid under the apron that hung down either side of the big red wheels. Just in time! I heard the crunch of a soldier's boot alongside the wall.

"Nothing here, sir!" he shouted.

"Would you like a fish? I have some lovely fresh cockles," said Mrs. O'Brien.

"Clear off," said the gruff soldier. The sound of his boots receded as he went back to his troop.

She trundled away with me concealed under the cart, scuttling under it like a dog.

We turned into Bath Avenue and when we reached the place where I'd left my bicycle I hissed at her to stop.

She lifted the tarpaulin. "Schooch!" was all she said.

There was no time to waste. As I pedalled the bicycle like fury, all I could think was Lees, Jameson. Jameson, Lees. Two sides of the same coin.

Chapter 7

A Visit to the Doctor

The short ride to Molly's lodgings in Rathmines was the longest of my life, sweating to reach her before curfew. I was scared to the pit of my innards, like a cow going to slaughter, yet relieved I hadn't had to face the Tans. Deep in my heart there was another feeling that was new to me. Shame. Shame at how we looked to the outside world. Not "a cut above" as Mother O'Brien called us. But poor people, all the more pathetic for pretending to ourselves that we were better than everyone else.

I faltered on Anto's borrowed bicycle. I wanted to go and get the gun and shoot Lees dead. But then the memory of my mother standing up to those thugs came back to me. She had only her words for weapons. If I shot a man dead she would feel worse than if someone killed me. This I knew deep in my heart. Dishonour, like they said in the comics, would be the real shame. Besides, I didn't have the courage. I hated that gun, its cold metal. My stomach gripped into a knot and I wanted to cry.

As I reached the house where Molly was staying in Rathmines, I almost collapsed off the bicycle. It was a respectable house with a small front garden and I felt out of place just as I had at de Valera's. My heart pounded as I raised the brass knocker.

I almost fell into the arms of her flat-mate, a newly qualified doctor called Dorothy.

"I saw you coming down the street, but I thought you were going to take flight, you were pedalling so fast!" She spoke with a posh English accent but her voice was warm and friendly, not all slithery like Lees.

She led me straight into the kitchen in the basement and gave me a warm mug of sweet tea.

"We better get you cleaned up," she said, peering at me through her glasses as she left the room. "You do smell!"

I'd only taken a sip when Molly strode in. I blurted out the truth. She was so angry I thought her red hair was going to shoot into flames like some Greek goddess from a myth.

Fool. Big-eared moron. Eejit. Halfwit. These were just some of the kinder names she shouted at me. She banged the table so hard that Doctor Dorothy ran in.

"Shush, Molly. He's just a boy. You'll bring the Tans here if you don't calm down."

Molly flushed red and paced around the room. The silence was more dreadful than her stormy rage. As I thought of poor Josephine whimpering in my mother's arms, the tears spilled out of my eyes.

This broke Molly's cyclone. She rushed to me and hugged me tight. "Hush, Dan, there now. We'll sort it out. Just like we did in the Rising. I'll sleep on it and we'll talk about it in the morning." Wrinkling her nose, she pushed me away. "You stink of fish!"

Doctor Dorothy filled a bath for me and gave me a bar of soap with the scent of lemons. It was just as well it had a sharp smell as I kept nodding off to sleep and sliding down the bath. It wasn't long before I was curled up like a baby in a cosy settle-bed in the attic.

Next morning Molly handed me a letter. It was addressed to "Mr. Field", Collins' code name. "You can join us at three o'clock. My tutor, Dr. Oliver St. John Gogarty's house, 15 Ely Place, just off Stephen's Green," she said crisply.

"But I don't even know where to find Collins. He's the Scarlet Pimpernel. Never in one place twice. "

"Start with your friend MacBride at Noyk's Solicitors. You'll find out if he really is a big shot."

"But it's Collins, Molly! In broad daylight. He's a wanted man!"

She sighed like I was a fool and said her tutor's house was a safe house. She explained that there was a narrow, hidden passage leading to the back garden of the house. It was between two buildings in a terrace facing onto the Green. "If anyone stops you, say you are lost and delivering a letter to another house. Or pretend to be a halfwit. You won't even have to let on!" She told me I'd have to scale a wall and drop onto an oil drum by a large ash tree.

"Will the doctor know we'll all be dropping in?"

She laughed. "He likes a bit of excitement, does Dr. St. John Gogarty. He's a famous wit and writes poetry too. He was one of the founders of Sinn Féin and at first didn't support violence. Then the Tans nearly killed his little daughter Brenda in Stephen's Green and he's helped the movement since. He's great friends with Collins."

I left immediately to go to Noyk's on College Green to see if they could get a message to Collins. It was so early there were only a few milkmen rattling their churns on the street.

As I got close to the office, I could contain my curiosity no more and huddled in a doorway to peek inside the envelope.

Jiggling it about without taking it out, I read a few lines: *"It is vital that you meet with us . . . important information . . . Jack the Cat . . . and my cousin might be in danger . . . I will repay the favour . . . your old friend, Molly."*

Molly had a bit of pull with them as she'd spent a lot of time in the GPO in Easter Week. She was only twelve at the time. The age I am now. I felt a bit funny. I was annoyed she was interfering in my important work for Ireland. But a little part of me was relieved she was asking Collins to look after me and protect the family.

There were only a couple of clerks in the office and they

told me Noyk and MacBride were at court. The younger fellow left to take the note to them to pass on to the Big Fellow. The elderly clerk gave me a load of filing to do, which I was glad of. It took my mind off all the troubles and meant I was able to lie low.

I left myself with plenty of time to get to Ely Place through the secret route. I couldn't find it at first. But then I noticed the narrow gate between the Board of Works and the neighbouring house.

I opened the gate and crept down the passage. I saw the large ash tree swaying in the breeze. I scaled the back wall of the garden. Then I dropped onto the oil drum.

The first thing I saw in the long grass was a football – beautiful leather with stitching – and a goal with a net at the other side of the garden. I couldn't resist practising my left corner shot. I pictured the net as a grid and aimed at the corner, pretending I was lobbing a bomb at Captain Lees. I was raising my arms in victory celebration when a doctor in a white coat shot out the back door and kicked the ball out of the goalmouth.

"But risen from the grave it's that old Bohemian, Dr. Oliver St. John Gogarty!" he exclaimed. "Can he take on the Young Pretender?"

I tackled him and he gave me no quarter. For an older fellow he was light on his feet. But I feinted, pretending to go one way while swerving round him, and left him for dust.

"The youth of Ireland take liberties with their elders –

the likes was never seen in the days of St Patrick. Did you know that Bohemians' sacred grounds in Dalymount Park used to be known as Pisser Dignam's Field? It was where the farmers relieved themselves on their way back to the country from market." He spoke in a loud confident voice. "I also played for Preston Reserves while a student at Oxford. A game of poetry and beauty is soccer. And you are a veritable poet of the ball. "

"Some of them think it's a garrison game."

"*Gah!* What do you think, young lad?"

I shrugged. "A ball is a ball. There's no use in having a free Ireland if you can't play a simple game."

"So your brains aren't only in your feet, Danny Boy."

He led me to the kitchen and left me there while he dashed off to see a patient. At the big table was a serious little girl of about nine or ten. She was eating a piece of bread and butter while drawing a swan. It was a very good picture.

"I'm Brenda. Are you ill?" she asked me.

"I'm with my cousin Molly," I said.

Her face brightened. "Molly looked after me when the horrible Black and Tans scared me in the park," she said. "I won't go out now." She continued to fill in the feathers. "I would like to be an artist," she said.

"I saw a man killed at Stephen's Green during the Rising," I said.

She looked at me with rounded eyes.

"Did you get nightmares?"

I nodded. "Still do." I didn't want to lie to her.

Her lips trembled, on the verge of tears.

"But you get over it," I said. "It doesn't go away but you learn how to push it out of your mind."

"Did you . . . do the things babies do?"

I knew what she was asking me. Did I wet the bed?

"For a bit afterwards. But not any more."

"What did you do to forget?" she asked me, her eyes opening wide.

"I spend a lot of time kicking a ball," I grinned. "I got good at it and that makes me feel better."

A big smile broke over her face, like the sun bursting out of the clouds. "I'll get good at art!" she exclaimed.

We heard a flurry of footsteps and voices raised from upstairs. The two of us were dying of curiosity. So Brenda and I tiptoed from the warm kitchen and made our way up three flights of polished stairs to the top floor. We snorted, trying not to laugh, as a floorboard groaned like a toad being trod on.

On the top floor, the door was ajar and we sat on the top step earwigging.

"You sure are the Big Fella now. With your 'Twelve Apostles' and a price on your head." Molly sounded scornful but Collins laughed.

Brenda and I froze like two mice trying to avoid a cat.

"He is a brave boy. He helps support the family," Molly continued. "Remember the words of poor Francis Sheehy Skeffington. It is better for us to live for Ireland than to die for it."

"The British government has declared war on our people, Molly. We elected a government and they refused to recognise us. Even jailing our acting president Arthur Griffith."

"The people didn't vote for gunmen, Michael. But for a political party and peaceful resistance," said Molly evenly.

"The British Empire is afraid of coming apart and we are taking the war to them. We only eliminate crown officials, spies, legitimate targets," said Collins in a matter-of-fact voice.

"Yes, when they are out picking blackberries or seeing girls home after a night out. I know everyone thinks the Tans are scum but they are flesh and blood. Whipped up like rabid dogs to do a politician's bidding." Molly sounded passionate now.

"You are right there, Molly. Reprisals are an official policy of His Majesty's government."

"Where will it end, Michael? When we're all dead? They killed McCurtain, the Lord Mayor of Cork – you had the British commander who ordered the hit, shot with McCurtain's own gun. Now eight thousand people in Belfast have been burned out of their homes."

"The Irish should govern themselves. It's that simple," said Collins.

Molly was having none of it. "And when we have our new country. Then what? What if we can't agree among ourselves? Already they say you and de Valera are at each other's throats. How will you settle your argument then?"

"We'll worry about all that when we get freedom. I leave

the dreaming to others." Collins was pacing the room. "I have no taste for killing. I like the English. Didn't I live among them for many years? I give you my word, Molly, when we have a half decent chance for peace, I will take it."

"What about Dan? Will you keep him and his family out of harm's way?"

There was the sound of church bells. A nursemaid called Brenda's name and she scuttled down the stairs.

"Come in, Dan, I know you're outside," came Collins' voice.

I went in to face the music.

"Tell me about the strange fellows who you keep bumping into."

I told him how the rough sailor who was obsessed with his fortune bore the same tattoo as the sleek officer with the gold-tipped cane. Could they be in the same gang? Or be the same person? But I couldn't quite believe that – they were so opposite. Maybe Jameson told Lees about the stamp. I didn't tell Collins about the upside-down King George stamp rotting with the gun in Ringsend Park.

"I'll get our intelligence officers to keep an eye out," said Collins as Molly's eyes bored into him.

"What about my family? Will they be safe?" I asked.

"Your mother has family in Kingstown. She may go there," Collins said. It sounded like an order.

I was surprised he knew this, but then he seemed to know everything.

There was the sound of a telephone and footsteps on the

103

stairs. Addy his secretary ran in with a note and gave me a wink. He must have had his staff with him. He raked his hands through his thick head of conker-brown hair, something I'd seen him do before when he was worried.

"Michael, you better get going," Addy said, giving Molly a quick hug. She handed Collins a message.

He cast his eye over it and handed it back to her.

"Dan should make himself scarce for a bit," said Collins. "Molly, I need to ask you a favour. You will have to trust me. It's nothing to do with fighting. I need you both to go down the country. Walk out with me through the front door and I'll brief you. Dan, you cut back through the Green. The best place to hide is under the light!"

A white-faced Molly gave me the tram fare, telling me to meet her back at her digs. She left immediately with Collins. I wasn't sure she was best pleased but I was excited – a trip! They went down the stairs ahead of me. Collins asked Molly to teach First Aid to some of the Cumann na mBan girls and country fighters.

"You can attend to a few wounded volunteers if you don't mind. They don't trust doctors. But they'll trust you, Molly," he said.

Molly nodded her head gravely.

"I'll be sending your friend Dr. Dorothy Stopford on a similar journey soon. It's a straight-up mission of mercy."

There was no way Molly would refuse him. She looked up to Doctor Dorothy.

I would have to face my fears and cut through Stephen's

Green as ordered by the Big Fellow. I nipped back through the passageway and, seeing the coast was clear, ran across the road into the park. I hugged into a tree and looked all around. Collins, to my surprise, had also entered the park and was close behind. I melted into the bushes, not wanting him to think I was following him like a puppy.

Collins, light on his feet for such a big man, went into the bandstand in the centre. I tracked nearer. He stuck out his hand in greeting to someone who had entered from the opposite side. Then I saw that O'Reilly and another of Collins' men were sitting on a bench facing the bandstand. I crept closer and closer through the bushes.

Through a gap in the foliage, I saw a polished shoe and the tip of a gold-topped cane flash in the winter sun.

To my utter horror, our leader was meeting Captain Lees.

"So you reckon you can get us the dogs," Collins said. He spoke in normal tones.

'Dogs', I thought. That's what they called their guns.

"I will need funds," said Captain Lees.

There was a brief whispered discussion but I couldn't hear.

I was too confused to concentrate. Did Collins not listen to a word I said? Were Lees and Jameson our friends or foes?

I went back to Molly's digs in Rathmines and headed the ball that they had in the house five hundred times. Have you ever been in a hall of mirrors in a circus? That's what it felt like. First you look normal. But move closer and you distort, bigger or smaller, fatter or thinner. So you can't even trust your own reflection. All I could do was keep my head down and hold my nerve.

Chapter 8

Flying Columns in Tipperary
December 1920

I watched the countryside speed past through the rain-spattered window. Cows and sheep, trees and bushes turned into green blurs as we clattered along. This was the longest train journey I had ever taken. I checked the timetable as I was jolted in my seat.

We were on the premier line to Cork and were to disembark at Limerick Junction where someone would meet us. Molly sat opposite me reading a medical textbook. The title was *Delorme's War Surgery*. Every so often she lifted her head to scowl at me. I was still in her bad books, no matter which one she stuck her nose in.

Just before we left Rathmines, MacBride had turned up with some clothes for me. I fancy they were his hand-me-downs for he was a swell and wore only the latest fashions. Molly just took them drily, observing that such a fine fellow thought rather a lot of himself. But I was more than satisfied with my new "Right Posture" tweed suit and the Burberry raincoat. I was wearing long trousers for the first time! My legs were so happy!

He had taken me aside. "There's a few documents sewn into the lining of the jacket. One for the Tipperary commander Breen if you meet up. And one to be dropped at Cork Station if you get there too."

"Molly won't be best pleased," I said. But all I thought was that we might be going to Cork as well! It would be as good as a holiday.

"They're legal documents. But what she doesn't know won't hurt her." He gave me a wink.

MacBride had made the travel arrangements and to our delight we had first-class tickets. At first we thought it was a mistake but then Molly figured he came from rich people so he assumed that was how one should travel.

I spread out like a king sitting in our own carriage. The black-painted locomotive that pulled the train belched steam as it chugged along. Our carriage was the lap of luxury, with high leather seats facing each other and polished wooden edges. I felt like the quality.

"Did you know there are three thousand four hundred miles of track in Ireland and no town is more than ten miles from a railway station?" I tried to make conversation with Molly but she scowled back at me over her book.

Brother Carmichael at school was a steam-train enthusiast. His lessons made me yawn. But sitting in a

108

proper carriage it all came alive. I mentioned the refrigerated carriages transporting eggs from little farms all over Ireland. The others speeding fresh fish from the coast. I asked her if our train had come from the Inchicore Railway Works. It didn't work.

"Just be glad the train is running. There have been some stoppages with Irish railway workers refusing to carry troops," said Molly.

Lulled by the steady rhythm of the wheels, my eyes closed. But a sudden commotion outside wrenched me from my doze. There were shouts of "God save the King!" and "Come out, you godforsaken rebels!" Troops had boarded the train after all! I felt my insides go cold. What if they found me and the letters?

"Relax, Dan," Molly said. "They're drunk. They won't be searching for rebels in first class." She pulled down the blind and stuck her head in her textbook.

On the spur of the moment, I took the soccer ball out of my bag and just to annoy Molly blew it up under her disapproving nose. It was one of the ones made with an inflatable pig's bladder. Doctor Dorothy had given it to me. It had been her cousin's who died in the war and I think it made her happy to have someone make use of it. To calm my nerves, I rose and did a few knee-kicks. I got bolder and began to bounce it off the ceiling. Molly intercepted one bounce and elegantly headed the ball back to me.

We were friends again, playing header, when there was a sudden knock on the door. The guard entered with an old lady and a gentleman. He looked military and carried a large leather folder. I had to make a dramatic save to stop the ball from lamping them.

Molly was mortified. I was worried I'd get chucked off the train. But the guard fawned on Molly. He asked if the two passengers could join us to avoid what he called the rabble in the dining car. Molly nodded assent. He was too busy addressing the woman as "My Lady" to even notice me. He almost genuflected and scraped the ground as he put their bags and the large folder on the racks above our heads.

When he left, the elderly woman looked at me with a twinkling smile.

"I am sorry we nearly hit you," I muttered. "Are you a real lady?"

She put out her hand to shake mine. She had a sharp face but kind eyes and silver hair like spun sugar. "No need to apologise. I am indeed Lady Butler but my maiden and professional name is Elizabeth Thompson. I am a war artist. I have even painted soldiers playing with a football when they shouldn't at the Charge of Loos last year!"

Molly and I looked at her with astonishment.

"This is my son, who fought at Ypres." Her son nodded to us. "Patrick, be so kind as to take down my art folder."

She took out a painting of a group of soldiers painted in muddy browns, charging through a mist. They were so lifelike I thought they were heading straight at us. The main soldier in the picture had a rifle in his right hand, his left hand raised and on the inside of his right boot . . . a football!

"The London Irish had a first-class football team. They were keen to score a goal in the German front-line trenches," explained Lady Butler. "This is a print. The real painting is in their mess in Camberwell in London."

"Maybe they were thinking of the famous game during the ceasefire at Christmas Eve 1914. Both the Germans and the English came out of the trenches for a kick-about," said her son. He moved stiffly – perhaps he had been wounded in the war.

"That's Sergeant Edwards," Lady Butler pointed to the player. "When the whistle for the big push sounded they defied orders and booted the ball out of the trenches with a cry of 'On the ball, London Irish!'"

I gazed at the picture. "He wants to pass and is signalling for a comrade to take the ball," I said. "Maybe he senses danger and wants to keep the ball in play."

"Spoken like a real footballer!" said Lady Butler, her eyes shining.

"What happened to him?" I asked.

"Edwards dribbled the ball for twenty yards before he went down injured. Shot through the thigh. His friend stopped to fix a tourniquet to the wound and saved his life." She looked over at my cousin and glanced at her textbook. "You look like you would know all about that, young lass."

"I am a medical student at Trinity College, your ladyship," Molly replied.

"Just like my young self, a woman prepared to make it in a man's world. And you will!"

Molly beamed.

"What happened to the ball?" I asked.

"It was pierced on barbed wire on the German front line. They took it back to the Sergeant's Mess in Camberwell in London."

We gazed at the picture in silent admiration.

"There were over a hundred thousand casualties at Loos," said Patrick. "For what! The battle was a disaster."

"War is hell," said Lady Butler. "There's no glory. Only the heroism of ordinary soldiers. That's what I paint. Imagine them doing something so brave in the face of death."

"When I am frightened, I often kick about with my ball," I said.

"These are men with no taste for killing," Molly said.

"They wanted to face death doing something they loved – as a team," said Lady Butler, smiling at me.

"Now the whole of Ireland is a battlefield. Tipperary is a dangerous area," said Patrick Butler, lowering his voice. "We are trying to persuade Mother to live with my sister at Gormanston Castle in Meath. But she is having none of it!"

"My husband General Butler was a famous soldier. But he got into trouble because he sympathised with the Boer rebels in South Africa against imperial power." Lady Butler packed away the picture. "We are Catholics and my husband deplored how the British treat the Irish. He hated war, in fact, as soldiers often do. But I am staying for the soft light of Tipperary!"

"Stop changing the subject, Mother! I spoke to a police officer in Dublin who was at Croke Park on Bloody Sunday. He said it was the most disgraceful show of lawlessness by the Black and Tans he had ever seen. It's getting worse."

I felt clammy at the mention of Croke Park and a sudden jolt of the train made me gag.

"Quick, open the window," Lady Butler said.

I took some deep breaths of fresh air and managed not to vomit. Molly mopped my brow with her handkerchief. Mr. Butler gave me water from his flask.

"My cousin and I were at Croke Park that day," said Molly in a low voice.

Lady Butler held my hand.

"What happened to the footballers at Loos?" I asked when I felt a little better.

"Maybe the game saved them. All those in my picture survived," she said. "Private Edwards is making a good recovery. He has joined the Military Police, I believe. Heart of a lion that boy has!"

"Maybe countries should just face each other on the sports field and not the battlefield!" I burst out.

Lady Butler clapped her hands and the others nodded in agreement.

The train, shuddering to a stop, threw us out of our seats with such force we all collided. We laughed, changing our mood to a happy one.

"I pray we meet our earthly destination before our final one," said Lady Butler.

We were at Limerick Junction, our stop. Our new friends were travelling on to Tipperary town.

We waved them a fond goodbye from the platform. I longed to head the ball to stop me thinking about how knotted up everything was, like a big messy ball of wool. But I forced myself to untangle my thoughts. Lady Butler was British but she wasn't my enemy. She was a Catholic married to a general and she had painted for Queen Victoria. She painted British soldiers being brave but hated war. Molly was right about me looking up to Michael Collins. But what he said wasn't true either. It wasn't just a simple matter of having a job to do to free the country. Bullets could hit the wrong people. And why was he talking to devils like Captain Lees who scared me more than anyone?

Perhaps because I was thinking of that horrible man I started having a waking dream. The train pulled out, the last carriage shrouded in smoke. But I could have sworn I saw a man with a narrow moustache, leaning over the back rail, miming shooting at me with a gold-tipped cane. I rubbed my eyes and when I looked again the train was gone.

It was early afternoon when we were met by a gap-toothed old fellow with a pony and trap. His name was Mickey Joe and he hunched his shoulders like a heron. He crooned some old rebel song as we trotted along the country roads. It was chilly and bleak in the danger zone of Tipperary. I imagined Dan Breen and his flying column round every bush.

"Do you know Dan Breen?" I whispered to Mickey Joe when we hit a broad stretch of road.

"Sure didn't I meet him the morning of the very first ambush at Solaheadbeg last year – two RIC constables were killed," he said through his gappy teeth. "'Twas the very day the Sinn Féin parliament met up. He got away clean that time. But he's taken quite a few bullets in other shootouts. And left more Tans and Auxies dead. He's a legend!"

I was half terrified and half excited that I might meet this outlaw round the next bend. Or that he might shoot us by mistake!

I asked Mickey Joe if he knew Ryan, the Tipperary player from Croke Park who'd gone on the run, but he shook his head. "It's hard to keep track of them all."

We plodded through lush green fields, aside a dark ridge that thrust from the landscape. The Galtee Mountains, Mickey Joe said.

We headed into the gloom of the dense wooded slopes. Trees took on twisted shapes in the dusky light. The wind in their bare branches was the high scared cry of ghosts or the banshee. A trailing branch brushed against me as we took a corner and I near jumped out of my skin. Molly too was nervous and we huddled together under the rough blanket, our knees knocking and our teeth chattering.

On and on we plodded through many miles of rough roads and twisted boreens that doubled back on themselves. At last at nightfall we came to a flat valley nestled in the foothills. A dim light in an isolated farmhouse among fields was like a lighthouse beam. A smell of fresh air, hay and milk.

The farmhouse was like a fortress, surrounded by mountain on three sides.

As we passed a barn, there was a strange horrible moaning sound.

"The Banshee!" I cried out.

Mickey Joe laughed through his crooked tombstone teeth. "Gosoon, have ye never heard cattle lowing in a barn?"

Ahead of us was a large whitewashed farmhouse. Further away several old barns and outhouses loomed in the darkening night. Mickey Joe explained they were a threshing barn for hay, a stable and a broken-down old barn used for storage.

The woman of the house appeared at the door. "Come in, and it's welcome you are surely," she said in a friendly voice, wiping her floury hands on her apron. Mrs. Prendergast had a mass of salt-and-pepper curly hair pushed into an untidy bun, crinkly eyes and a big smile. She showed us straight into the large kitchen and sent the old man to carry our bags into our rooms.

We sat at a worn wooden table in the cosy kitchen warmed by a roaring fire. There was a dresser filled with crockery, with a picture of the Sacred Heart and a calendar from the local creamery on the wall. The air filled with the smell of freshly baked bread as she took several loaves of soda bread out of the big old blackened range. She broke one of the steaming loaves into four sections then cut them into thick slices and placed them with a dish of yellow butter and two knives on the table. Then she poured us two glasses of fresh milk from an enamel jug with a thin blue rim that was chipped here and there to black. The butter melted straight into the soft bread and the milk was frothy and sweet. It was the best bread I'd ever tasted.

She enquired after our journey and told us they'd all be arriving after sundown for the First Aid lesson.

"I'll just fetch my kitbag," said Molly, "and we'll be ready."

"There might be a few need a bandage or two," Mrs Prendergast said.

She gave each of us an oil lamp. A tall lanky farmhand, a young fellow a few years older than me, called Paudy, joined us. We set out across the field to the large storage barn. Our lamps guided our flickering procession across a rough path, creating large shadows.

"Scared, are you, young jackeen?" Paudy said to me. He put the lantern under his face and loomed in at me, looking like a ghost on Halloween.

"Whist, Paudy! He's just a lad," said Mrs. Prendergast.

"This is a man's game," he said, swaggering.

I wanted to tell him that Collins trusted me to smuggle secret documents but I bit my tongue.

The outside of the barn looked patched and almost derelict. Inside it was clean enough with several broken carts in various stages of repair. But there was a strong whiff of hay and feathers.

Paudy pretended to attack me with a dangerous-looking metal contraption with teeth. I reared back.

"It's only a plough and harrow for digging up clods of earth, you amadán!" he said.

Mrs. Prendergast told him to stop. He rolled his eyes behind her back.

"You city skelps would have nothing to eat without our dairy and wheat and potatoes," he boasted. "We do have the threshing machine for threshing days."

"Aren't you great," I said, sarcastic.

He picked up a scythe, a curved blade on a pole, and loured over me like the Grim Reaper.

"Be careful in bed tonight," he taunted. "*Ahoooo!*"

I clenched my fists and thought about that gun in Ringsend Park. That would shut him up.

Mrs. Prendergast pulled out a small wooden table and bade Molly to put her doctor's bag on it. There were also a few hay bales and little wooden milking stools along the walls. She placed the oil lamps in aluminium basins, explaining she didn't want to run the risk of knocking them over.

The lamps created an eerie atmosphere. Within seconds ghostly shapes rose from the four corners of the room. I thought I was at Hell's Gateway. But as the shapes sat on

118

the hale bales I realised my error.

These were men – most in their twenties but some not much older than me. They were unshaven and one or two had boots hanging off them, like tramps. I was looking at the "invisible army' – the foot soldiers of the Irish Republic – the most wanted men in the British Empire. They stank like drains.

A massive ghoul rose towards me. I shrank back. A booming voice rang out as he clapped me on the back. "If it isn't my young comrade from Bloody Sunday!"

It was Thomas Ryan, who I'd lost sight of in the dung heap! My fear melted away. He explained that he'd been on the run since I'd last seen him. He certainly smelled like he'd been sleeping in a ditch.

I asked him in a low voice if he'd dropped his gun back in Dublin when hiding in the dung heap.

"No," he said, "and I've got what I need here."

He raised his hand from his side and I saw he was carrying a rifle.

Mrs. Prendergast coughed and introduced Molly who was standing at the desk.

"Molly is here to lecture you on First Aid," she said.

The tired and pale men gazed at her with open curiosity.

"What's a biteen of a girl going to show us? We don't need to learn sewing," a big fellow remarked.

Molly glared at him. "You might be glad of it to sew up your gaping wounds. But the first thing is how to stop you bleeding to death in the first place."

The big brawny fellow stood up and ripped off his coat. He pulled up his filthy shirtsleeves and displayed gigantic biceps.

"Can you stop the blood flowing through that? I bet you a shilling you can't."

She gave him a tight smile. "Why, you're a perfect dummy to demonstrate on – what's your name, sir?"

"Mossie," he said.

"Someone give me a belt," said Molly.

Ryan took the belt off his Macintosh and she instructed him to feel his comrade's pulse on his wrist.

"Leppin' like a hare," he said.

Molly tied the belt extra tight above Mossie's elbow, the muscles standing out like boulders. He winced but winked at the assembled volunteers.

"This here is the brachial artery." She pointed out a large raised vein like a gnarly branch.

Molly placed a pencil on the knot and tied a loop of the belt over it. She twisted the pencil several times. Mossie's face went red. He gritted his teeth.

"There's no pulse," Ryan cried out. "Bedad, she's stopped the blood flowin' all right!"

Mossie cried out. "I can't feel me arm!"

There were a few guffaws.

Molly suppressed a smirk as she released the pencil and Mossie banged his arm to get the blood flowing again.

"Anyone else like to be a guinea pig?" she said, sweet as sugar.

None of them came forward.

"You may only be a slip of a girl, but you're good enough to be a doctoreen!" one of them said from the shadows.

"I'm still only a student," Molly said as they all clapped and whistled.

Molly showed them some simple dressings and talked about the use of alcohol in wound-cleaning. But about halfway through her lecture, it was clear most of the men were too busy scratching themselves to pay much attention. The room stank like a pigsty. Molly wrinkled her nose.

Thomas excused himself to check on the lookout.

"When is the last time any of you washed?" Molly asked in the middle of showing them how to make a sling.

They all looked down, shamefaced.

"Two weeks. It's hard when you're on the run," one of them mumbled. "We're all driven half mad with the Volunteer itch. The only thing we can do is take off all our clothes and shake the lice out of them."

She examined their hands that were covered with little red pinpricks.

"You're riddled with scabies. You all need a good scrub! And treatment with sulphur powder."

"'Tis worse than the Tans and the Auxies put together!" one of them exclaimed.

"Forget about the powder nonsense – what we need is a plentiful supply of home-made wheaten bread," came a deep sonorous voice from the back.

"Dan Breen!" one of the fellows called out. "If it isn't the second most wanted man in Ireland!"

All the Volunteers stood up and threw their caps in the air, welcoming the new arrival with shouts, whistles and catcalls.

"Pipe down," called out Mrs. Prendergast, "or you'll bring the Tans!"

Dan Breen strode in and plonked himself down on Molly's table. She tapped him on the shoulder but he ignored her, taking out a wanted poster and putting it up beside his face.

"Is that what I look like? A sulky bulldog?" His comrades roared with laughter as he read from the poster. "'*Wears his cap down low on his head and looks like a blacksmith coming home from work.*'" He pulled his cap down low on his forehead and capered about, causing them to double over with hilarity.

Molly waited for the laughter to subside. "I'd like to continue my instruction with some advice about cleaning a bullet wound."

"What would you know about that?" said Breen. "Do you know how many times I've been plugged?"

"Is it four, Dan?" Mossie spoke up.

"Let me see. Once at Knocklyon rescuing Hogan from the train. We got two RIC men then. Another time in Dublin attacking Lord French. We didn't get the Lord Lieutenant but rubbed out one of his bodyguards. Got a few wounds meself, and took me three months to recover from that. Then a couple of bullets at the Fernside shootout. The man of the house was shot dead by the cursed Tans."

The assembled volunteers regarded him with awe.

"I was in Dublin in 1916," Molly said. "I saw many people who lost their lives. It's not something to be spoken lightly of."

I marvelled at Molly's courage in speaking up.

Breen smiled in a way that sent a shiver up my spine. "If anyone comes into my house or my country I'm going to get rid of him, and I'll use any means to do it. I'm not one bit sorry about taking out the enemy. I'll face my Maker with a clear conscience."

"Hear, hear!" someone shouted and there was a round of cheering.

"We need to shake things up a bit around here, get a proper Flying Column going. Not just bits of raids like you've been doing. Anyone want to join me?"

A forest of hands shot up. Volunteers shook their firearms and hollered assent.

I sat on my hands.

Molly's hands trembled as she packed away her First Aid kit. Dan Breen annoyed me for being such a show-off. So I helped Molly put away the bandages and slings.

"Glad to see we're all real men here," said Breen. He scowled over at me. "Not yellow jackeens tied to women's apron strings."

As the men cheered, Mrs. Prendergast drew us away to return to the farmhouse. I glanced back and saw Breen take out his revolver to clean it. Now was my chance. I went towards him, the letter from MacBride concealed in my hankie. During Molly's talk, I'd worked it out of the lining of my new raincoat.

"Use this," I said.

He took the hankie and felt the letter. His expression changed.

"Not tied to the apron strings after all," he said with a smirk.

"They're just excitable boys at the back of it," Mrs. Prendergast said as she led us back across the yard.

"That's exactly the problem." Molly shook her head. "Easter Week 1916 wasn't the glorious sacrifice that everyone is inventing now. Lots of innocents got caught in the crossfire."

Mrs. Prendergast looked at her with respect. "It's different here in the country. The Tans and the Auxies get away with more. There aren't any newspaper men or witnesses even."

"Nothing seems to stop them these days," said Molly.

I was squashed into a tiny settle bed in a teeny attic room. But at least I wasn't sleeping with the itchy Volunteers. As I lay in the dark I started to think about all they were giving up and I felt like a coward. Breen impressed me even if he scared me. He was on a wanted poster and all. I thought about all the bullets that had riddled his body. Was I brave like that? I couldn't even hold a gun for long. Maybe I wasn't a proper man.

I couldn't sleep. I lit the candle and saw there were a few books on the shelf. I picked one at random and opened it on a poem by John Masefield, "Sea Fever". I knew the name. He was a friend of my father's. They had both trained as merchant navy men on the *HMS Conway* in Liverpool.

"I must go down to the seas again, to the lonely sea
and the sky,
And all I ask is a tall ship and a star to steer her by."

My father had sailed from the Cape of Good Hope in Africa to the Bering Strait of Russia. How I missed him! He would know what to advise. He did not approve of fighting, that I knew. He had grown up in India – a "child of the Empire" he called himself. He loved the sea with the fever described by the poet. Not for him a quiet life behind a desk or tied to the earth. I did not share his passion. The few times he'd taken me out on boats I got sick as a dog. But he never made judgment, just laughed and mussed my hair and told me to keep heading the ball. Now he was lost somewhere in the vast ocean. I prayed he was alive, maybe drinking from a coconut on a South Sea Island or watching colourful shoals of rainbow fish. I pictured him like this and fell asleep.

A hand shook me in my dream.

"Dan, whisht!"

It was my tormenter, Paudy.

"There's a job on. Do you want to come and be a lookout?"

I didn't want them to think I was a "yellow jackeen". I jumped out of bed.

"I can't go. Me leg's lame." Then the cheeky beggar got into the warm bed I'd just left! I ached to say something to him about it being a "man's game" but kept quiet. He was just like that fellow Pus-Face that got me mixed up in it all in the first place.

In the kitchen, I grabbed a piece of bread and butter and downed a mug of cold tea. There was no sign of Molly. My heart thumped against my chest like a startled bird in a cage. I didn't know if I was more excited or afraid. I was going on an ambush and would see a Flying Column in action.

Chapter 9

The Ambush

A caterpillar of ten lads crept through the open countryside from gorse bush to hedge to ditch, Dan Breen, my friend Thomas Ryan and big Mossie among us. It was pitch black. Our breaths froze in the air. We were ordered not to make a sound. We hadn't gone far when we halted at a thicket of trees.

Breen called us and we huddled together in the pale moonlight.

"Another group of Volunteers has been out destroying the bridges on the main road. That's to force a convoy of enemy troops onto these by-roads. Our mission is to attack just up ahead."

I could see the excitement and fear in the other members of the column.

Breen asked Ryan to brief us on our position. He told us

we were midway between Cahir and Clogheen, which were garrison towns full of British soldiers. We were heading on a by-road to a crossroads.

We reached the crossroads, a bleak no-man's land in the middle of nowhere with stone walls and high hedges.

Breen signalled for us to stop so he could brief us again.

"Mossie, stay here and be lookout so we know when the other posse has forced them off the main road. When you see our target coming onto the by-roads, give a loud whistle. Then run up to join us. Me and the rest of the column will be waiting at the next bridge to attack the convoy."

Breen was sharp and direct. A leader.

We scrambled through gorse for a quarter of a mile to lie in wait for the convoy at the next bridge. I felt scared. The cold sliced us in two.

Breen issued more orders as we huddled under the bridge near a wood.

"Ryan, go ahead to figure out our escape route," he ordered. "Dan, you stick with him in case we get separated. You can be a messenger."

I was only too happy to stick with Ryan on a scouting mission. I preferred the risk of being fired at in open countryside to ambushing British soldiers armed to the teeth. I cursed Paudy and his mor-yah gammy leg.

There was a rustle nearby. Breen cocked his gun.

"Don't shoot!" It was one of our own who had run to intercept us. "The military are coming! But they're not in a convoy – they're spread out in small groups combing the countryside! They're on horseback and there's a cycling corps in the rear."

Breen cursed. "They must know I'm in the area. They want my scalp!"

"We can't win if it's hand-to-hand combat," said Ryan. "We'll all be destroyed."

"Get us to safety and we'll decide our next move," commanded Breen.

Ryan acted fast. He cut out through the woods and led us through a gorse-field. The branches clasped us like witches' hands and the thorns caught us like claws. But we moved fast with the fright of encountering the enemy. We went down a boreen bordered by a high hedge. Then crossed a river called the Thonogue. We were now in a high wood in the foothills of the mountains, breathless and afraid.

"There's a concealed cave opening just at that cliff – you'll be safe there," said Ryan to Breen.

"Where's our lookout Mossie?" asked Breen.

They counted the men. They'd forgotten about Mossie.

"Ryan, you and the boy better go back and find him," said Breen. "The troops will have moved on by now but it's too dangerous for us to move around as dawn will be breaking soon."

Ryan explained to Breen that I was only filling in for Paudy who'd hurt his ankle.

"When you find Mossie, he and the boy can go back to the farmhouse, get supplies and wait further orders," pronounced Breen. "You can come back here and we'll regroup."

Ryan and I inched back the way we had come. Ryan had his rifle loaded and at the ready, halting to listen every fifty yards. When we reached the crossroads where we'd left Mossie, I saw a movement behind a low stone wall and tugged Ryan's arm. A head was bobbing up from the wall.

"Halt! Throw out your weapon, raise your hands and come towards us or I'll shoot!" shouted Ryan.

There was no response. He repeated the challenge.

"Halt, are you friend or foe?"

The head rose up for the third time but whoever it was didn't surrender his weapon.

Ryan opened fire.

The noise was terrible as the bullets clanged against the cold stone. The recoil of his weapon threw Ryan back. He fired twice more. Again no response. We waited. The sound echoed for miles. I was scared the army would come find us but I climbed up on a rock to get a view over the wall.

"I don't think there's anybody there!" I hissed at Ryan. "He must have fled. What will we do?"

"That's the first time I've ever fired a gun in combat," he said. He looked badly shaken and regarded his rifle in wonder. "The farmhouse is only a quarter of a mile from here. Just follow the boreen there. It goes up by a quarry and there's a cut up to the farm. Tell Mrs. Prendergast to sort out some food."

"Where's Mossie?" I asked.

"He might have been captured, or made his own way back to the farmhouse," said Ryan.

He sped off immediately. With heavy heart and legs, I followed the boreen. The cold dawn light was breaking through the grey clouds now.

Now I was in the quarry, gravel crackling under my feet. I couldn't think of a more desolate spot on earth. Beneath the crunch of the stones, I heard a low moaning sound. I crept closer, sure it was an animal.

At the bottom of a gravel pit, about five foot down, lay Mossie, cut up and bleeding.

I bent down. "Are you shot?"

"I don't think so, but I'm cut to bits by the gravel and the brambles. I ran like the clappers through the bushes when the shooting started."

It had been Mossie's head behind the wall!

"Why didn't you show yourself?"

"I thought you were the other side," he moaned.

The sides of the gravel pit were steep. If I tried to haul him up I might end up in it myself. So I searched round and found a rope. I tied it around my waist. Then I threw it around a tree so I could lever him up. I threw him the other end of the rope.

"Come on, Mossie, use your brawn to haul yourself up," I urged.

With much grunting he pulled himself up on the rope and out of the hole.

Then, with his bulk leaning on me, we stumbled through

131

the cut back to the farmhouse. He'd injured both his hands and fallen on his leg so had to limp along. His clothes were badly torn and blood seeped through the rips.

As we got to the outer buildings, a pale yellow sun was struggling to rise. All the energy went out of Mossie so I left him in the barn where we'd gathered but a few hours before.

I ran into the kitchen, almost knocking over Molly who was pacing the floor like a caged tiger. I told her what had happened as Mrs. Prendergast joined us.

"Keep him in the barn. There's a hidden dugout under it," Mrs. Prendergast instructed. "There's an entrance to the dugout under the hay bales by the left barn wall. The military might search the surrounding areas if they heard the shots."

In the barn, Molly cleaned and dressed Mossie's wounds. "You need to rest up for a while," she told him. "No flying columns for you."

"Thank you, doctoreen." Mossie sounded like a little boy, pale and worn out.

I pushed back a big bale of hay by the barn wall. Under a pile of straw and dirt there was a small trapdoor concealed under matting. I raised it and a drop-down ladder led to a wooden chamber taller than a man, with room for ten rough beds. There was another trapdoor at the far end leading up to the yard as an escape route. There were loads of boreholes to let the air in. I lit one of the candles with the matches that were scattered all about.

No sooner had we settled Mossie in the dugout than we heard raised voices in the yard.

I crept up the ladder and heard Mrs. Prendergast shouting, "Both my sons were killed in the Great War! One in Passchendaele and one in Flanders! Sure look anywhere in the farm!"

The sound of rushing feet.

"Would you like some tea?" Mrs Prendergast sounded desperate.

"Men, search the house first," I heard a posh English voice command.

I gasped in terror. I clambered back into the dugout, extinguished the candle and pulled the door down. We stayed in the dark, trying not to breathe too loud, straining our ears. Mossie lapsed into a sleep, and moaned once or twice softly.

After what seemed like hours, Molly wanted to see what was happening but Mossie held her arm in fright. I was scared stiff, fearing that Mrs. Prendergast, Paudy and old Mickey Joe would be dead. But I forced myself to investigate.

As I peeked out the barn door, a convoy of troops in an armoured car went off down the boreen. I breathed a sigh of relief.

I crept closer to the farmhouse. At the woodshed I hunkered down among the logs. I was right to be cautious. Through the half-door, I saw an officer with three other Auxies and Mrs. Prendergast.

"Apologies for the damages. Troops get a bit frustrated with the Irish. Don't know friend from foe," he drawled.

I saw his white glove on the door. My blood went cold. Captain Lees!

"Next time I may not be able to restrain them. If you see the girl or boy, send word to the barracks. As for the other outlaws, Breen and Ryan, it's only a matter of time before there's a noose around their necks." He laughed as he went out the door and jumped into the waiting car with the other Auxies.

I watched as the car sped down the lane and waited until it disappeared.

Mrs. Prendergast was in the kitchen. She threw her arms around me and sobbed.

"Thank God you're safe! And the others?"

I told her Molly and Mossie were in the dugout. The others were hiding in a cave.

"That officer thinks I'm a loyalist on account of my poor dead boys," she said. "The cursed Tans wrecked the house but didn't find a thing. I'll get word to our lads to come back here tonight, as this will be the safest house in Ireland. They won't search it two days in a row."

In the sitting room her grandfather clock lay smashed on the rug. The sofa was slashed to bits, its stuffing bursting out. In the kitchen all her good china from the dresser lay in smithereens on the flagstones and the milk churns were emptied all over the floor.

"Your house!" I said.

"'Tis only things. Thank God they didn't search the cart. It's full of ammunition Mickey Joe brought from the station just now, hidden in egg boxes."

I looked out to the yard and saw him unloading the cart. He raised his cap and gave me a salute. Another person I'd underestimated. They could have thrown him in prison or worse if caught smuggling arms.

"Mickey Joe will take you to the station."

He came in with a newspaper. It was a few days old, dated the 28th of November.

The headline read: STORY OF KILMICHAEL AMBUSH.

It was a report on the Cork raid I'd heard the stop press about, just before I'd run into Lees at my house. The attack was in a place near Macroom. Seventeen auxiliaries were dead. Ambushed by a flying column led by Tom Barry. There was going to be another crackdown.

Mrs. Prendergast looked at the paper. "All hell will be let loose now! Tom Barry trained with the British Army. That boy won't take any prisoners for sure."

Molly looked distraught. "It's going to get bad in Cork."

"We can't stay here if Captain Lees is on our trail," I said.

Mickey Joe came back. He handed her a letter sent by train.

Molly read it in a flash. "It's from Dorothy. God knows how she got this to me. The military police raided the house, so she can't leave Dublin. But they need medical help in Cork. I am to deliver the First Aid supplies to Cork Railway Station, leaving them at the guard's office. "

As we clambered into the cart, Paudy shot out, no sign of his lame leg. He looked at me shamefaced and handed me a package.

"I heard you were there on Bloody Sunday. So was my uncle and he picked this up as he ran out. He gave it to me. But you deserve it more."

I peeked inside the paper. It was a battered, laced GAA ball, the last thing touched by Hogan before he died on the pitch.

Chapter 10

Escape to Cork

At Limerick Junction, the Cork train was already on the platform. Mickey Joe ushered us to the guardroom and introduced us to Joseph, the train conductor, who was to look after us. He was a large, baldheaded man from Northern Ireland with a strong handshake. We helped load the supplies on board.

Then Mickey Joe came back with a load of new luggage for us to add to our own. We now had a few extra bags, a couple of medium-sized wooden grocery boxes marked "Provisions" and of all things a violin case.

I put the GAA ball in with our luggage. I didn't want to hold it yet. It just brought back all the fears of that day. It was ghoulish even, the last thing handled by Hogan before he took a bullet. I half expected blood to pour out of it.

Molly turned to me and held me by the shoulders.

"I think it's best we go to Cork," she said. "It might be the frying pan into the fire but we'll be away from Captain Lees."

I wasn't as surprised as she was about Cork. She didn't know about the documents given to me by MacBride.

I looked at the train to take my mind off it all. The locomotive steam engine was a dark grey, almost black. Passenger carriages were a deep purple with crests on the lower panels. At the back were grey wagons for goods. Joseph checked the underside of the carriage of the guard's van. He pulled out a leather tube. Inside it was a rolled-up letter.

"So that's how we got the message from Dorothy," Molly said.

He chuckled. "Ach, we're as good as the Post Office."

He told us to travel with our luggage in the guard's van.

"Will there be any military?" I asked.

"I hope not. The military are avoiding the trains since a few lines were blown up. They've taken to the road."

He pointed out a small wooden cabin at the top of the brake coach – the "birdcage". He could look down the whole of the train exterior through a trapdoor in the roof.

"I'll see them coming," he said.

I felt relief – for now.

"Why do we have a violin case?" I asked.

"It has a false backing with medicine hidden in the panel," he explained. "And you never know when you might need a tune!"

138

Molly sat on the leather seat. I stretched out between two strong boxes and snoozed as we chugged towards Mallow. It was a slow journey with frequent stops and Molly was soon deep in conversation with Joseph.

Joseph was from Enniskillen and knew some of Molly's mother's people who were well known Quakers in the area. After scores of people were killed in riots in Belfast he'd moved his family to Tipperary.

"The government is making a mess of the whole situation," said Joseph. "I supported Home Rule. But then the government didn't give it to us. They're even throwing many of our new leaders like Griffith in jail. And he's a moderate."

"And yet we cannot stay in this state of lawlessness forever," said Molly. "All our leaders need to find a way to peace."

"Amen to that," said Joseph.

At one small halt, someone handed Joseph a beer bottle through the guard door. I watched through half-closed eyes as he pulled out a twist of paper from inside it. A message in a bottle.

"You are to transfer onto the Bandon Train in Cork," he said. "Someone will meet you in the station office."

"There must have been a change of plan," Molly said. "It's a wonder they reached us."

"There's a friendly postmistress near here who sends on phone messages," he said.

We pulled into the Cork Terminus. Joseph rushed us off

the train with our trunks before the other passengers came for their luggage. He led us to the station office, where the Station Master gave us some tea. We were told that two women would come from Cumann na mBan to take care of us. Joseph asked us what our cover story was.

"The truth, sir. I have letters from Dr. Ella Webb of the Adelaide Hospital, saying I am carrying some medical supplies. And from Professor Mahaffey, saying I am a student at Trinity College Dublin who needs to be able to conduct her business."

"The station is watched," said Joseph.

He showed us into an inner waiting room with a glass window between it and the outer office so we could see people coming and going.

"There's patrols of Tans outside the station and there's an RIC barracks just up the road," he said. "But since the Kilmichael attack they're only venturing out in groups."

Through the partition window, I watched a train guard raise an almost invisible trap-door in the floor in the outer office. He dropped documents straight in. A teenage boy turned up and gave him some post that went the same way. More foot soldiers in Collins' intelligence network.

We sat on the high leather seats listening to the ticking of the clock. Every footfall made me think Lees was on our trail.

"I'm glad Lees didn't see us. He's dangerous," I said to Molly. "He's some kind of double agent. I saw him offering to buy arms for Collins. I don't understand it at all."

Molly bit her lip. "These are dark dangerous times."

"How did he know we'd be in Tipperary?" I asked. "We went there on Collins' orders. Do you think Collins –"

"Don't be stupid, Dan," she cut me off. "Spies might have seen you at the station in Dublin. And he might have followed you."

I remembered the vision of him on the back of the train. It was the most likely explanation.

I took out the soccer ball and blew it up. Worrying about Lees was making my head hurt. There was the sporadic sound of gunfire. But we were so used now to volleys, we scarcely mentioned it.

Molly grabbed the ball from me, annoyed, and held it out of reach. "If you weren't such an eejit we wouldn't be here."

"Hey, give me back my ball. I thought you believed in non-violence!" I cried. Laughing, she stood on a chair. I tried to jump up but she was too tall.

"I'm going to push you off," I said. "You've been warned."

"See what comes with hanging out with thugs and corner boys!" She wagged her finger at me. "I'm teaching you decency."

I caught her by surprise by tickling her under the arm and the ball fell into my arms.

I gave her my hand. "Come on, I'll show you how to spin the ball on your foot."

And that's what we were doing when two young

women walked in. They introduced themselves as Maud and Kitty, two Cumann na mBan women. They would travel with us to Bandon.

Kitty looked closely at Molly. "'Tis right young you are for a doctor," she said. "They only just about accept Doctor Dorothy and she's nearly thirty."

"I'm only a student," Molly explained, blushing.

"Molly was in the GPO with Connolly and Pearse," I said.

They looked at her with respect.

"Things are very tense here since the Kilmichael ambush. Those shots you hear, that's the Auxies and Tans just firing into the sky," said Maud who had a friendly face and dark hair under her hat.

"There's a new curfew of ten o'clock," said Kitty who was fair and sleek, like a well-fed cat.

I loved the lilt of their voices.

As we were about to go, I remembered the other letter sewn into my jacket lining. I let Molly go a little bit ahead with the others, then poked it out of my coat and popped it in the invisible trapdoor. I immediately felt lighter under the roof of Cork's main station, as high and wide as a cathedral.

We took a tram and rattled over the first of two iron bridges spanning the branches of the River Lee on our way to the Bandon line station. They were called Brian Boru Bridge and Clontarf Bridge after the old hero who drove the Vikings out of Ireland at the Battle of Clontarf.

"These two bridges are special," said Maud. "They were built to accommodate four types of transport. Can you guess?"

"Rail, vehicles and foot passengers?" I replied, stumped about the fourth.

Maud smiled. "Sea! Both of them flip open to let ships through. Aren't they a wonder!"

"I bet Brian Boru would be happier if they kept the invaders out," I said and they laughed.

Kitty pointed to where small houses jostled together up steep hills, above the river on the northern side. I really liked the look of it.

As we crossed Clontarf Bridge she pointed out the grand City Hall to us on the opposite bank of the river.

"We have a City Hall, an opera house, a university, a Grand Parade. 'Tis better than Dublin we are surely!" she said with a glint in her eye.

"The Liffey is way stinkier than the Lee," I said, wrinkling my nose.

"*Corcaigh* – the Irish word for Cork – means 'marsh'," said Kitty. "Most of the city centre is on reclaimed land. It's actually an island as you can see from all the bridges."

"Our grandfather's people came from Cork," said Molly.

Kitty patted my knee. "You are one of us!"

The station for Bandon at Albert Quay was a squat rectangular stone building with a few platforms. There were few passengers in the late afternoon. It was bitterly cold and we were glad to get into the wooden carriage of the waiting train with several passenger seats facing each other.

Kitty was a student nurse and she and Molly found plenty to discuss, dropping their voices as other passengers joined the train.

We set out at last and it turned out to be a really exciting journey.

First of all, about two miles or so out of the city, we crossed a cast-iron four-span bridge about a hundred feet up!

"This is the Chetwynd Viaduct," Kitty told us. "Lads have great sport round here trying to lob their bowls over it."

We gazed out the window, thrilled with the sensation of being so high up. But there were more thrills to come. Not long after, we went through Goggin's Tunnel – the longest in Ireland – a thousand yards!

After Kinsale junction, there were only a few other passengers left, a sleeping old man and a couple of older ladies.

Maud and Kitty glanced at the other passengers.

"There are quite a few loyalists in Bandon. It's a garrison town," Maud whispered.

In Bandon station another old fellow in a horse-drawn cart was waiting for us. There seemed to be an endless supply of these old men, all creaky and gnarled like old trees.

Maud explained it was better to avoid the main roads

with the Tans and Auxies looking for a fight. Many of the roads were blocked with trenches dug by the boys from the brigades and several bridges had been blown up.

We went on another roundabout route up boreens and down by-ways through green countryside. The air seemed balmier here.

"You're in the heart of the war now," said Kitty. "Major Perceval, the local military leader, is a torturer as well as a murderer. Word is he's setting up a mobile unit – their own flying column to fight fire with fire."

Across a field, a herdsman rounded up a field of cows. On the roadside, a bent old woman in a shawl gathered firewood. The war seemed a world away but was all around us. I longed for my football that was deep in my luggage again, the one thing I could get a handle on in this spinning world.

Chapter 11

With the Guerillas in Cork
December 1920

We stayed for a few days at a thatched farmhouse with a family called O'Neill in a place called Maryborough. As well as farm workers, there were quite a few young people coming and going. Such was the bustle and activity I never quite fixed the names to the various faces. They hurtled about the newly whitewashed kitchen as we perched on low wooden stools. Day and night, a turf fire burned and a high round pot oven bubbled on the edge of the fire. Flitches of bacon hung from hooks in the ceiling. As I tucked into the big feed of brown bread and rashers I listened to their talk. They were all "in it" and spoke in code. A hand grenade was now an "egg". An ambush was a "job", a "hit up" or a "lash". They referred to documents and papers as "dope". They talked a lot about "war flour" and "Irish cheddar". When I asked Maud she told me they meant explosives.

I helped a bit on the farm and Molly gave lots of talks and instructions in neighbouring farmhouses and saw quite a few patients.

A few days in, we were taken some miles to a large manor house that was all boarded up. The rain was so cold it almost scalded my face. We were told that an absentee landlord owned it – the family name was Winthrop-Sealey – and the tenants had been frightened away by all the ambushes and raids. The caretaker was secretly sympathetic to the Republicans and turned a blind eye to the use of the several buildings.

"There are seven battalions here in Cork, organised around each of the main towns," Maud explained. "Tom Barry has set up a few flying columns that are on the run, moving from place to place every few nights."

There were about sixteen young women and teenage boys gathered in the barn to listen to Molly's lecture. She was much more confident here than she'd been in Tipperary. They were fascinated when she showed them how to clean a bullet wound to prevent infection and use anything that lay to hand as a splint. You'd think it was a theatre show. But I got a bit bored halfway through and snuck off with my ball.

I had just perfected my "figure of eight" where I bounce the ball on my head, shoulders, knees, feet and chest when a movement caught my eye on the brow of a hill. It was a group of cyclists coming our way! I wondered for a minute if it was a Flying Column, but then saw their tin hats and the blur of khaki.

"Scatter!" I ran into the barn full pelt. "There's a pile of them on bicycles!"

"Oh no, it must be Perceval's mobile unit!" cried Maud.

Great confusion! Girls grabbed their coats. One burst into tears.

"They'll arrest me. My brother was at Kilmichael and my parents sent me away since!" shouted one tall lanky fellow. "That will be enough to get me killed."

A young lad with a shock of red hair went outside and climbed a tree.

"They have us surrounded! We're goners."

A couple of the boys picked up pitchforks. "They'll murder us all in revenge."

The seconds felt like hours. We were sitting ducks.

Molly grabbed the violin case and opened it. Inside was a battered old instrument. She stood on a chair. "Anyone here play the fiddle?"

A boy who was holding a pitchfork put up his hand. "I've started learnin', Miss."

"We're all going to stay here," Molly commanded. "If you run outside, they'll shoot you for running. If they're going to kill us, they'll have to do it in cold blood. Let's make it hard for them. What's your name, boy?"

"Jemmser, Miss."

"Play a jig. If we're going to die at least let's go out dancing!"

I smiled. Molly was remembering the footballers at Loos. I picked up an old basin and a stick and started to beat out time.

Jemmser's hands were shaking but he struck up the chords of a lively tune – "Baint an Fhéir!" he called out – bringing in the hay.

Kitty immediately grabbed one of the lads, and Maud another. Soon two lines were facing each other with Kitty calling out the moves.

Molly hid her First Aid things and, taking out a pocketbook, began to make notes. I wondered what she was writing as I threw myself into the beat.

A shot rent the air!

One of the girls screamed and I felt an acute pain in my foot. I thought I'd been shot but I'd just dropped the basin on my toe.

The barn door shook as they battered it in. A group of soldiers with blackened faces burst through. Bayonets pointed at us and revolvers aimed.

"Halt! Put your hands up or we'll shoot!"

Everyone froze, motionless. One of the boys reached for the pitchfork but Molly calmly walked up to the barn door.

"Have you come to join the céili?" Molly's voice was controlled but her hands were shaking.

"What the 'ell's going on 'ere!" a tough-looking soldier snarled.

Molly took out a letter from her leather satchel. "Why, sir, I am a student at Trinity College Dublin conducting a study of folklore. This is signed by the Provost of the College, Professor Mahaffey." She waved the letter. "Perhaps the senior officer out there would like to read it."

The snarling soldier was about to snatch it but Molly pulled herself up to her full height and looked him in the eye.

"I want to hand it to the senior officer. Tell me your name and rank."

We all stood as still as statues, petrified with fear, barely able to look at what was happening.

I glanced up for one moment. I thought the soldier was going to strike her. But Molly didn't flinch. He dropped his hand.

"Captain Montgomery, come 'ere!" he growled.

A senior officer strode in, all squeaky leather and spruce uniform. He scanned our frightened faces with an almost amused look. He had a strong face, a small moustache and a devil-may-care air. When he saw Molly's outstretched hand with the letter, his lips curled into a smile. He took it from her hand, every inch the gallant. For one mad moment I thought he might join her in a dance. He ran his eye over the letter, tossing it to the ground, a thing of no account.

"You, Miss O'Donovan, should clear off. Our orders are to search the place." The smile of amusement curdled on his lips, his tone was clipped and his eye severe.

He turned on his heel and walked out.

The soldiers barged about, overturning farm implements and wooden pails, roughly brushing aside anyone unlucky enough to be in their way. The officer stayed outside, keeping his distance.

A soldier shouted out to their superior. "Nothing found, sir!"

"I could arrest the lot of you for breaking and entering!" said the senior officer, standing at the barn door once more.

"Except we're not," said Molly evenly. "The Winthrop-Sealeys are my cousins. They said I could use the premises, as it is so hard to secure other venues. Young people won't gather at the crossroads any more."

"Go home, the lot of you!" shouted the officer as they left.

None of us moved.

After a few minutes, I went to the barn door and watched them disappear over the brow of the next hill.

"They're gone."

Molly's legs collapsed from under her and Kitty caught her by the elbow. But with one motion, the entire company broke into applause. We all burst into hysterical laughter and excited talk.

I picked up the letter the officer had thrown on the ground. It was indeed from Professor Mahaffey and said she should be allowed conduct her business as a student. That she was a scholar of exceptional ability.

"This daylight mobile unit is a new tactic," said Kitty with a frown. "The troops usually wait for nightfall to ransack our homes."

"Someone must have welched on us," said Maud.

"There's a quare few loyalists in Cork."

"I don't know. Since Kilmichael they're hitting every boreen and backwater at random," said Jemmser.

"You need to learn semaphore and Morse code so you can have a good signalling system," said Molly. "That way people will know when patrols are in the area." She told them how she and her brother Jack had a simple code based on prisoner's knocks, tapping out letters of the alphabet. She said she'd send them coded instructions when she got the chance. Then she tapped out about sixteen times, explaining that was G-B-U. God bless you.

We went back to the farmhouse. It was decided that after we'd had something to eat it was best for us to get back to Dublin.

We'd only just finished a feed of Irish stew and gathered all our things when a young boy called to the farm. He'd run a fair way.

"Maud's brother Michael is shot!" he gasped. "A skirmish last night near the coast. They're hiding in a dugout in a farmhouse. The wound's in his jaw and he's very bad!"

Maud let out a scream. Then she pulled herself together. "Molly, will you see to him? There isn't a doctor for miles around."

Molly, though tired, agreed without hesitation.

It wasn't far off our route. After the detour to the hideout, we'd travel on to Bandon.

A farmer, Mr. Doyle, took us by pony and trap. We had

a good story. If any troops came upon us again we would tell them we were on our way to catch the train at Bandon but the farmer had to call in on a sick cow at a place called Cloundereen. He was well known in the area for his expertise.

When we drew near to the safe farmhouse where the unit were hiding out, the farmer dropped us off. A girl was waiting and took us across several fields. The only real place of danger was crossing over the road that went to Bandon, where Black and Tan lorries sometimes passed. We were in luck. The windswept road was clear of traffic. We went down a deep cutting of furze, most of the blossoms dead and withered. There was hoar frost on the bushes and the puddles were iced over. Then we crossed over a fast-rushing stream, picking our way over slippery stones.

The thatched cottage looked deserted and was in a large field down a deep incline, hidden from the roads. About fifty yards from it, the girl whistled, a trill like a blackbird's. That was the signal. Two volunteers met us at the door. Both were about twenty and had firearms in holsters under their tweed jackets.

Maud's brother, Michael, was lying on the table, his jaw covered by a blood-soaked bandage. He moaned, his breath jagged. Maud ran to him and kissed his brow and he murmured in a half sleep.

"Best hold his hand," whispered Molly as she busied herself taking out her First Aid kit.

"But you're just a wee girl," said one of the volunteers.

"This 'wee girl' just saved the life of a group of us surrounded by a cycling corps, George," Maud said.

Molly ignored his comment and asked what they had done to treat Michael's wound. They said they'd poured some whiskey on it but there was none left.

Molly went to the patient. He was almost unconscious, moaning in his sleep. She cut off the bandage.

"He's got some fragments lodged in the soft tissue. It must have been quite long range," she said.

She deftly removed the bullet fragments with a tweezers and then bathed the wound in disinfectant.

"The wound needs to be kept clean and wash your own hands," she instructed.

"Will he be all right?" Maud asked, her face ashen.

"I think so. It's lucky it wasn't the bullet itself," Molly said. "Change the dressing daily. Feed him liquids only – soups and broths. Then try to get him to a hospital to make sure no infection sets in."

"Maybe you stopped the bullet with your teeth," Maud said to her brother.

He opened his eyes, rallying for a moment, but didn't attempt to smile.

Maud started fussing then about getting a stretcher. Molly said all they had to do was make a "chair" with their arms to carry him. She made them less anxious by showing them the correct way to hold him.

"Don't mind what I said about you being a slip of a girl," said George, exhaling with relief.

Molly smiled. "If I minded that I would never have enrolled in college."

"We'd be lost without the women of Cumann na mBan and the youths. We can only do it because people are willing to hide us in their homes and act as lookouts and carry dispatches. We have the support of the whole country."

Molly frowned but didn't respond. "You should make sure to have a First Aid kit available in as many houses as possible," she then said.

She told them about the supplies she'd brought. She also spoke to them about scabies and applying powder and they laughed – eager to be rid of it.

While he was sorting out the First Aid supplies, George came across the GAA ball given to me by Paudy. I'd almost forgotten about it. He tapped me on the shoulder and led me outside, blowing it up as we went using sheer lung power.

"This one's been through the wars," he said.

I nodded but said nothing. I didn't want to have to talk about Croke Park.

We practised drop kicks and watching the arc of the ball made me feel better about the empty loneliness of the countryside.

"You've a good left foot on you, boy. But you've the set of a soccer player," said George as I went to tackle him.

"I like the ball control," I said.

He kicked the ball up high and ran forward to catch it.

Then he paused and tossed the ball up and down.

"The Gaelic games are handed on from ancient times. When a fellow plucks a ball out of the sky, it's like an old Irish God has come back to earth." He kicked it to me. Then he scurried into the barn and came out holding a hurley and a sliothar. "This is what Cúchulainn used to slay the hound of Culainn. And some say hurleys were used in ancient battles. That's why the British banned them. Trying to break the link with our past."

"I'm quite keen on the future," I said.

"City boy," he said, mussing my hair.

Molly called us back in as it was getting late. Maud stayed to tend her brother and we retraced our steps to the farm with the girl who could whistle like a blackbird. The farmer was waiting to take us to Bandon.

The route was perilous. Stones were scattered all over the road from torn-down walls. We had to go around a couple of crude barriers made by Volunteers – felled trees with barbed wire around them.

As we got closer, the roads improved. Farmers were driving cattle to market and bringing goods to town on carts. "Gee up!' they said on the road, pushing cattle and horses. Harnesses creaked and whips cracked.

"Paddy, have ye heard they declared martial law yesterday?" said one skinny old fellow in a battered cart, showing our driver, Mr. Doyle, a newspaper.

I read it. Law and order was now in the control of the armies. They could punish you if they even *thought* you were helping Republican forces. That could mean us. Trying to save someone's life, or even giving them a drink of water was an offence. It was cruel.

Bandon station was thronged with people sending supplies from the market into Cork city. But there was an unnatural hush. We soon saw why. A band of soldiers patrolled the platform. A couple of soldiers speared bags of flour with bayonets and threw boxes of eggs onto the tracks.

Molly and I stayed with our luggage at the far end of the platform, in the shadows. Noticing us, a group of farm-women seemed to sense we didn't want to draw attention to ourselves. As they waited to load vegetables onto the train they silently massed in front of us. An old tramp went up to beg from the soldiers, getting a cuff in the ear. The train pulled in and we jumped on, heaving our luggage on with us. We waved our wordless thanks to the women from the train window.

Once on the way to Cork, in a crowded carriage full of ordinary people, our exhaustion caught up with us. We dozed on each other's shoulders.

We awoke with a start when we got to the Cork terminus. Time was tight. We would be lucky to catch the evening train to Dublin. But Molly reassured me that Kitty had given her the address of her family home, in an area called Montenotte, if we got stuck. At the Albert Dock Terminus in Cork we hurried to the tram, weighed down by our luggage. The tram would take us across the River Lee to the Glanmire Railway Station. Soon the Auxies would be prowling but in the late afternoon people were still going about their business.

I was glad to be back in the bustle of the city. The ebb and flow of people, the sight of houses huddled together, was a tonic even if there was an air of threat.

As we crossed the first branch of the river, a Crossley Tender roared alongside the tram track. It was followed by an open lorry stacked with several cans of petrol. People who had been chatting about their Christmas shopping in Cash's and Roches Stores stopped cold. The chatter picked up again when the lorry passed on. One woman said the shops were jammed, even though there was martial law.

Another studious-looking man with glasses said he was going to look out for the Aurora Borealis at night. It had been over Cork for a few days, he explained. "A green jet of light after a magnetic storm, also known as the 'Northern Lights'. Rare this far south."

I longed to find out more, but stayed quiet in case my Dublin accent attracted attention.

Intermittent firing crackled as daylight faded. But we had got so used to that, we didn't even remark on it. I was so accustomed to being frightened that all I felt was numb. I thought about football moves in my head, thinking through the best goals I'd ever seen scored. I froze them as pictures and thought about the plane geometry of the ball that Willie explained to me from his maths book. Like a parabola he'd called it, a curve in the air, good for getting over a wall of defense in a free kick. You see, football is a game of angles that's all about timing. Even the pitch is symmetrical, composed of quadrilaterals, right angles and rectangles. I like maths and when it relates to football I like it even better. Thinking about this made me feel better inside. Even Molly stopped scolding me for my foot jiggling.

But we were too late! When we got to the station we saw the train to Dublin disappear down the track. We would have to wait until ten o'clock for the next one. We were starving hungry. The ticket seller told us everything was shut but there was a hotel at nearby Luke's Cross that did food and was safe enough to get to. We waited for a while but were weak with hunger. I whinged so much that Molly gave in at last and we nipped out. It was half past eight on the station clock.

We walked fast, Molly cursing me under her breath.

We got only part way up the hill towards Luke's Cross when we heard an almighty bang.

A woman hurried down the street. "The Volunteers have lobbed a bomb at the Auxies at Dillon's Cross! Go home!" she said, pointing back up the road.

We hurried back towards the station, glancing around nervously. There was a glow in the sky.

"Is that the Northern Lights they were talking about?" I asked.

"It's fire!" Molly said.

Bullets rang out loud and clear in the cold night. The

smell of burning singed the air. We were glad to get inside onto the platforms.

Soon people poured into the station, fleeing from trouble. A woman ran in with blood streaming down her face.

"The Auxies are burning our homes in Dillon's Cross!" she wailed.

Molly took her to the Guard's Office, where there was a First Aid station, and attended to her wound.

"It was the bomb thrown by a Flying Column at Dillon's Cross that set them off," the woman gabbled. "The Auxies said the Volunteers had killed one of them and wounded six and Cork would pay. When I got to the bottom of Summerhill they opened fire at the corner on this end of King Street. Women and children were crouching in doorways. I got hit by the butt-end of a rifle."

Molly bandaged her head wound and told her to rest.

Another woman in tears described how she'd seen a party of Auxies throw petrol into houses. They'd stopped anyone who tried to rescue their property.

Molly moved among the people, bandaging their wounds. Some of them were more shocked than hurt and she bade me fetch them water mixed with a little brandy from the stationmaster's supply. But many were bleeding and bruised – beaten by Auxies.

I looked up at the board. Our train was due in but there was no point in even trying to leave. The station was a milling scene of confusion, just like Croke Park had been that day. Molly was needed and here she would stay. I tried to stop the panic rising up in my chest by keeping busy.

Around ten o'clock a respectable man carrying a briefcase dashed in. A tram had been burnt out on Patrick Street, the main shopping street in Cork.

"They dragged us all out of the tram and beat a priest with the muzzles of their rifles. Then they told him to run and fired shots at him. It's a mercy he escaped!"

People rushed onto trains to get away, not caring where the trains were going.

A woman with a young boy ran in distraught. "My daughter, I've lost my daughter!"

Molly told me to give her brandy and water. She wailed as her boy clung to her.

"She was just outside, my beautiful child with the golden hair – please, I must go find her!" The words tumbled out of her. She squeezed my wrist so hard it was as if some force was summoning me. "And her wearing her new red frock and all."

"I'll go," I said, without thinking.

Outside, I could see a red glow in the sky across the river in the direction of the city centre. Fire must have been spreading in every direction. There was a strong wind blowing, fanning the flames. I pulled my collar up and pressed on through the station forecourt onto the street. The smoky air stung my throat.

Outside on the street – chaos. Under an abandoned cart nearby, I thought I saw a flash of red. I heard a whimpering

161

sound. It was a small child, maybe four years old, her bright hair tumbling around her tear-stained face. She clung to the wheel. I ran over to her just as a group of howling drunk Auxies lurched up the street and made for their lorry parked halfway up.

I was holding my hand out towards the child as an arm grabbed me. I followed the frightened gaze of the cowering child.

A crazed Auxie thrust his blackened face towards me. His eyes were cold like steel. He wore a bandolier, a shoulder belt with loops for gun cartridges, over his trench coat and held a long firearm known as a carbine in one hand.

"I know you! Fenian brat!" He was stupid drunk, half mad.

But I knew who it was. Captain Lees. The cut of him. That cruel voice.

"Still got that stamp, you little blighter?"

There was no doubt now who it was. He thrust his face into mine and opened his mouth wide in a snarling laugh. A sudden flare in the sky lit up his crazed face. I saw the glinting gold tooth in his mouth. Then before my eyes he seemed to shapeshift like a werewolf. His voice deepened – gravelly and coarse – "Hanging around huckster shops listening in to men's fortunes!"

Jameson! Then he pulled himself back up to his full height and raised his hand.

But before he could strike me, I kicked at him with all my might, winding him in the stomach. He doubled over. I grabbed the little girl, yanking her by the arm, and ran back towards the station.

"You'll pay for this!" Lees roared as one of the other Auxies grabbed him and pulled him towards their lorry.

"Come on, let's go loot the jeweller's!" his friend yelled.

I brought the child back into the station and reunited her with her mother. The little girl was dazed, heaving dry sobs, unable to speak.

The station clock said it was half past midnight. A man said one whole side of the main street, Patrick's Street, was a mass of flames.

"There was a crazed band of them, about fifty Auxies, setting the department stores on fire," said a woman. Her leg gushed blood from a fall as she'd fled across the river. "The fire brigade contained the blaze at first, but then they set fire to the Munster Arcade and Cash's!"

People called out the names of shops and premises on fire. Egan's Jeweller's, Saxone Shoes, Burton's Tailors, the Lee Cinema, Roche's Stores and Sunner's Chemist's. They told terrible stories. The woman whose wedding ring had been torn off her finger as her house burned. The father who had to run into a burning building to rescue his son. The old man forced to sing "God Save the King" as Auxies fired bullets at his feet to make him dance.

I fell asleep at one stage but awoke from a nightmare of a blackened face leering at me as I was thrashed with a gold-topped cane.

I lost track of time. Molly kept me busy helping at the

First Aid station, passing her bandages, fetching water. She sent me around the building to see if I could find chairs. People were huddling on the platforms, trying to sleep.

Somewhere in the early hours, as people sank into fitful sleep, someone called out my name. I reared back, terrified it was Lees coming to get me. But it was our friend, the train guard, Joseph. He led me to a storeroom and we carried down some chairs back to the guardroom.

"All of Cork will burn," he said. "The Auxies are shooting at fire officers. And their one steam fire engine has broken down! They've telephoned to Dublin to send motor pumps by train. It's on its way. We should get you and Molly on that train when it's returning to Dublin."

As we looked out the window, there was a massive explosion across the Lee.

"City Hall and the Carnegie Library are blown up!" a man shouted.

The sky filled with blue, purple and orange flames, wondrous and terrible.

A journalist called in to speak to our conductor friend Joseph. "The Auxies are cutting the hoses so the fire brigade can't put out the blaze. The commander of the Fire Department says it's worse than the night Dublin burned in Easter 1916."

Molly looked out the window and I could see her recoiling as though she was up right next to the fire. She had been at the GPO when O'Connell Street burned all around her and the rebels had to evacuate under sniper fire.

She had a terror of flames.

"Molly, you and the young lad should come with me back to Dublin on the special train," said Joseph.

Molly refused at first, but a group of Cumann na mBan then arrived to help so she gave in.

We boarded the train. As we came out of the tunnel and looked back, the sky glowed red like some terrible sunset as the city centre burned to the ground.

Somewhere in that mad rampage, Lees was on the loose. I had been right. Lees and Jameson were one and the same. But he was in Cork and I was on my way out of it.

We were safe for the time being. I was on my way back to Dublin. Home.

Chapter 12

The Thomas Whelan Case 1921

I was in shock after Cork. I was brave enough during the day. But at night rampaging snakes striking out of burning buildings invaded my dreams. Lee/Jameson. Jameson/Lee. A snake with two heads.

There was the big war. But Lees and I were having our own war. It worried me that he was still after that Indian stamp with the King's head on upside down. He could want it all he liked. It was still buried with the gun in Ringsend Park.

With my dad still missing, we had the most miserable Christmas ever. But one good thing was we moved again.

After Lees' visit my mother didn't like being trapped in a cul de sac any more. So we took new lodgings just around the corner in a cosy little cottage in Bath Avenue Place. If Lees came around again he wouldn't think we were so near by. Our road ran between Bath Avenue and South Lotts Road so there were two lines of escape.

On New Year's Eve I knocked the worry out of my head with fifty straight headers in the little back yard.

Then my mother called me in, her voice cracking with nerves. She held a paper or letter in her hand, and was turned towards the fire in the kitchen so I couldn't see her face.

"It's a telegram from your Uncle Edward," she began.

My heart stopped.

She turned round, not smiling exactly but relieved. "'False arrest in NY. Deported to Caribbean. I am on way.'"

"He's . . . still . . . ?" I asked, hope rising in my chest.

"Yes," she said, hugging me. "He's still alive. That shipping clerk was right when he said they were arresting Irishmen on suspicion of gun-smuggling. They've deported him from New York to the Caribbean as it's a British colony and there was a special order to send him there. Uncle Edward is going to rescue him. He's innocent. They'll have to let him go."

I gazed into the fire, relieved. But the flames reminded me of Lee's blackened face snarling at me in the ruins of Cork. I wondered if he had ordered my father's deportation.

"Dan, promise me you'll stay out of it. If you get into any trouble it will be harder to get your father home in one piece."

I nodded. But I had to let someone on our side know about Lees in Cork.

I soon got my chance. On the first day back at school,

Seán MacBride, dressed smartly as ever, fell into step with me as I turned into Brunswick Street.

"Hello, stranger," he said. "Need to earn some money?"

I shook my head. I didn't want to get pulled back in.

I told him about Lees in Cork and he thanked me for the information.

"I don't trust that fellow. He's supposed to be helping us get arms, as some sort of double agent. But I think he's a spy. I'll tell Mick. He'll turn the air blue when he hears. But Mick knows how to play those fellows at their own game."

I walked on to shake him off but he continued to chat.

"De Valera's back in town. Came back from America disguised as a priest. Someone said to him Collins was doing a great job and he struck the guard-rail of the deck and said 'We'll see about that!'. The Big Fellow and the Long Fellow are deadly rivals, that's for sure. My money's on the Long Fellow. He's full of fine talk but has the cunning of a snake."

I laughed. MacBride cocked his head and smiled back.

"Collins thought you might like to run messages out to Dev. His wife said you were a great lad or some such guff." He smiled again and cuffed me on the shoulder, trying to charm me.

But I resisted. I'd promised my mother. I told him so. He just shrugged as if that was a thing of no consequence.

"Do you think the war will be over soon?" I asked.

He snorted like a horse. "It's going to get worse! The British have passed a law to divide Ireland. They want to give the North of Ireland their own parliament for the Unionists and we would have another here in the South. But we want a united Republic. It's not theirs to give. It's for us to take."

MacBride acted like he was in the know about everything.

Then he bent down and spoke softly. "We need someone with your steady aim. We're lobbing Mills bombs at British Army trucks patrolling the city. The little bombs that look like pineapples." When I didn't answer, he went on, "You do what feels right with your conscience."

We walked on and I wished I could get away from him.

Then he said, "Your friend Whelan will be coming to trial soon, you know. And we'll see how British justice works then."

"I'm helping Molly with some Quaker yoke on Saturday. It's for all the thousands of people burnt out in Cork," I blurted out.

"Ah, yes. My mother is involved in that too. Give Molly my regards," he said and turned heel.

It was true. On Saturday we gathered at the house of Alice Stopford Green who was Doctor Dorothy's aunt. She lived on Stephen's Green so her address was easy to remember. They were setting up a "White Cross" organization to help people affected by the war, like those burnt out in Cork. There were lots of Quakers coming along. Alice Stopford Green was a grand lady who wore cloaks and fancy jewellery and wrote big fat books about

Ireland. I was happy to help put out chairs in her vast drawing room.

"Why, if it isn't Dan! Last time we met you were stinking of fish!" a woman called out.

It was Doctor Dorothy, who came in holding a tray of biscuits.

"They're hoping to raise twenty-five million pounds in America," she told me. "John McCormack the tenor has been putting on concerts."

"He'll end up hoarse," I said.

She laughed and handed me a letter. "My aunt wants you to take this letter to the post office, special delivery. It's to General Smuts, the Afrikaner general who fought the British in the Boer war. He is something of a statesman, trusted by both sides. She hopes he can help broker peace."

I was only too glad to get out of hanging around for a boring meeting.

Then that afternoon my mother asked me to call in to Nanny's shop in Ringsend to get some smoked fish.

"Well, if it isn't the bauld Dan!" said Nanny when I came into the little whitewashed cottage with the green half-door. The paraffin lamp guttered in the corner.

Bridie came in from the back kitchen. Her smiling face made me happy inside. It was like a sparkling rainbow through the sun and rain.

"That horrible man with the tattoos came round again," she said as she measured sugar in the scales. "But my Aunt Nanny chased him away. He wants to know what she saw

170

that time in his hand. He thinks Nanny put a curse on him."

My scalp prickled in fear and I felt my insides go weak.

Nanny just pursed her lips and picked out pieces of fish and wrapped them in newspaper.

There were headlines of more atrocities wrapped around the fish. British troops at a checkpoint on O'Connell Bridge had opened fire. Two passersby were killed, another five wounded. Six Irish policemen were killed in an ambush in Clare. The British then burned over twenty homes. On and on, until we're all dead.

Nanny asked me to run a message. "Dan, could you ever find out for us if that young fellow Whelan is safe? He's popular round here. Went to Mass every week. When he laughs, you know the fibre's not as hard as in some of them. Writes to his mother, a poor Galway widow woman, every day."

I told her that MacBride had said the case was coming up soon.

"Some of them witnesses are getting cold feet," she said. "Maybe someone's warned them off."

Lees crossed my mind. Maybe that was why he was calling around again. But I shut out the thought.

So after school on Monday I headed to Noyk's offices in Stephen's Green. As I waited in the reception room, I chatted to his typist Brigid. Her brother Mick Malone was a famous rebel who had died in the battle of Mount Street 1916. She told me her sweetheart was in a Flying Column.

"His name's Dan Breen. We're to be married this year."

Dan Breen! I nearly fell out of my standing. Hadn't I met him in a barn in Tipperary! I told her about the failed ambush and how we were lucky not to get caught.

She threw her arms around me. "He'll be the death of me," she said softly. "Lord protect him that the Tans don't get him."

I felt myself going red to the tips of my hair. She let go of me and blew her nose. That pulled her together.

Mr. Noyk spied me through the door. "Come in, young lefty, and liven up my dreary life of courts and court martials."

I shimmied him the ball that was in the wastepaper bin and told him my errand about Whelan.

He looked sad. "I've just been to see him. He's a soft country lad with a beautiful character. But he's been caught in a trap."

"But he's innocent – at any rate of Bloody Sunday!" I cried.

"The Commandant there, Maye, a slippery character, said to him, 'I admire you as one soldier to another.' Whelan told him proudly, 'I was a soldier for a free Ireland.' He joined the Irish Volunteers only for a short time. He isn't active now. But that's enough to hang him."

MacBride came in with the file. "We had some great witnesses that saw him at Mass. But they've all got scared to testify. Maybe if they would come to court there might be a slim chance?"

So Nanny had been right. Maybe Lees had got to them.

Noyk scratched his head. "It wouldn't be the first time

witnesses have been scared off. It wouldn't be easy to change their minds."

"You live near there, don't you, Dan? Could you show me their houses?" MacBride piped up.

"I'll race you!" I said.

We tore down the stairs and I ran out the door, way ahead of MacBride who'd paused to grab his coat and hat. But at the top of Brunswick Street, coming past Trinity College, he raced past me on a bicycle. He turned round to look back at me. Cocky so-and-so. But that was his undoing. He hit a rut and was thrown over the handlebars. I helped him to his feet. He wasn't seriously hurt, just bruised. Laughing, we agreed to call it a draw.

The first address was Mrs. Mann, Whelan's landlady in Barrow Street. She was making a stew and her apron and hands were covered in blood. Her face was closed when she saw MacBride standing on the step. But she smiled when I stepped forward. She recognised me from the shop. She asked us in as she was great friends with Nanny and went to her for fortune-telling.

At first she shook her head. An officer with a gold-tipped cane had called round and told her she could go to prison for harbouring a rebel. But a tear fell from her eye when MacBride told her it was a matter of life and death.

"I adore young Tommy," she said, wiping her face with the bloody apron. "He's much steadier than his flat-mate, Damien."

My heart sank. Damien – Pus-Face – was a total gom.

173

Too yellow to do anything. Like when he chickened out of being a lookout on Bloody Sunday and pushed me in his place.

"Can we speak to Damien?" MacBride asked her.

"That bowsie left the day before Bloody Sunday. Did a runner without paying the rent and all," she said.

He'd gone back to his family down the country who'd recently moved. Mrs. Mann didn't have a forwarding address. I was relieved he was out of it.

MacBride left his card. "Don't worry about the threats," he told her. "Half the landladies in Dublin would be behind bars if that was the case."

Our next call was to Dinah, the girl who sat beside him at Mass. Lees hadn't got to her but she was afraid her new boyfriend would be jealous if she said she was sitting beside Whelan in Mass. I thought she was stupid but MacBride flattered her into testifying.

Then we called in to see a man who was a foreman at Boland's Mill, Mr. Lacey. He was reluctant too. Lees had called to his employer saying he was a Sinn Féin sympathiser. And even though his employer took no notice, Mr. Lacey didn't want to chance it. But when MacBride explained how much was at stake, he said he wouldn't see a man sent to the gallows because he'd been a coward.

I took MacBride in to meet Bridie, as she was always curious to see people she'd heard me talk about. She asked him wide-eyed about his mother who was supposed to be the most beautiful woman in the world and for whom Mr. Yeats wrote all the poems.

"Does your mammy mind you doing all this work?" she asked him.

He winked at me. "She's happy about all the stuff she knows about."

He no more tells his mother what he gets up to than I do!

"You must do everything to help Mr. Whelan," Bridie said. "For we all love him so. He brings me apples from the market as he knows I'm partial to them." She went into the kitchen and fetched a little package. "I have embroidered a handkerchief for him. Please give it to him if you visit the prison."

MacBride went back to Mr. Noyk, triumphant, convinced we had a strong case once again.

"You can be our Court Martial Messenger at Dublin City Hall," he told me.

I was thrilled. I could earn a few bob for my mam in the most guarded place in Ireland!

Chapter 13

The Trial
February 1921

On the morning of the trial in February, I walked through the doors of Dublin Castle, that hated place, to get to the court in Dublin City Hall. I was wearing MacBride's old suit and my mother had washed my face red raw. Everyone was on edge. There had been a new development. Someone had been arrested who had vital testimony. But the prosecutors wouldn't say who. I hoped it wasn't Pus-Face.

I carried rolls of documents behind Mr. Noyk who wore a long flowing cloak and a short white wig and Mr. James Williamson, King's Counsel, who was our barrister for the defence. He wore an even bigger wig and longer flowing black robe. MacBride walked beside me, sober and spruce in a black suit. He carried large files and a briefcase.

"Smart move of Noyk's to ask a Unionist to defend Whelan," said MacBride.

We passed through a barricade with Auxies posted as sentries. They had us in the sights of their rifles and they scrutinised our passes with a sneer. Mr. Williamson the Unionist was haughty with them. Guns were trained on us all the way through Dublin Castle Yard.

We entered the council chamber of the City Hall. At a long table sat the Court: five officers each with a revolver in front of him and a Judge Advocate.

"Revolvers at the ready," remarked MacBride. "So much for British justice. "

Noyk scanned the room crowded with men in trench coats. "It's full of secret service men," he said. He pointed towards the other barrister, a stern-looking fellow with a thin, clever face. "Their prosecutor is Travers Humphreys. He's famous for convicting grisly murderers – a poisoner known as Crippen and another devilish chap who killed several wives."

I couldn't help gaping at him.

Whelan was on trial with a Dubliner called Boyce. The charge against Boyce was murder of Captain Baggallay on the 21st November 1920 at Lower Baggot Street.

Whelan stood up. He looked fresh-faced and pleasant despite everything. He wasn't accused of murder but of "carrying a revolver". His case was much less serious. I felt a bit cheered up.

The first witness for the prosecution was a lodger in the same house as the dead captain. He had been in the bathroom and swore that both Whelan and Boyce had pointed guns at him.

"But sure wasn't I in Mass at the time back in Ringsend!" said Whelan.

The second witness was a young dispatch rider from Dublin Castle who swore he saw Whelan near the scene of the crime.

The third witness was a medical officer who gave evidence of the wounds.

Whelan made a statement in his soft Galway accent. "I got out of bed around eight thirty in time for nine o'clock Mass at Ringsend Chapel. I came home for some breakfast, then after about twenty minutes I went to the Eye and Ear Hospital with another chap who had a toothache. That was about a quarter past ten. Then we went to Clarendon Street Chapel for eleven o'clock Mass. And then I went to Haddington Road to meet a girl who was going to be confirmed. I went home for me dinner and then I went to Croke Park."

It was all so boring it sounded true.

There were lots of murmurs from the secret service men at this. "Bet you fired on us," I heard one say under his breath.

The judge told them all to be quiet.

I clenched my fists. I had seen Whelan on the way to Mass. Then at Croke Park with my own eyes before all hell broke loose. I wished I could speak up but my mouth was dry.

"I left about five o'clock owing to all the trouble," Whelan continued. "I spoke to me neighbours and went home for tea."

They called the first witness for the defense. Mrs. Mann

came out and she gave me a little smile. She was wearing her best suit and her hair was scraped back neatly in a bun. No sign of the bloody apron.

She explained that Mr. Whelan paid thirty shillings a week and took his meals in the kitchen with the family. "Sure he's like one of the family," she said.

"Please confine yourself to factual statements," the judge warned.

Mrs. Mann accounted for almost every minute of Whelan's life. She knew what time he got up at, twenty to nine. What time he shaved at, that he had rashers and sausages for his breakfast. He'd bought a hat the day before. He'd been wearing his new fawn hat and brown clothes when he went out. He wrote a weekly letter to his mother. He was a frequent communicant. She was so exact and precise, the prosecutor scowled and MacBride, grinning, gave me the thumbs-up.

The next witness up was Miss Dinah Deegan. She had sat beside him at him at Mass, in the sanctuary, the section to the left of the pulpit. "I once went to a play with him," she blurted out, blushing deep red.

Whelan gave her a friendly smile.

She then added she had another appointment with another boy to go see the crib in Inchichore.

"She's trying to make him jealous," MacBride whispered to me.

Mr. Humphreys didn't bother-cross examining either of the women.

"Is that good?" I asked MacBride.

He looked thunderstruck. "It's their way of undermining their evidence. They think they're just no-account women."

The officers with the revolvers looked at the women with stony faces. Anger flushed up through me. I knew how brave the women had been to come forward. Especially Mrs. Mann who'd been threatened by Lees.

Our third witness was our trump card, Mr. Lacey. We had proof he was telling the truth.

He was sweating and scratching his collar as if he was the one accused.

"I've never been in court before in me life," he said in a quavering voice. But he explained how he had been to Mass too and saw Whelan coming from Barrow Street towards the church just before quarter to nine. He knew him because he used to be his boss at Boland's Mill.

Mr. Travers Humphreys rose to his feet and jabbed his finger. "A typical Irish alibi!" he thundered. "Everyone's at Mass, praying to God. How could they lie! Well, I contend you are making it up!"

Mr. Lacey quaked. "I'm not. I said 'Good day' to him and all. I was all nervous as I had to give me cousin's daughter away in marriage that afternoon. I'd called in to get my own baptismal certificate and a holy medal from the priest. I saw Whelan as clear as the nose on your face!"

One of the officers tittered at this, as Mr. Humphreys does indeed have a rather large nose.

Our counsel Mr. Williamson rose to his feet, calm and polite. "Please show my learned gentleman the copy of the baptismal certificate and the parish ledger."

Mr. Lacey handed Mr. Humphreys the documents. The priest had written the time in the ledger when he issued the baptismal certificate – 9.50 a.m.

"A priest swears a sacred oath of honesty. This proves Mr. Lacy is telling the truth. This is no mere 'Irish alibi',"' said Mr. Williamson.

Surely, I thought, they'd have to believe all the Mass-goers now.

But the officers didn't even glance at the document. They had already made up their minds not to trust the word of any Catholics.

But there was still hope. The final witness was a well-known Dublin architect and a Unionist. He had done some work on the house and said it was impossible for the man in the bathroom to identify anyone! It was too dark and the passage was too narrow. I thought he was a clincher, as he had no reason to help Whelan and Boyce. And he was one of their own.

I began to hope they would both get off.

"Fingers crossed for Whelan," whispered MacBride as the judge rose to sum up. Even a crooked court was up against overwhelming evidence.

The judge looked thunderous. He convened the military martial officers around him.

I crept closer, pretending to pick up papers. There was

lots of terse whispering. "We'll have to return innocent verdicts," I heard one of the officers say.

But then someone came in wearing a trench coat, his face obscured by a low hat. He carried a document. The judge glanced at it and a smile broke over his face. A smile of doom.

The judge, who was supposed to be holding the scales of justice, glared at the accused men. He then held up the document.

"Some new evidence has just been presented to court. A witness who cannot be named has made a signed confession that Whelan admitted the crime to him." The whole room let out a gasp.

Mr. Williamson rose to feet. "Let me see that document! This is an outrage!"

There were murmurs around the room. Some brave soul shouted, "It's a fix!" only to be grabbed by a sentry and hustled out of the room. All the secret service men gave themselves away by slapping each other on the back. MacBride watched them with narrowed eyes, noting every single one of them. I too scanned the room. There was something familiar about the man in the trench coat. I had a cold sick feeling it was Lees.

Mr. Noyk shook his head. Whelan looked thunderstruck.

Mr. Williamson examined the document. It was typed on Castle paper. "Lord Judge, I urge you to adjourn the court while we take this new evidence into account."

The judge banged his gavel. "My learned friend, I am

fully satisfied that this is legitimate evidence in a legitimate court."

Mr. Williamson slumped in his gown, like a bird shot down from flight, and withdrew from the table where the court sat, revolvers at the ready.

The judge rose and began his summing up. "I pronounce a verdict of innocent on Boyce."

My hopes rose. Boyce's face broke into a grin.

"And in the light of the new evidence, guilty for Whelan."

There was an audible gasp from our team.

"The accused will suffer the full penalty at our disposal. Execution."

The word hung in the air, Whelan's friends in the courtroom too stunned to react. Only a woman's voice cried out, "Oh no! My beautiful boy!"

The officers at the desk smiled like devils at Lucifer's feet. Boyce threw his friend a stricken look.

It was as if all the air was knocked out of me. Whelan's face went pale and he clenched the table with whitened knuckles. But within a split second he righted himself and looked the judge in the eye.

"They must have tracked down his roommate," MacBride whispered. "They've beaten the confession out of him."

Pus-Face, I thought, my stomach clenching. He hadn't even been in Dublin and had done a runner, Mrs. Mann had told us. Mother of God, I prayed, I hope he said nothing about me. Then I felt terrible for here was Whelan going to the gallows and all I could think of was my own skin. And poor old Damien, he must have been terrified.

As we gathered up our papers, I heard Noyk say to Mr. Williamson. "At least we got one of them off!"

He replied with great feeling, "It is like comforting a father when one of his two sons has been saved from death." Even a Unionist was ashamed to see an innocent man framed.

Mr. Williamson then went to the back of the court to an old countrywoman dressed in a shawl, with a gentle, dignified face. It was Whelan's mother, Brigid, who had cried out. Her face was ashen as she fought to hold her tears.

The stern lawyer and the old countrywoman embraced.

Someone roughly jostled me in his haste to leave. The man in the trench coat with a hat pulled low over his brow. He opened the door with an ungloved hand. There was a sharp writhing movement as his fingers flexed. The head of a snake curling around his wrist. That cold fist in the pit of my stomach curled tight. Lees. He had framed Whelan. I knew now why he had been hanging round the shop, trying to find a weak link. And when they couldn't, they beat a false accusation out of stupid old Pus-Face.

After we left MacBride pulled me aside. "Do you remember that gun you told me you had hidden after Bloody Sunday?"

How could I forget it? "Yes, I buried it."

He spoke with quiet menace. "It's time it rose from the grave."

Chapter 14

The Gun

I crept out of the house at first light and met MacBride down by the sea wall on Pigeon House Road near our old cottage. There was an early morning sea mist, cold and clammy, salty to our breaths. We scaled the wall without a word. I saw the X marked on the tree with the stone at its centre and took three steps. MacBride had a shovel under his coat. It felt like we were pirates digging up buried treasure. Several feet down, we hit the tin lids and sacking covering the overcoat. We took it from the cold earth without a word. MacBride gave me the shovel to hide.

"That fellow Damien, who they beat the confession out of, went crazy last night when they told him Whelan's to be executed. They've put him in the madhouse. Guess who made him give a false statement?"

"Lees." I didn't have to guess. "I hate him." Poor old

Pus-Face. I thought. I didn't like him but I took no pleasure in his pain.

"Lees will get what's coming to him," MacBride said. "My mother is starting a campaign to get Whelan's sentence commuted. They've already applied for leave to appeal. She feels it bad on account of my father."

"Is there any hope?" I asked.

MacBride unwrapped the gun. He held it in his hand.

"My father had one like this in the Boer War! This is our justice." He checked there were bullets in the barrel and handed it to me. Then, pointing at a shrivelled apple on an old apple tree about ten feet away, he said, "Bet you couldn't hit that."

I took aim and fired. The bullet smashed the apple to smithereens. I was thrown back but righted myself quickly. There was a sharp smell from the discharge that hurt the back of my throat.

"Beginner's luck," said MacBride.

Birds had risen in the air at the sudden sound. I was annoyed at MacBride being all superior. I followed one with my aim. The sound screamed though the sky. The bird fell with a thud. We ran to the clearing where it had come to earth.

There in the early morning frost lay a dead blackbird, its chest exploded open, its neck broken. The colours were vivid. The white of the frost, the black of the wing, the red of the blood. MacBride leant down beside it and whistled.

"You're the best damn natural shot I've ever seen."

I too knelt down beside the bird on the grass. I was sure it was the blackbird I'd heard on that cold November day when I'd buried the gun. He would sing no more. Huge heaving sobs came out of me. And snot. MacBride took the gun that was dangling from my hand. I felt broken up inside. He handed me the little handkerchief Bridie had made for Whelan and I wiped my nose.

If it was this awful killing a blackbird, how could I ever kill a man? I didn't want to look at MacBride's face, to see his contempt. But to my surprise he put his hand on my shoulder, like a brother.

"You have to go away and think if you can face this. Everyone has to decide that for themselves." He took the gun and left me there.

I wrapped the blackbird in the old coat. My fingers touched the outline of my grandfather's letter that had the stamp with the King's head on it. Upside down, like the world. My grandfather had been a brave man, tending to the wounded in battle. I thought maybe it would give me courage. So I took it out and hid it in the lining of my coat. I buried the blackbird where I'd hidden the gun. I said a little prayer for it in my heart.

I sat on the harbour wall for a long time, gazing at the waves breaking on the shore. If my father was here, he could tell me what to do. But he wasn't.

I found it difficult to concentrate in school. My feelings were all mixed up. I was dead inside, winded like I'd been kicked in the stomach. I shivered so much even Brother Disgrace noticed and sent me home early.

I walked up the road with a heavy tread. I didn't even notice that someone had come up behind me and fallen into step with me.

"Off any place special?" said a cruel posh voice.

I jumped. It was Lees. He loomed over me, like a spectre. My breathing went shallow. It took all my power to walk on. I turned up my collar and shrank into the side of the buildings.

"All the girls sad about Whelan? Eh? Won't look so pretty with a noose around his neck."

I raised my fists to strike him but he grabbed one of my hands and crushed it.

"Maybe you could deliver a message to some of your pals?" he said in a low voice, more menacing than if he'd shouted. "Collins doesn't turn up to our meetings." He laughed – a harsh grating sound. "Heard I was in Cork lighting fires. Thinks I burnt down his dear city. How silly. How could I be in two places at once?" He pinned me against the building. "Some little blighter said he saw me the night Cork was burned."

I was whimpering in pain. "Please, Mister. Don't hurt me."

"Give him a message from me. I want the money and safe passage out of here. He gets what he wants." He took a step back, then viciously lunged at me again. "Sailors can be arrested in foreign ports, detained as enemies of the British Empire, you know."

I felt a spurt of anger. "Have you hurt my father?"

He laughed in my face. "Don't get uppity with me, brat. You do whatever I tell you or I'll make it my business to hurt everyone you care about."

He lifted me up by my coat collar and flung me roughly into the road. His grip was strong and I smelt whiskey on his breath. I crumpled like a sack and lay cowering in the gutter. Snivelling. Like the coward I was.

I didn't go home. I went to MacBride's house on Stephen's Green, round the back, and threw a stone at his window. I gave him the message from Lees.

"I'm seeing Collins tonight at Vaughan's hotel in Parnell Square. I'll pass it on."

"Those Mills bombs you want thrown," I said. "You're on."

One hour later we were perched on a rooftop on Brunswick Street, watching the traffic go by. I liked being up on the rooftops. I thought about my cousin, Jack the Cat. He had leaped from chimney to parapet all during Easter Week.

An open-topped Crossley Tender came round the bend. MacBride took out the Mills bomb, a grenade that fitted into my hand.

It was perfect. There was no other traffic, and the Crossley had stalled. But just as I was about to pull the pin, something caught my eye.

There was a sign on the truck. "**Bomb Us Now**." Strapped to a seat in the open back of the truck was a little girl dressed in white. Bridie.

189

I dropped my hand.

"For God's sake, Dan . . ."

MacBride followed my gaze. "That's really low," he said. "They are using innocent civilians as human shields to stop us bombing them. I'm going to get my foreign journalist friends to report that."

I had come close to bombing my best friend. The sickening feeling it gave me churned me up inside. Maybe even if you hated the person it would feel the same. Just plain wrong. I knew then I wouldn't even want to bomb my worst enemy – Lees. I had come too close to the fire.

I dropped down from the roof and followed the vehicle. It drove up Brunswick Street, past Boland's Mill and into Ringsend, dropping Bridie outside the shop. I watched as she skipped in, unscathed, for all the world like she'd been out on a jaunt. My heart was on fire.

I did something I'd never done before in my life. I went into Ringsend Church just to say a prayer.

To my surprise it was half full. There were all kinds of people there, not just the usual shawlies and oul fellas, the "god-botherers". But respectable ladies from Sandymount sat by clerks in their suits. Young office girls, their faces red with crying, were comforted by old women from the markets. In among them was Mrs. Whelan, Thomas's mother, turning a handkerchief over and over in her hands.

"Hail, Holy Queen, Mother of Mercy, we pray that you will spare our son Thomas. Or if it is thy will to take him, may he meet his Maker, in the fullness of your love."

They were holding a vigil. On a stand surrounded by candles was a smiling picture of Thomas. He looked radiant.

I was taken aback to see my own mother there, her hands joined in prayer, her head bowed. I slipped in beside her and she put her arm around me. I felt the warmth of her, the love, the life. She whispered to me that no application for a reprieve would be accepted. There was no chance of a retrial.

The words were like nails. There was no hope.

Chapter 15

The Execution
March 14th 1921

It was the day of the execution. My mother and I left in the early hours before dawn. The streets were already thronged along the route to Mountjoy Jail on the northside. Ordinary life in Dublin came to a standstill under the grey skies. Sacred pictures and candles were set up in the streets and people prayed and sang hymns.

Outside the jail thousands gathered. My mother, who was uncomfortable in crowds, knelt at the back with Nanny and Mother O'Brien. Bridie was there and she slipped her hand in mine. But MacBride saw me and called us forward to stand right outside the gates. We joined Maud Gonne, Mrs. Whelan and the family in prayer.

Mrs. Whelan wore a grey tasselled shawl with embroidery on it. My mother whispered to me that it was traditional dress for women in the west of Ireland. Maud

Gonne was all in black and wore a veil that fell behind her. She looked like a figure from a Greek tragedy that we learned about at school. It was all so sad it hurt the back of my throat. MacBride told me another prisoner had seen six coffins delivered that morning from the carpenter's workshop.

A nun spoke to Mrs. Whelan. "He told me that today he would start a new life that will last forever," said the nun.

A sob broke from Mrs. Whelan and Maud Gonne comforted her.

"He sang 'A Shawl of Galway Grey' for me last night," his mother said and she began to sing through her tears: the sad song of two broken-hearted people saying goodbye to each other.

> *"Twas short the night we parted,*
> *Too quickly came the day,*
> *When silent, broken-hearted,*
> *I went from you away."*

Everyone joined in. Seán MacBride and his mother clung to one another – it must have reminded them of how Seán's father died.

As we left, Nanny took Seán aside and held his hand. "You cannot help poor Tommy now. Study the law and put down your gun. Then you can really help other poor mothers and their sons."

Much affected, he kissed her on the cheek and promised he would. Some day. That "some day" made me feel cold inside.

The bells tolled at six o'clock in the morning for the execution. Everyone fell to their knees to pray for the dying. Mrs. Whelan bowed her head and clutched her prayer book.

"He's gone," she said, her voice breaking, wiping her tears away. *"Slán agus beannacht*, my beautiful boy."

A decade of the rosary swelled up.

> *"As it was in the beginning,*
> *Is now and ever shall be,*
> *World without end. Amen."*

We left for home. The crowd remained. Five other men were still waiting to be hanged at hourly intervals. We could take no more.

"They're trying to arrest me. So I can't carry that gun," said MacBride as we slipped through the crowd. "I've hidden it in my mother's garden under the rose bush. But I need it tonight. Will you at least collect it and do a drop at the Catholic Boys Club on Great Brunswick Street? I'm going there now. Even if you get caught, I'm sure they wouldn't hang a kid."

This was serious stuff. I thought about Whelan, gone now, my stomach lurching. I wouldn't be pulling the trigger.

"Okay, I'll call by."

I could feel my mother's eyes burning into the back of my head. Even if she couldn't hear us against the murmur of prayers she knew something was up.

"Good man." MacBride gave me a slight smile and

melted back into the crowd.

There was no school that day. We went down to Sandymount Strand. I sat on the rocks for a long time. I watched the clouds running their shadows over the water while my mother walked the shore. It was bitterly cold but I didn't care. I wondered if my father was drowned, fishes swimming in and out of his skull. At least he didn't have to live in Ireland. Or die for it. But would he kill for it if he were in my shoes?

I took off my socks and shoes and waded into the water.

Maybe the sea could wash all my troubles away. The freezing cold water shocked me. But I waded in further any way. The salt water cut my legs like knives. I could feel the tug of the outgoing tide.

"Dan, Dan!"

I heard my name called but I ignored it. I was up to my waist in water now. I was about to plunge in, when two arms grabbed my shoulders.

"Dan! Come back now, you'll catch your death!" It was my mother. Her arms were strong as she dragged me back to the shore.

We stood shivering on the bank, both of us in tears.

A woman ran down. "I saw your poor boy from my window. Come back to my house now."

Within minutes I was seated in front of a roaring fire, a blanket around my shoulders, a mug of tea in my hands. The woman of the house had lent my mother some clothes. She was one of the women she'd skivvied for.

My mother stroked my arm. "Oh Dan, what were you thinking?"

I bit my lip. "I was just wondering what it was like to be dead. To feel nothing."

"Poor Thomas Whelan," said my mother. "He died a noble death."

We gazed at the crackling fire, the logs flaming blue and red.

"What's it like to kill someone like that?" I asked her.

A tear slid from my mother's eye. "What terrible times we live in that a child is thinking of what it's like to die and kill," she said.

A log settled, burning hard now.

"Has Father been arrested for smuggling arms?" I asked.

"Your father would never do that," she said. "Do you not remember why he jumped ship when he was young? It wasn't just for adventure. His father got him a commission in the Royal Navy but he refused to take arms. He hates violence."

I rubbed my knuckles that were feeling raw now from the rapid changes of cold and heat.

"I can only tell you what it's like to live," said my mother. "Feeling pain inside isn't a good feeling. But it's part of life. Sometimes you think you are broken but you are being broken open to new things, to grow."

"Some of the lads say they don't feel anything when they pull the trigger. Others have nightmares, feel blood in their mouths," I said.

"If you cannot feel pain, it makes it easier to inflict it. Dan, you are not a killer. It's not in your nature," she said.

"I'm too weak," I said.

She held my face in her hands, her eyes searching into my soul. I looked deep into her eyes full of love.

"No, Dan, you are too strong. You feel other people's pain. That is strength. May God preserve and keep you so." She embraced me tight. "We cannot go round it. We must live through it. The only way we know how. Respecting other's humanity and dignity no matter who they are."

I started to shiver again and felt like crawling under a rock. "It's all very well for Father to have such fine feelings. He isn't here!" I cried.

She touched her own chest and then mine. "He's here in our hearts," she said. "When we married, your father and I swore we would always love our children no matter what. And not expect them to live in our images. I know some people think I am too soft on you. But I want you to learn to make up your own mind."

We sat there for a long time. The clock struck two o'clock in the afternoon.

"I'll need to get back to Josephine," she said. "Our neighbour, Mrs. Burke, is minding her and I don't want to impose."

At the bridge, Mother turned in the direction of home. I ran the other way towards MacBride in Brunswick Street. I didn't turn round but I felt her eyes burning into my back all the way down the street.

197

Chapter 16

The Drop

MacBride was in the back of the Catholic Boys Club near the Carnegie Library. He was in his element, issuing orders to a group of men. I wasn't sure if he was really in charge or just acting like he was. He took me out onto the roof. We surveyed Great Brunswick Street, the big long length of it that stretched all the way from Ringsend Bridge to College Green.

"We're laying a trap for the Auxies and Tans," he said in a quiet voice. "Tonight, we'll extinguish all the lights and get them to call here. We'll be waiting for them all right. Around thirty men posted inside and outside the building – no escape. Can you do the gun drop just after seven?"

He took my silence for assent. We went back downstairs. Someone called his name.

"You're a good enough shot to fire," he said to me. There

was an edge in his voice, like he was issuing a challenge.

I heard a clock ticking on a mantelpiece. I saw pictures of priests on the wall alongside Pearse Connolly and Clarke. All those leaders executed in 1916 for their part in the Rising. I caught my own eye in a large mirror. I looked like a skinned rabbit.

My mouth was dry with fear. "I can't come," I said.

A flicker went across his eyes. "Then Traynor the bootmaker will do the drop," he said coldly. "Even though he has ten children to support, he wants to do his bit for Ireland."

I turned to leave.

"Each to his conscience," he said, steel in his voice. "You're just a little boy still."

"So are you," I said.

I passed one of the brigade. Seán Dolan, whose brother was in our school, was assembling a crude bomb of gelignite on the billiard table. Above it was a large picture of the Vatican where the Pope lives.

I heard MacBride's bitter laugh as I pelted down the stairs three at a time.

My mother was relieved to see me when I walked through the door. And when I told her I thought I was like my father, she was elated. I didn't have to spell it out. She knew I meant I didn't want any part in using guns. In the evening, we played card games, gin rummy and "twenty-ones", after Josephine fell asleep.

I heard the roar of a bomb and guns ricochet late in the

night. But I was so tired I fell into a deep dreamless sleep.

"Read all about it! Gun Battle in Brunswick Street! Hand to hand fighting between Auxies and Rebels!" the paperboy on the corner of Ringsend Bridge yelled as I passed him on my way to school.

He called me over.

"Janey Mac, the bullets were leppin' off the pavement last night. Seven dead!"

Fear gripped me but mostly relief I'd had no part in it.

"A bomb went off right outside the College Street Police station. Blew a man's leg off! Then two truckloads of Auxies drove up outside the Catholic Working Man's Club and the Volunteers were waiting for them."

I gulped. I'd seen Dolan assemble that bomb.

"There was a terrible gun battle. Blood all over the street," the paperboy continued. "The Auxies caught one of them – Traynor, a bootmaker – with a gun in his hand. He'll hang for sure!"

A pang struck my heart. The man who took my place.

The paperboy added in a half whisper, "MacBride got away."

I couldn't help going to have a look at the scene of the battle further up the street. There were long streaks of blood along the grey pavement where the dead and injured had been dragged away. Groups of people were gathered round in knots, talking in excited whispers.

"Pitch black it was," said an old shawlie. "They shut

down all the streetlights and you couldn't see your hand. I heard at least a hundred shots!"

"The manager of the Sinn Féin bank was caught in the crossfire – riddled with bullets!" exclaimed a fruit seller.

"A fella was shot dead in the neck when he stopped to help poor old May Morgan who'd been badly wounded. Ex-soldier and all, just bein' a Good Samaritan," a young mother, her baby on her hip, chipped in. "Two Auxies, three ordinary people mindin' their own business and I heard two of the Volunteers. All dead."

More numbers to add to the balance sheet of war.

I buried my head and worked extra hard at my maths in school.

I took a different route home, going round by Mount Street. But near Haddington Road, Anto, fit to burst out of his Findlaters messenger-boy uniform, pulled up on his bike.

"Can you get Molly? It's urgent."

He told me why in gulps. His ma, Nancy, was a cleaner in Mercer's Hospital. They had brought in the bomber, Seán Dolan, after his foot was blown off by his own bomb. Said it was a tram accident. The matron found the splinter of a bomb and rang Dublin Castle to come and arrest him. But Nancy overhead the conversation and sent word to Anto. He went with MacBride and a few others in a car to rescue him.

"The matron picked up the phone but I ripped the phone off the wall!" he exclaimed. "Big Jimmy lifted Dolan straight out of the bed. There were spikes stickin' out of the stump of his leg. That's why we need Molly! I know she can fix him."

"She's probably at a lecture," I said.

We rushed round to Trinity College. She was just coming out the side entrance, the one reserved for female students. She agreed without hesitation and jumped on her bicycle. She gave me a lift on her handlebars.

The safe house was at Beechcroft Avenue in Ranelagh. The owner was a Protestant lady who had turned against the British government after losing her three sons in the war. In a stable out back, Dolan lay groaning on some sacking. Molly gave him a tincture that settled him. I didn't want to see his leg with the spikes so I kept lookout in the back lane, just a boy kicking a ball. It was a fine evening. There were tiny buds on the branches, birds with twigs in their mouths building nests – a taste of spring in the air.

"Dan!" MacBride was calling me from a woodshed.

I ducked in. He was shivering, hunched in his overcoat. Not the cocky fellow I was used to. Face the colour of ash. He was the frightened boy now.

MacBride stared at his hand. "We were lying in wait on the road. Sparks were hopping off the pavement. An armoured car was only twenty yards away. We had to retreat. I shook my comrade Leo. But my hand was full of his hot blood. He was already dead." He rubbed his hand on his jacket. "I hid, covered in his blood, until first light." Covering his eyes with his hands, he continued in a low voice. "My father's death, all those who have fallen. They weren't real for me, you know. But last night, death was beside me. It's not what I thought."

"I'm sorry," I muttered.

"I was hard on you yesterday," he said. "You were right to stay away. It's no place for boys. I need to have a good hard think myself."

We fell silent, each lost in his own thoughts.

Time passed. Then a horse whinnied, startling me.

I looked out and saw Molly's flaming hair in the twilight as she left the stable.

"Be careful on your way home," MacBride said. "They're out for blood."

Molly wheeled her bicycle and we walked home together by the canal.

"Do you know MacBride well?" I asked.

"He's asked me out a few times," she smiled, blushing red to the roots of her hair. "He's not my type. A bit too full of himself."

"At least that explains why he's always asking me to run messages," I said.

"Ah, poor Dan!" She pulled my ear. "You thinking it was your fast legs and your amazing ball skills!"

We decided to both go home to Mam to keep each other company. But we walked straight into a barricade across Bath Avenue. The Tommy manning the station gave us a nervous nod as he let us through. We were in the middle of clambering over it, when a cold voice rang out.

"Detain those two!"

I saw the shiny boots before I spied the spruce moustache.

Captain Lees smiled his devilish smile. "Search their bags."

Schoolbooks, my bible, torn to shreds all over the road. Lees gave a look of triumph when he pulled out Molly's cloths that were covered in Dolan's blood. Caught up in them was his bloodstained puttee that soldiers wear around their legs. And right in the bottom of her bag, his volunteer badge that he'd asked her to give to his girl.

"You are under arrest, Miss Molly O'Donovan, for aiding and abetting enemies of the state. Take the boy in for questioning."

"You have no grounds!" cried Molly.

Lees smiled his venomous smile, his eyes flashing yellow like a snakes. "The beauty of martial law is I don't need to have." He struck her hard across the face. Then stroked her hair.

Her eyes blazed at him as she reared back.

I hated him more than I hated anyone ever. I picked up the bicycle and with all my might threw it at him and the squaddie.

"You little . . ." A shot rang out.

Lees had fired at my feet.

"Arrest that boy!" roared Lees, his temple bleeding, his face contorted with fury.

"Sir, they are just kids!" The squaddie, a teenager himself, stood there, bewildered.

"Run, Molly, run!"

But she didn't.

Lees grabbed me. I wriggled and struck out like mad, but he got me by the throat.

"Leave him be!" Molly threw her whole body at Lees. But he was solid muscle. She bounced off him. Then she tried to pull me away from him. Lees struck her once more about the face. Blood ran down her lip.

"Do something, you idiot, or I'll have you court-martialled!" Lees roared at the squaddie. But when the squaddie did nothing, Lees put his gun to my temple.

"Don't shoot! Please God, no!" screamed Molly.

The squaddie cocked his gun at her, the bayonet shining. Tense now, coiled and ready to fire.

Lees tossed Molly a filthy rag. "Tie it round his eyes."

Before she tied the knot, Molly put her fingers to her already swollen lips, urging me to silence.

Lees checked the blindfold then bundled me roughly into a car.

"Take her into custody," he instructed the squaddie.

The engine fired and we sped off to God knew where.

Chapter 17

Hostage

My left temple throbbed. The taste of blood was metallic in my mouth. I moved my tongue around the back of my teeth with difficulty. But they were all still there. I think I must have bitten my cheek in fright. The worst thing had been the rats gnawing at my bare feet. But after a while I couldn't feel them as my feet went numb.

I was blindfolded, tied to a chair, no idea where I was. The rough hemp of the rope cut into my hands and legs. My neck felt like it would snap off.

Wiggle your big toe, then the next one, I told myself in my head, willing the life back into my feet. Pretend you've got a tiny football and you're trying to pass it back and forth between your left and right. But it keeps getting lost in your toes.

My left foot was throbbing. But at least I had a left foot.

Not like poor Seán Dolan with his dodgy gelignite bomb.

I had no idea if I'd been there days or hours. I heard a blackbird's call, then a robin's chirp. There was more light, even under the blindfold. A cold dawn. Then a knocking sound. I told myself it was a branch against a window. I strained my ears for other sounds but there was only a high, howling wind above the dawn chorus.

I ached with loneliness. But at least Lees wasn't here. Or I couldn't sense him. I was still alive. For now. That was something. And I hadn't squealed on my comrades. Of that at least I was sure. Or I hadn't squealed yet.

I tried not to think about what Lees had done to me. He'd driven like a maniac for about twenty minutes. I'd counted out each second in my head. Then I lost track of time. I didn't think we were in the mountains because the car hadn't gone uphill.

When we arrived at this place, he'd stuck a gun in my back. There was a crunch of gravel under foot. Then rough branches. Brambles grabbed at my clothing. I sensed utter darkness. I smelt pine and leaf mould. Another salty smell. The sea nearby. My guess was we were in a wood near the coast. A fumble with keys. A faint scent of apples. The creak of a door opening.

He dragged me inside the building and tied me to a chair.

First he'd tried to wheedle me. "Where are they? MacBride? Dolan? All those rebels who killed my friends?"

"I don't know, sir."

"What were you doing in Cork? In Tipperary?"

"I don't know, sir."

"What's in those messages you deliver to de Valera?"

"I don't know, sir."

"Where's that little villain, MacBride?" he roared in my left ear. It was still ringing.

"I'm just a messenger boy."

"Just a little messenger boy, are you?" he cruelly mimicked my voice that hadn't yet broken but got high when I was nervous. "But you're not innocent, Dan, are you? You're a little thieving gunrunner. A sneaky little rebel!" He was screaming now. Unhinged.

I flinched at the slobber of his spittle on my throbbing face.

"That's my gun now, you know, that you gave to MacBride to shoot us. I got it off that stupid bootmaker Traynor we caught after the Brunswick Street massacre." He slapped me across the face.

I tried not to cry.

"What's Collins up to? Trying to negotiate, is he? You delivered messages to that Archbishop. Clune. That's right. The one whose nephew got killed. Set up meetings with the big General Smuts. You filthy little cowards want a truce."

My tongue was swollen now. I couldn't speak.

"Well, some of us don't want a truce," he ranted, stamping about. "Some of us like the war. We want to smash you into the ground! Kill every single one of you. We want to finish what you started!"

208

He put my feet on a low stool and beat the soles with a leather strap. It stung. But I was used to leathers from the Brothers. I could take it.

I began to replay matches in my head. Bookman's brilliant cross. Bohemians' victory over Luton. That pass . . . to . . . I thought of keepy-uppy moves . . .

After a bit, he got bored with beating me. I could hear his panting as he tied my feet to the chair.

He moved his head closer to mine, his whiskey breath making me heave.

"What are you saying? Speak up! "

"It was a classic drop-kick move . . . Darcy took the free kick . . ."

"Think that's funny, do you? Do you? Shut up, you little sniveller," Lees said calmly. Then he leaned in close and whispered in my ear. "I'll show you. You're no match for me and the might of the British Empire. You puny little piece of dirt."

SMASH!

Me and the chair crashed to the cold flagstone floor. The back of the seat broke my fall but my head was hurt. I cried out in pain but my cry was muffled by my swollen tongue.

"Think it's funny to taunt me?" I felt his breath as he whispered in my ear. Then his voice changed to Jameson's harsh gravel tones. "Thieving little stamp collector!"

The sour smell of whiskey made me gag. He hauled me and the chair back up. I was close to passing out.

"Ah Dan, don't fall asleep on me. We've only started."

He threw a glass of cold water on my face. He was back to Lees again. "Is Griffith having secret meetings with the Prime Minister to arrange a truce?"

I laughed, despite myself.

"'Ow would I know . . . ?" I tried to mumble but my tongue was thick.

"I was genuinely trying to help at first. Earn some money. Get you lot some arms. You scratch my back, I'll scratch yours. But you put paid to that, Dan, didn't you?"

"No, sir . . ."

"Now Collins won't see me because of you. He thinks I burnt down Cork! Now where did he get that idea? Who was it I ran into in Cork?"

For a horrible moment it was as if I was back there. I saw in my mind's eye his twisted features in his snarling face as he'd rampaged in the burning inferno.

I started trying to do big sums in my head. What's forty-five times fifty-seven? What's an isosceles triangle? What's the square root of three million and a hundred and eight?

"What are you mumbling now, you halfwit?"

I must have been speaking aloud.

"Let me show you something." He spoke with quiet menace, more scary than his rants.

He left. A door opened. A cold rush of wind. The heavy tread of boots as he came back in. Then a nauseous, filthy smell. He pulled the blindfold off me. My eyes swam, the candlelight danced as I tried to adjust my sight after so much blackness. His devil's face was in an evil grimace in the yellow circle of light. There was a revolting smell of rotting flesh. He pushed a vile bloody, decaying mess of twisted bones and singed flesh under my nose. I saw maggots crawling through it.

"Know what this is?"

I shook my head. He got angrier if I gave no response.

"Why, it's only Dolan's foot! Where is he so I can give it back?"

He dropped the seething mess onto my lap. I screamed.

He laughed then. Like a madman. Like the vicious devil he was.

He took the limb away and put it back in a sack. Then replaced my blindfold.

"Just like that stamp that disappeared with the coat, Danny boy. I was seeing things then. You're seeing things now."

"Will you let me go . . . for the stamp?" My voice was small and thick from my swollen tongue, wheedling.

He thrust his face into mine. I couldn't see him but I could smell him.

"I won't make any promises." His voice pushed against me in the darkness.

"Coat lining . . ."

I heard him tear at the coat, the crinkle of paper. He let out a whoop of joy.

"Me go," I moaned.

"You stupid little fool. Didn't your mother ever tell you not to trust strangers! It's probably a fake anyhow from a filthy thieving little scumbag like you."

I heard the crash of glass.

"Now look what you've done. I've run out of whiskey."

Rustling sounds, heavy breathing. A door creaking open. A gust of wind that carried a faint tang of salt. We were definitely somewhere near the sea.

"Don't get too comfortable. I'll be back. To finish you off."

His evil laugh rang in my ears as the door clanged shut. The sound of a bolt in a lock.

I was alone. I cursed myself for giving him that stamp.

I must have passed out at some stage. But now I was awake. My swollen mouth was parched. I wanted a drink of water more than anything. I had to move.

The blindfold was looser than before. He had pulled the chair closer to the wall after he'd righted me. If I could tip it back, I might be able to rub the rope against a jagged stone. I strained my head back but felt only air. Using all my strength, I wriggled the chair back towards the wall, then tipped back. I felt the wall's rough texture with relief. There was the sharp edge of a flagstone level with my hands. I angled my wrists and snagged the rope on it. The pain in my arms was excruciating. But I kept at it, sawing and rubbing. I imagined my father's patience when he made his ships in the bottle. How he would construct little balsa boats then work for hours to ease them in at the right angle.

I sawed for what felt like hours. Just as I was about to

give up, the rope sprang apart. My hands were free! I pulled off the filthy blindfold. Then clapped my hands to bang the blood back into them. My eyes were blurry but I could make out my surroundings. A candle guttered on a table. There was a patch of light through a window. I was in a rough stone building, flagstones beneath my feet. One end had farm tools and seemed to be some sort of disused workroom with old broken-up machinery.

The knot around my ankles was tied with a vengeance. A double figure of eight cinched in the middle. Then a few rounds of rope to bind my legs to the chair secured with a stop knot. My father could tie knots like that. And so could I. I felt the rough cord with my throbbing fingers to work out if it could be unravelled. It was hopeless. It would have to be cut. I cast my eyes around the room. There was a large glass shard from the whiskey bottle several feet away near the table. Summoning all my strength I inched the chair towards it. At this rate it was going to take forever. I couldn't pause, couldn't give in. I was half a body-length away. If I threw myself and the chair on the floor, I could reach it with my arms.

I tilted to the right and landed side on. The pain pierced like knives. With a bit of sliding I reached the glass shard, and cut my finger. The blood felt sticky, creamy almost. I got to work, sawing at the rope.

But just as I'd sawed through the cords, the bolt clanged in the door. The pale light pouring in was like a slap. I put the shard in my pocket. If he came near me, I intended to use it.

"Dan! Jesus preserve us! What has that animal done!" Within a heartbeat, Molly was beside me.

I tried to speak but my tongue was too swollen.

"Help me get him up."

Two men had come in with her, their faces covered by scarves.

"Did he say he'd be back?"

I recognised the broad Dublin accent. Vinnie, one of the Squad.

"Water," I murmured.

Molly fetched me a cup from somewhere. It was the sweetest water I ever tasted. I was too dazed by its fresh pure taste coursing down my throat to wonder how they'd found me.

The other fellow pulled his mask down and grinned. "I'm here to pay back a favour."

I couldn't focus my eyes. But I knew who it was. Charlie, the gunman I'd saved when I skied the ball, that time when I'd come from school.

"Listen, did he ask you anything?" he said.

I could talk a bit better after the drink. I told him about the questions about my messages. MacBride, Dolan. Why Collins wouldn't see him. I mentioned the stamp but they just shrugged at that.

"He's spooked all right," said Vinnie.

"His number's up," said Charlie. "Even his own side want to see the back of him."

Charlie searched the room. He found a cache of papers

behind a stone in the workroom.

"Bingo!" he said. "Lees knew I wanted to get these files back. These were his bargaining chip."

"He showed me Dolan's foot." I gestured towards the sack in the corner.

They looked at me in amazement.

Vinnie poked inside the sack and let out a short laugh. "I didn't know Dolan was half pig!"

Charlie and Molly peeked in. They caught each other's eye, then fell about laughing hysterically.

"I can verify that Dolan's foot is in fact a pig's trotter," said Molly, trying to rein in her laughter.

"It's not funny," I said, but even I started laughing, though it hurt my ribs.

There was a screech of brakes.

"He's back!" said Charlie.

The laughter stopped.

"No violence, please," said Molly. "I asked Mick not to kill him."

Charlie and Vinnie waved us back as they went out and crouched down behind a woodpile. We hunkered by the wall near the half-door. Molly put her arm around me to stop me shaking.

There was a hail of bullets, the crunch of brakes, an almighty crash.

"You can come on out!" shouted Vinnie.

We peeked over the half-door. The car was crashed into the side of the building. The windscreen smashed to pieces.

Lees was slumped over the wheel, blood spattered everywhere.

Charlie looked inside. "Job done," he said.

Molly went out the door and looked at Vinnie and Charlie, horrified. "But I asked –"

"There's a war on. He pulled his gun. It was self-defense. He must have suspected something," said Vinnie matter of factly. He stopped, like a fox, listening to some faraway sound. "Crossley Tenders patrol near here. There's a car waiting for us. We have to go." He tossed me a gun. It was the .455 revolver. The one Lees had got from Traynor. The one I'd hidden in Ringsend Park.

"If he's still alive, use this to finish him off."

They took a path through the woods. As soon as they were out of sight, I dropped the gun down by the water butt and left it there.

I winced with each step. So Molly led me back inside where she bandaged my feet and put ointment on my head. She gave me another drink of water.

"The squaddie was disgusted by Lees arresting a boy," she said. "He let me go. Told me where to look for him and all. It was brave of him. Lees is – was – considered a loose cannon. The regular soldiers don't like him."

"How did you get the Squad here?"

"I cycled straight to Collins in Vaughan's Hotel in Parnell Square. He sent the boys to help." She helped me up. "You could say it killed two birds with one stone." Her voice was bitter.

We came out the door. The daylight was so bright it stung my eyes. Molly fetched her bicycle from around the side. I tried not to look at the car. I was too tired and cold and sore to feel anything, not even relief.

But just as we passed the car and I tried to sit on the saddle of Molly's bike, we heard a low moaning sound. A gurgling noise like someone choking on blood. Molly froze.

"It's him!" She roused herself and approached the car.

"No, Molly! He might be armed!"

But she was already at the door.

I picked up the gun and covered her. Just in case. But it shook so much in my hands I couldn't even get my finger in the trigger, let alone fire it.

Lees' left temple was pumping blood and there were wounds in his shoulder and breast. His face was covered in cuts from the glass. Molly examined him. His face was already turning blue.

He gripped her arm. "Sing to me . . ." His voice was husky, slurred. "Please . . ."

"Sir, you are mortally wounded," she said.

"Sing," he insisted. "The witch in Ringsend . . . a crown . . . she saw it . . . this is not it . . . king's ransom they promised . . . I'll ransom the King . . . between war and peace I'll . . . stop them if it takes the king's head . . ." He faded a bit. Then came back with a menacing cry. "Sing for king and country – Danny Boy!"

Molly nodded at me.

"Oh Danny Boy . . . the pipes, the pipes are calling . . ." My

voice faltered.

"We need to get you to a hospital, sir," said Molly. "Give you some morphine, dress your wounds."

"Morphine – please –" he said, his mouth full of blood. His hand grabbed her arm, the tattooed snake uncoiling and recoiling.

Molly thought for a moment. "There's a convent dispensary near here. They won't ask any questions. You stay with him, Dan."

"Don't leave me with him," I pleaded. "I'll come with you."

Molly cast around and found a rug on his back seat. She covered him and made him comfortable. She was so gentle. Even though I knew she hated him as much as I did. But I felt sorry for him too. I did not like to see him suffer.

She nodded. I sat on the saddle. She stood to pedal the bike. I hid the gun back behind the water butt.

We got outside the demesne. The convent was only five minutes away. We were in Clontarf, I realised, on the northside, right beside the bay. I knew it from looking across from the Pigeon House. The salty breeze whipped us in the face.

She left me outside while she knocked on the door of the convent and was immediately admitted by a kind-faced nun. I got the impression this wasn't her first visit. Molly wanted me to stay behind with the nuns, but I wouldn't leave her. It was harder pedalling back. Driving rain came in off the sea and a savage wind lashed the waves. They rose above the sea wall and threatened to crash onto the road.

When we got back to the building I knew something was wrong. We tiptoed towards the car. But Lees wasn't there! We followed a trail of blood, through a short, densely wooded path, then found ourselves crossing the road by the sea wall. The wind howled now, surf splashed over the side. The trail of blood ran out at the wall. There wasn't a single living soul to be seen.

"He's been swept out to sea," Molly said.

My enemy was gone. I felt nothing.

"God rest his soul," Molly said, clasping her hands in silent prayer.

I kept my hands at my sides. "Why did you try to help him, Molly? After everything."

"When I become a doctor I will swear an oath to care for the sick and not let them suffer. I will not be worthy of my calling if I do not learn to treat even my enemies."

"I still don't want him back," I said.

Molly gazed out to sea. "It's really hard," she said. "But if we become like them, they've won. They can take everything else, even my life. But I won't lose my humanity. That's my victory."

She was shaking. She fell to her knees and rocked, crying and crying. I crouched down beside her and put my arm around her. After a time she smiled and we got to our feet to continue our journey home. We were both too tired to cycle. My feet hurt like hell but I wanted to get away.

As we came down by Fairview, a Crossley Tender slowed down. We glimpsed a group of Black and Tans seated on boards. It passed us by. But just as we thought it was moving on, it screeched to a halt.

Black-capped Tans got out, searched Molly's bag. Threw bandages, needles, books all over the pavement. At the bottom they found Dolan's blood-stained puttee and his Volunteer badge for his girl. In all the excitement, Molly had forgotten to dispose of them.

"You are under arrest for coming to the aid of enemies of the State."

"But she just tried to . . ."

Molly put her hand on my arm before I said too much. How could we explain our mission of mercy for Lees without betraying everyone else? Including the brave squaddie who'd let her go.

Too weary to argue, Molly followed them into the tender. Of all the sad sights I've seen, a defeated Molly was the worst.

Chapter 18

Inside the Joy
May 1921

"You've got to go back for the gun," Molly told me when we were finally allowed in to visit her two months later in Mountjoy Jail.

She looked well despite her ordeal, though thinner and older somehow. She'd celebrated her seventeenth birthday in prison.

I tried to change the subject.

"I'm back playing ball. I've got a new game. It's called 'Danball' and uses all three balls: rugby, GAA and soccer." I started to explain the rules to her and how girls could play too but she gripped my hand tight.

"Throw the gun in the sea!"

I shook my head. "Nah. No way am I going back there."

"You can have my bicycle!"

That clinched it. Her bike was a beaut! I'd left it back at

her lodgings in Rathmines after her arrest in the hope she'd come back.

When I called to pick it up, her friend Doctor Dorothy was rushing out to the dispensary. She told me Oliver St. John Gogarty, Molly's tutor, wanted to go to the newspapers about her case. But Molly wouldn't let him. She was afraid the publicity would be bad and they might throw her out of college.

I wasn't too thrilled about going back to Clontarf where Lees had held me. But on a sunny May morning, the place looked different. I scaled the wall into the old demesne and was relieved it was still deserted. I saw through the trees that the main building was a ruin. I had been held in a ramshackle flagstone building in a rundown old apple orchard surrounded by a wood. That explained the scent of apples. There was no sign of the car. I searched all around, and behind the water butt but there was no trace of a gun.

I went back to Ringsend Park where I was due to play a game of Danball. Bridie was there and McIlroy and his gang. Even my brother Willie turned up. Another fellow of about seventeen called Dan Head joined us. We nicknamed him "Head-the-Ball". He was always trying to get information out of me about jobs. I told him nothing. He asked me about Bloody Sunday, Croke Park, Tipperary, Cork. But I just shrugged and headed the ball to shut him up. He was older than me, about seventeen, but I felt like he was younger. Desperate to see some action.

Boys treated me differently, I noticed. With a certain distance and respect. I asked Bridie why.

"Do you know what they're singing?" she whispered.

"What?"

"Dan, Dan, killed a man,

Beat him on the head with a frying pan."

I gasped. "If only they knew, Bridie!"

"I knew you wouldn't kill someone," she said in a happy way. She knows that inside I'm as soft as butter.

Willie and I picked the teams and I explained the rules.

"You have to keep the three balls in play and you can score with any of the balls. But only according to the rules of that game. So no holding the soccer ball or slide tackles for GAA."

"There's no referee," added Willie. "Anyone disobeying the rules has to take time out to the count of sixty. It's a game of honour."

It was gas fun. Bridie was very handy as a winger because the boys didn't bother marking her. We ended up with a 30-point draw, all falling about the place laughing.

As we were leaving the park, Willie took me aside. He told me one of the brothers had asked him to carry a message. To de Valera in Greystones later that afternoon. I didn't like it.

"If you get caught, you might lose your scholarship."

"If I don't go, I might lose it too! Some of the brothers are on the side of the rebels. I'll be honest – I don't want to get involved."

I didn't want Willie getting involved either. He was my

mother's pride. If anything happened to him, she'd never recover. It was bad enough with me. But I didn't have much to lose.

"I'll do it," I said. "I know the way and I'm younger. I won't get into as much trouble."

He smiled with relief. "I owe you one. But come and see me play first."

So despite my promises to myself, I was back in it. But first I went to see Willie's match in Blackrock. It was the Leinster semi and Blackrock were six points down going into the second half. It was grim going. The pitch was mucky after a shower of hailstones. But they came out roaring.

"It's worse than the Somme!" someone roared in the crowd when Blackrock emerged like mud monsters from a scrum.

But the lads dug in and came back at them. In the last minute Willie scored a try, shaking off the opposition like he was shrugging off a coat. It all rested on the final kick of the match. Willie lined up for the shot on goal.

At exactly that moment, one of the Brothers came up to me and, pretending to stumble, slipped me a letter hidden in his prayer book. I looked up in time to see the ball sail through the goalposts. They were still celebrating when I ran to the station.

I went into Dev's house over a neighbour's wall, just in case anyone was watching. I knocked on the back door. To my surprise it was answered by a tall lanky fellow: de

Valera himself. He lived up to his nickname – a "Longfellow" in every way. I am tall and even I had to crane my neck. His expression was long too, like a wet Saturday. His face was severe and scholarly, creased and forbidding as if carved in rock. In a faltering voice I explained I'd just come from Blackrock. He almost jumped out of his skin. The lines crinkled into a smile, like ice breaking on a lake.

"What's the result? No, talk me through the whole match, pass by pass."

So that's what I did, relishing every scrum and line throw. It was quite a while before I reached the climax of the game.

"There wasn't a breath in the stadium when Willie lined up for the conversion." I hammed it up, enjoying his anticipation. "He was calm and unruffled. This was Willie's specialty. He bent his head and joined his hands as if in prayer. Then a little run, his right boot shot forward and connected with the ball." Dev listened to me spellbound. "The arc of the ball was pure poetry – a parabola. It sliced though the goalposts as if a magic hand was drawing the perfect goal. Willie was mobbed by his jubilant team. The crowd erupted. Even the opposite team murmured, 'Great goal'. The captain of the opposition shook his hand."

De Valera jumped up and down in triumph and shook my hand vigorously. "Heroic! Well done, Blackrock!"

Síle, his wife came in with a plate of currant cake and a glass of milk. "I told you he was mad for rugby," she said with a wink. "Even though he hasn't been to a game since 1913."

"There's no football game to match rugby," he said. "If all our young men played rugby not only would we beat England and Wales, but France and the whole lot of them put together. Pity it's a garrison game."

"It's just a ball game, sir," I said. "Maybe if we get our own country –"

"If only if it was that simple," he cut in. "I told Síle to get rid of my ball so I'm not tempted."

Síle shot me a sideways look. I kept my mouth shut. I'd got good at that.

Then, shaking his head, de Valera read over the message I'd brought. He wrote out a letter.

"This has to go to Collins in person at Vaughan's Hotel," he said.

I nodded.

But, before handing it to me, he glanced over it.

"Can a bright boy like you memorise it for me?" he said, passing it to me.

I saw the schoolteacher in him.

I looked at the note.

"This is a direct order. We need extra paraffin for the agreed date. The added custom will create a favorable impression on our overseas friends."

He made me say it back to him then he threw it in the fire.

I thought about what he said about rugby as I sat in the train back into the city. Thought how stupid it was to want to ban it. What kind of Ireland was it going to be if you couldn't play any game you want? One thing for sure, I was never going into politics.

I headed into Vaughan's hotel on Parnell Square to see Collins.

"Aux," said someone to me as I went inside. That was code word for Auxies on the premises.

I could spot them easily. A group of loud officers near the door, red-eyed and smelling of beer.

I thought Collins would be hidden in the back but he was out front propped up at the bar, chatting to a couple of fellows. They were all hunched over the counter, watching the Auxies through the large glass mirror over the bar. But at such an angle their own faces were obscured.

Collins gave me a slight nod and led me out back to a small yard crowded with beer barrels and boxes. There was a yeasty smell in the air.

"The darkest place is under the light," he winked at me.

But when I delivered the message, he exploded with rage, letting out a string of swear words.

"Divil take that Long Fellow! It's suicide. We'll be lucky if anyone gets out alive!"

One of his companions came out to tell him the Auxies had left.

"What's wrong?" he asked with a second glance at Collins' red face. It was Charlie, who I'd last seen when they'd rescued me.

"Sheer madness! It'll be a mess like the Rising was!" Collins stopped himself and whispered into Charlie's ear.

My breath went shallow with the strain of listening.

Charlie let out a long slow whistle. "It'll make the front page of every newspaper!"

Collins bent down to me. "Keep your gob shut. But take my advice, Dan, and stay out of town on the 25th May. We're about to slit our own throats!"

Chapter 19

The Burning
May 1921

I tried to find out what was going down so I could warn people, but it wasn't easy. This was a massive job on – the biggest of the whole war, bigger even than the hits on Bloody Sunday. Everyone was under strict orders to keep their mouths shut. Try as I might I couldn't winkle anything out of anybody. MacBride, my usual source, was on the run. When I told a few people like Mother O'Brien and Nanny I was so vague they thought I was spoofing. Nanny's husband Mathew, known as "Achie", who worked for the Custom House, just laughed at me.

So I decided to keep my nose out of it. Collins himself had warned me to keep clear of town on the 25th of May. But there was a little worry-worm gnawing away at me.

Tuesday the 24th May was dry and we played a long game of Danball in Ringsend Park for my thirteenth birthday.

Head-the-Ball came up from Ballybough. He was full of himself for some reason and was keen to take me on, laying into me at every opportunity. He was a heavy tackler and I thought he was going to take the legs off me. He did his nut when I nutmegged him, put the ball between his legs and picked it up behind him! I still scored three goals. One from a corner kick with the soccer ball. The other the conversion of a try with the rugby one and the last one, a sweet little lob over the keeper.

Head-the-Ball slapped me on the back. "Happy Birthday! Bejay, someday we'll play alongside each other for Ireland!"

He wasn't a sore loser – that was for sure.

"I'm not sure which is more of a long shot – a free Ireland or Danball being its official game," I said.

He laughed.

He drew up his shoulders, looking all important. "I better get an early night. My company is on tomorrow."

He was talking about the big job, of course. He was finally getting his chance to impress everybody. I felt a chill in the pit of my stomach.

"You should stay out of it," I said.

"Turned yellow have you, Danny Boy? I'm a true patriot," he said.

I was annoyed after all I'd been through. I didn't like him thinking I was a coward, but I worried about what he might be getting himself into. A greenhorn like him.

I decided to bluff to see if I could find out what was

happening. "I'm to run messages, if I can get out of school. Maybe I'll see you there." Then after a beat I added, "Where's the meet-up?"

He took the bait. "Oriel Hall."

That was up on Saville Place, near where I used to live. I didn't like going back up there after Bloody Sunday.

"See you there – what time is it again?" I asked.

He gave me a hard look. He had a big open face and a trusting manner. But he wasn't thick. "Stay out of it, you young pup!" He laughed and cuffed me good-naturedly on the earhole.

I felt edgy and didn't know what to do. I waited until my mother was out of the house and took the ceremonial sword from the strongbox. I went back to Ringsend Park, to the copse of trees. I slashed and slashed at the undergrowth, until it was a patch of brown earth. I cut away the branches to let the sun shine where no light had been. So new things could grow.

I thought about it as I lay in bed, like a puzzle in a boy's magazine. But I couldn't figure out what the job was going to be. They needed a lot of petrol according to de Valera's message. Charlie Dalton said it would make the front page of every newspaper. Could they be planning to firebomb the GPO – the rebels' stronghold in 1916? But that didn't make sense as it was still being rebuilt. Fires weren't the usual style of the army of the Irish republic.

For added custom. Something in the Custom House? But

that was a vast building for boring papers about houses and roads and stuff. It was so unimportant the military didn't even bother guarding it.

I called by Nanny's shop in Whiskey Row the next morning to order more ointment for Josephine's chest. Bridie was nowhere to be seen. But Nanny's husband, Achie, was setting off for work on his bicycle. He was a clerk on one of the barges that inspected shipments at the Port and Docks Board up by the Custom House.

I bade him good morning and told him to be careful.

"I just keep my head down and my eye on my ledgers," he said.

I sat in class, lying low in case Brother Disgrace gave me the leather for not knowing my geometry. My head was taken up with a different geometry. Trying to figure out the target. If Oriel Hall was the muster place, I figured it must be on the northside of the city. Paraffin was used to light lamps. Or to burn things. Maybe they really were planning a fire? It seemed odd, not their way of fighting at all. But going on Collins' reaction this was de Valera's idea. Disgrace watched me like a hawk. I was trapped. For now.

At lunchtime, around twelve thirty, I felt edgy as we kicked ball in the playground. The school's secretary rushed up to Brother Disgrace. They gazed anxiously towards the city centre. Brother Disgrace scratched his head and blew a whistle.

"Boys, pick up your things, and make your way home. It's a half-day. Any boys who cross by Butt Bridge to the northside are advised to go around by O'Connell Bridge."

Everyone was too delighted to wonder why. But I knew what was going on as if an angel had whispered in my ear.

The target really was the Custom House! Right next to Butt Bridge. The last piece of the puzzle fell into place. That's where Head-the-Ball was going. He was in over his head and didn't have a clue about the risks he was taking. He'd never seen any active combat. It would be a suicide mission. Not some game of Cowboys and Indians. And Achie, Bridie's uncle, was working there. He could just get caught up in it. Collins had said it would be sheer madness. And he ought to know. I had to try to warn them.

I shot out of school like an arrow from a bow.

I slipped down Shaw Street towards the bridge, defying the Brother's instructions. The scene looked normal. But there were more lads than usual making their way over Butt Bridge and by Tara Street Station. They were trying too hard not to look like they were up to something, like drunks coming out of a pub trying to look sober. That was the dead giveaway. I could have sworn some of them were carrying tools. I even saw something like a hatchet peeking out of some eejit's coat.

The green dome of the Custom House rose over the quays. It was a large grey-stoned Georgian building from the eighteenth century when some earlier King George was on the throne. Very grand and fancy with columns. And those low walls running across the top of the building called parapets.

On the quay in front of the building big burly dockers unloaded barrels from a ship that had come up river from Dublin Port. They stacked them in neat rows. A man with a metal case in his front basket cycled by me. I thought maybe he was a photographer.

I crouched down between two rows of the barrels. As soon as I did, I realised how foolish I was. Even if something was happening how could I warn anyone? I had no idea where Head-the-Ball or Achie could be. The one could be off on a boat and the other safe at home having a cup of tea. While I like a gombeen was hiding between barrels. And would they just clear off on my say-so that there might be a big fire? They hadn't heeded my warnings before.

A policeman was patrolling on foot by Liberty Hall. I was as tense as a rabbit watching a fox. Several Volunteers dressed in ordinary clothes drew up to the side door. I recognised Vinnie from the Squad in his carpenter clothes. I knew by the cut of them that they were armed. I felt sick lurch up my throat. I needed to save my own skin.

I was just about to leave, when BOOM! An explosion threw me back against the barrels. I teetered on the edge of the dock and nearly fell into the barge that had pulled up alongside. But I righted myself in time. I was badly bruised. There was the sound of gunfire, then the harsh smell of smoke.

To my horror, three lorryloads of Auxies and Tans arrived. They were in a new kind of long armoured vehicle, shocking in its size. They piled out, just as smoke poured out of a window of the Custom House. The sharp smell of petrol caught in my nose and throat.

"Dan!" Achie was on the barge. "Jump in!" he shouted.

I threw myself down, sprawling onto the deck, but I was fine, no bones broken. More gunshot, shouting. This was a proper gun battle. Achie concealed me under sacking and gave a signal to the captain to leave. When I got out in Ringsend Basin, I saw billowing smoke hang over the city centre like a storm.

Chapter 20

Truce
July 1921

For five days a pall of smoke hung over the city as the Custom House burned. The fire brigade was held up by other Volunteer Units and didn't arrive in time to save the building. That made me feel a bit sick – remembering how the Auxies had behaved in Cork. De Valera issued a bulletin saying they regretted the destruction of a historic building. But the lives of four million people were more to be cherished than any historical masterpiece. That didn't include Head-the-Ball and eight others who died.

Poor stupid old "Head-the-Ball" threw the bomb that knocked me back and was killed in a hail of bullets. I felt sad about him dying. But the truth was I was glad I hadn't joined him. The score was nine dead, three of them civilians and four Volunteers. Four Auxies were wounded. Over a hundred Volunteers arrested. Including many of Collins' most trusted men. It seemed to me an own goal. And yet de Valera said it was a success. A spectacular show of force, like we were a real army. It made headlines all over the world.

I felt guilty. I did so much header practice, I gave myself a headache. I should have tried harder to put Head-the-Ball off or something. The smell of burning and petrol lingered for a long time. I took to calling into Saint Andrew's Church after school to say a prayer for peace – or a pause or something. Just to give us all a break.

The nightmares returned. Grim flickering flames and devils with black caps and bayonets instead of pitchforks invaded my sleep. I awoke at every loud noise, every bump in the night.

In one dream a grinning Captain Lees tied me to a burning goalpost with live snakes instead of ropes. I avoided reading newspapers, crossed the street rather than chat to the newsboys. Even Nanny's shop became a trial as Bridie was always reading out the latest from the papers covering the fish.

A week after the explosion, at the beginning of June, Josephine took ill. We didn't have the money for the doctor. So Mam sent me to Dr. Ella Webb's dispensary to ask for medicine. I queued up with old fellows with gout, girls with wracking coughs and mothers clutching sickly babies. I was almost embarrassed by my own good health.

The doctor on duty was Molly's friend, Doctor Dorothy. "Dan!" she exclaimed.

As she prepared the cough mixture for Josephine, she lowered her voice and gave me some startling news. "You should be proud of yourself. You know that message you delivered for my aunt to General Smuts from South Africa? It has borne fruit. He has been a good influence on the King, I hear. The King has promised to help bring peace to Ireland if he can."

I shrugged. "As if Michael Collins or de Valera would listen to the King."

"Everyone is tired of the fighting. General Smuts fought against the British in the Boer War. They all trust him," she said. "Keep your eyes on the papers."

I offered her a penny for the mixture but she waved the money away. "You can pay me back by helping Aunt Alice with some filing. Her papers have come back from Dublin Castle in a shocking state. She will pay well."

Summer holidays were coming up. I would be glad of the money. Dad was still missing even though Uncle Edward wired us some money.

I saw the headlines on the way home: "**King Calls for Peace**."

The king gave a speech on the opening of the new parliament in Belfast on June the 22nd. He called on "all Irishmen to pause, to stretch out the hand of forbearance and conciliation, to forgive and to forget."

Easy for him to say, I thought. He never had to deal with the Tans or the Auxies. Or Lees. You would never have trusted him even if he'd stretched out his snaky hand.

Then just before our school holiday on the 11th of July, I called into Nanny's shop for a message. Customers were clumped together as usual in the fuggy warmth, all talking at the same time. Bridie, on the counter, was hidden behind the newspaper.

"**TRUCE**" it shouted in big letters. I didn't believe my eyes.

Bridie sprang down, grabbed my hand and led me outside. "Listen. Can't you hear it?"

"I can't hear anything."

"That's the point! No gunfire. No Crossley Tenders. No shouts from Tans. Peace." I grabbed her hand as Nanny stood at the half-door.

"We'll be back in half an hour," I said.

Bridie jumped onto my crossbar and we sped off as church bells rang out across the city.

Crowds were already clogging Dame Street, all the way up from Trinity College. I used the bicycle as a battering ram to force my way to right outside Dublin Castle. I had to pinch myself. The Auxiliaries were sharing a joke with Anto of all people.

"Heh, Mister, what do you get if you cross a Tan with an Auxie?" he called out.

"A bullet in the head!" said one dirty-faced urchin.

Everyone laughed. Nobody got shot. A miracle.

One laughing Auxiliary held a golf club while a fellow officer snapped him with a camera. It was like a dream. There was no sign of weapons. A press photographer ushered a large group in front of the Olympia Theatre for a photo. Shop-girls, shoeless kids, schoolboys, working men, bakers and soldiers – all smiling for the peace. Bridie and I stood on the edge. I kept a tight hold of my bike as one young fellow was taking more interest in that than the camera!

Small boys crowded up close to the Auxies, mouths open to get a close look at them, like eejits in the front seats of the cinema. Adults hung back a bit, more cautious. Like they still expected to be shoved up against a wall and searched. Or dragged inside for an interrogation. Or shot in the back.

A couple of people wept.

'If only my young Peter had lived to see this day," said a middle-aged woman, shaking the hand of an Auxie, a smiling schoolmasterly-looking man with a sunburnt face.

I felt my chest expanding. I breathed in the deep air. Freedom! I gazed up at the Castle. There was a flicker on the edge of my vision, like a cross ball in a game. I could have sworn someone was scanning the crowds with an eyeglass. But there was nobody there.

Chapter 21

The Code
October 1921

Molly was still in prison. My father was still lost somewhere between the devil and the deep blue sea. But there was quiet on the streets of Dublin as we breathed in the new air of the truce – for now.

Collins and President Griffiths led a delegation to London to negotiate our freedom. Their pictures were all in the papers wrapped around the fish in Nanny's shop. Kids ran about the streets and "oul wans" once more gathered for a gossip on street corners.

But I was stuck in a library on Stephen's Green shuffling papers, dreaming of knocking a ball about outside.

Don't get me wrong. I was glad of the work. Doctor Dorothy was as good as her word and here I was sorting papers for her aunt, Alice Stopford Green, who wrote big huge history books that would knock the block off you if they fell on you. I seldom saw her. When I did, it was like seeing someone come to life from a book. She was an ancient old lady who wore old-fashioned clothes and a large cross that she told me came from Venice. In her long cloak, she was like a wizardess who could do magic spells and conjure up spirits. But it was I who was expected to do the magic. The twenty bundles of papers that had come back from Dublin Castle were in a right mess. They'd been seized because they thought she was conspiring with the rebels. When all the time she'd been working for peace. It was such a big job, I continued all through summer and even at weekends when I went back to school in September.

I loved sitting in her book-lined library, but her papers were in a shocking state. There were torn notes on ancient Irish civilization, old Irish forts, Celtic crosses. Old letters, even some curious medical notes. All in her tiny handwriting, or typed close together. I'm sure it was all clever stuff, but the papers made me sneeze and I only glanced at the contents to sort them into piles.

Then one day, as I worked through the blizzard of words, I came across papers in a different hand. Some were even printed on Castle notepaper. I looked with longing towards Doctor Oliver St John Gogarty's house and wondered if he was outside kicking a ball. I pictured taking a bouncing ball to my chest and knocking it into the sweet spot on the right-hand side of the net. Before I knew it, I'd crumpled up a few pages and was heading them towards the window. A sudden noise stopped my prank. I rescued

242

the papers and tried to uncrumple them, praying they weren't the most important pages in her book.

Something caught my eye as I unfurled a marbled paper, crowded with small print. It was torn and I realised it was some sort of letter, undated and written in code. I was excited. I loved puzzles. It looked like random letters of the alphabet. But I soon picked out the pattern. There was a small red dot under certain words and letters.

I saw straightaway it was written backwards. Maybe because I'm left-handed and so my brain works the other way round, I found it easy to spot. I held it up against the mirror. There was half a sentence: **"An attack on his Imperial. Maj–"** Then a date. **"Nov 1921 anniversary of bloody Sunday . . ."** In the right-hand corner there was a small handwritten note. *"The officer has been under considerable strain and an honorable discharge should be considered."* There was also some sort of diagram and an official crown stamp. These were Castle papers about the British army!

I put it to one side. I shuffled through another group of papers. I found a torn fragment dangling from a ledger book. It was the same marbled paper. I put it with the other sheet. The watermark was complete! I felt a prickle on the back of my neck. The rest of the sentence matched. "**An attack on his Imperial Majesty would be blamed on the Irish and discredit their cause forever . . . All Soul's Day, significant for Irish. Same month as Bl . . . Sun . . . afternoon.**"

Same month as Bloody Sunday.

Then my eye was caught by a symbol. A snake, its body curled round two initials. "CL".

Captain Lees. It had to be. But he was gone. Wasn't he? But who knew what plots he was spinning before he died. I went to crumple up the papers. But I heard his sneering voice taunting me. 'You're no match for me and the might of the British Empire.' I remembered his ravings as he lay bleeding to death. He was going on about the King then. The man was cracked. Only a lunatic would come up with such a hare-brained scheme.

I decided to obliterate it forever. I would show it to Bridie and then we would burn it in Ringsend Park.

I whistled as I walked up Whiskey Row. But I stopped in my tracks when I saw Bridie's white face over the half-door. She put her fingers to her lips and glanced at the inner door.

A hunched figure sat brooding at the table. His hair was cropped close to his head. His right arm was laid palm upwards. He turned. The guttering paraffin light snagged a scar that ran down his cheek. I would have known him at the gates of hell. But how could he have returned from the dead?

"I told you never to darken my door!" It was Nanny's voice, cold and insistent.

"Just read it." The loathsome drawling voice. Captain Lees – a Lazarus returned from the dead.

"I need more light." Nanny rose to get a candle.

As her figure crossed the doorway of the back room, I entered the shop, easing the half-door to avoid the familiar creak. I eyed the shovel for the coal and picked it up. Bridie cocked her hand, thumb up, index finger pointing. I strained my eyes. He had a gun.

The lamp cast a pool of light in the inner room.

"You are going to cross water," Nanny said. "I see a crown."

Lees exhaled.

"I see an arc, something aimed and shot . . ."

"Does it reach its target?" Lees asked, his voice raised.

Nanny held his hand to the light. "Yes," she said. "And no."

"Don't try to fool with me, witch!"

"I am telling you what I see. A crown and something reaching a target. Something finished."

Lees leaned back with satisfaction. "That's good enough for me. I'll show that Collins blighter who's the boss!"

"I've already told you that you have a short life line," Nanny said. "You won't live. I'll tell them what you've done."

He laughed, a strange strangled sound, like a maniac. "Nobody will believe you. I'm officially dead."

A door slammed. There was a shivering silence.

Bridie and I looked at each other, thunderstruck, terrified that he would discover us.

But it was Nanny alone who came out, grabbing her coat in a rush. Lees had slipped out the back way. We looked at her. But her face was closed, giving nothing away. She left the shop without a word to us.

I showed the letter to Bridie and explained the message.

"He means to do a very bad thing," she said.

"I think he wants to kill the King and blame it on the Irish," I said.

Bridie's eyes widened. "And only you can stop him."

"But no one will believe us, Bridie, a bunch of kids. Maybe Collins would, or MacBride. But they're both in London with the delegation negotiating the treaty for freedom."

"Send them a message." Bridie frowned.

A customer came into the shop and we continued our conversation in whispers.

"If we send them a message they'll think it's a joke: a man has come back from the dead and wants to kill the King!" I said.

Nanny rushed back into the shop. "I just went to see a policeman. Says I to them, there's a dangerous fellow on the loose. But they said the jails would be full if they were to arrest every madman in this country."

Nanny went out to the yard.

"Told you no one would believe us," I said.

"Molly would believe it," Bridie said.

"But Molly's in prison," I said.

"Then you'll have to get her out."

I looked at Bridie and smiled at her joke. "The only way would be if she was found innocent at trial and Molly hasn't even been charged with anything."

I decided to check with Mr. Noyk if Molly might come to trial soon but he was visiting courts down the country. His clerk just shook his head and said they were keeping everyone under lock and key to break morale. I had hit a brick wall.

Chapter 22

Halloween Escape
October 1921

The next day the papers swam before my eyes at Alice Stopford Green's. All I could think of was the devilment Lees would be spinning and no one to stop him. I was glad when Dr. St John Gogarty sent his driver with a note that he wanted to see me. Brenda his daughter showed me into his library. She was smiling and laughing and looked much better than the last time I'd met her when she'd refused to go outdoors because of the Tans.

"Isn't it grand there's no more fighting?" she said.

Before I even sat down a football bounced into the room. I caught it on my left heel. Dr. St John Gogarty bounded in, wearing his white doctor's coat. He fizzled with energy. I chipped him an easy ball to his feet and we passed it back and forth, only stopping when he smashed the ball into the window.

"What's all that commotion?" his housekeeper called out.

Luckily the window wasn't broken.

"Nothing!" he called, with a wink. He capered around with the ball, trying to spin it on his finger.

I snatched it and with a flick of my wrist turned it into a spinning globe. He laughed and recited a Limerick.

"There was a young fellow called Dan,
Who kicked a football with élan,
He played in Mountjoy
A diversion to deploy
And the girls out of jail they all ran!"

I looked at him, openmouthed. "A jailbreak!"

"Yes, indeed. Will you help?"

"On one condition. Molly has to be included."

He smiled at me. "Of course Molly can come with the other four girls. If you can persuade her."

"But how will they get out?"

"The plan is in place. Your role is to be a decoy."

I gazed at him, puzzled.

"The governor has said they can play football in the exercise yard. You bring in the football. Hang around, show off your skills."

He explained that keys were often left on tables by friendly wardresses who guarded the women. Some of the women prisoners had even made wax impressions from candles. These were smuggled out during visits and the duplicate keys smuggled back in on another visit. These

249

keys would give the breakout party access to the prison grounds so they could get over the wall.

He showed me the women's photographs in a newspaper. They were Linda from Sligo who had been caught smuggling guns; Aileen from Carlow who was charged with minding explosives; May, a Limerick woman imprisoned for passing military codes to the Volunteers; and Eithne from Donegal, who had smuggled documents. Women from the four corners of Ireland. Linda was the main organiser.

All I had to do was show up and tell Molly to join the escape.

"She'll have to go into hiding," he said. "Have you thought of a good place?"

"We need to go London," I blurted out.

He thought for a moment. "It's as good a place as any to hide. But you'll have to get to the mailboat and get past the security. A visiting student from India is travelling back. I can ask him to chaperone you."

I wondered about telling him that the real reason was to talk to Collins. To tell him about Lees rising like Lazarus from the grave and his strange plot to attack the King. But he bustled off before I had the chance. He'd have thought I was making it up anyhow.

The gate of Mountjoy Jail loomed like a fortress on Halloween, October 31st, the day appointed for the attempt. Somewhere inside the walls, the bodies of Thomas Whelan and all those other hanged men lay in unmarked graves. I feared seeing their ghosts ooze out of the grey walls. I had de Valera's old rugby ball, the GAA ball from Croke Park, and the soccer ball that had belonged to Dorothy's dead cousin killed in the war. All deflated in my knapsack. I had a vague idea of teaching the women Danball.

But just before I entered the gates, a fellow dashed up with a brand-new soccer ball.

"Dr. St. John Gogarty sent this to you for luck," he said and disappeared.

The guard let me in with a nod and handed me over to a wardress. She winked at me in a friendly way so I figured she had helped in smuggling the keys. It took an age to unlock and lock the doors through corridors of grey stone and steel doors with rusty bars. The walls sweated damp. Little prying windows set high above the doors seemed to spy back at me. The worst thing was the sounds: the jangling of keys, the tread of heavy footsteps, the shrill calling of far-off voices. I hugged the ball for comfort, smelling its odour of new leather, praying it would bring me luck.

We reached the yard and the sudden burst of daylight dazzled my eyes. The inner exercise courtyard heaved with excited women. I spied the five who were to escape. Eithne and May were laying out goal-mouths. Linda, the brains behind the escape, was covered in a blanket like she was unwell or was pretending to be. She was squatted down near another entrance door. Molly was tending to her, so I thought she must be genuinely ill. Molly was puzzled to see me there at first.

But she ran to greet me and gave me a big hug.

"When the game is in full flight, we'll sneak through that door where Linda is sitting. A ladder will be thrown over the wall by the canal. I'm going to help Linda to get over as she's unwell. I've given her a perfume bottle to throw over the wall to use as a signal that they're ready. Then, even if the guards come, I can delay them."

"You need to come too," I urged.

Her eyebrows shot up in surprise.

"No. I'm innocent. If I go they'll think I've got something to hide," she hissed.

I looked into her eyes, pleading. "Please, Molly. Lees has come back."

She was shocked but composed herself as I explained what had happened.

The code. Lees coming back from the dead.

"No," she said. "I am needed here."

I glanced over at Linda. "She looks ill. She won't make it if you don't help her."

She wagged a finger at me. "Dan, stop being cheeky. The other three can help her. Going after Lees is a wild goose chase. You don't even know if this plan was his."

"Come on, Molly. It was a letter signed with his initials with a snake around it. Who else?"

I wasn't giving in. I sidled over to Linda and whispered the whole story in her ear as quick as I could over the noise.

"I'll make her do it," she said. "Meet us at 30 Mountjoy Street. Do some of your fancy footwork now to distract attention."

I abandoned any idea of teaching the women Danball. They were all too fired up and ready to play soccer. A big strong woman blew a whistle.

"It's Cork versus the Rest of Ireland! Line up in your teams."

It might as well have been the Amazons against the Furies. It was the roughest, most raucous match I've ever seen played. There were about twenty players on both sides and new team members kept joining in from the sidelines. The women threw themselves into it. Making sliding tackles, run on goals, brazenly fouling and arguing loudly, hoofing the ball into the sky. The rest of the prisoners cheered as if it was Croke Park. I was supposed to be a linesman. But I kept getting swept up in the drama. It was hard for me to see Molly and Linda with so many heaving bodies in the way. But every time I glanced over, Molly was furiously shaking her head. We were going to have to drag her out of Mountjoy – kicking and screaming.

The whistle blew again. I provided the half-time entertainment. The women were so thrilled they grabbed me and gave me the bumps! Then, as the second half began, the jail-breakers seized their moment. A young Dublin girl ran on goal, and was brought down by a horde of wild Corkwomen. She took a penalty to rapturous applause. Nobody except me noticed the escapees slip away. An arm grabbed Molly but she resisted. I did what I had to. I lammed the ball in from the touchline. Then when the melée surrounded the ball, I rugby-tackled Molly through the door and put my weight against it. I breathed a sigh of relief when I heard her scuttle after the others.

Soon after, I left them playing and departed with my knapsack. It was beginning to get dark.

I cut down past the hospital to Mountjoy Street. The meet-up was in a house just past the Black Church, a low-slung building with a tall narrow steeple. They say if you circle it three times at midnight you'll see the devil. I quickened my step as it was Halloween. Though at that moment I was more afraid of facing Molly than seeing old Satan.

I arrived at the address, a two-storey Georgian end-of-terrace house to the sound of thunderous piano music. It stopped abruptly when I knocked. The door was opened by a smiling bubbly woman called Dilly. She had been practising the music for the silent films, she explained. That was her job in the cinemas in town. She was pretty enough to be in films herself.

"Come and join our recital. We're planning to sing songs of freedom!" she laughed.

Molly was eating a hot buttered scone in the back room as if it was manna from heaven. Her head was covered by a towel. She began chewing rapidly when she laid eyes on me, so she could clear her mouth to give me a tongue-lashing. But I thrust the torn document with the date and code at her. She frowned at it, dismissing it with her hand. But then I held it up against the mirror over the fireplace and called her over.

She and Dilly peered in close. Dilly's mouth dropped in amazement. But Molly looked blank, like she couldn't believe her eyes.

"Now do you believe me?" I urged her.

She blinked, taking it in. Then she nodded.

I sighed with relief. "I'm not sure anyone else will."

"Mick will believe you. It's many a time he's hid in our attic, so he knows the maddest things go on," said Dilly. There were some paintings of her around the walls, as "Innocence" in the dress of a shepherdess. She took out a little boot charm. "He gave this to me. I hear you are a lucky boot yourself."

Molly looked at the letter again. "That date looks like the 1st November – All Souls Day. Tomorrow! We have no time to lose! We'll have to warn Collins. But I can't go. I'm on the run. They'll be watching all the ports."

"Lees must be going to London. That's where the King is – and Collins. Someone has to go," I said.

"Molly, you are the perfect courier." Dilly handed her a false passport and pulled the towel off her now shoulder-length hair. "Who's going to recognise you?"

We gazed at her in the mirror with amazement. Molly was now blonde.

She put on a pair of wire-rimmed glasses, glanced at her passport, and said in a cut-glass English accent, "I'm Miss

255

Rosa Thompson. Newly returned from India."

Dilly's father ran in with a stop press. The women looked at it eagerly. It listed each of the escapees. The last line read: "Police are anxious to question a young boy who brought the football into the prison."

Dilly sized us up. "The Castle will still have men watching the boats. You can't travel together."

"What about a disguise for me?" I asked.

"We could dress you as a girl," said Molly.

"Or a nun," speculated Dilly.

"No way," I said.

Dilly's face lit up with an inspiration. "We'll just have to post you!"

Chapter 23

London November 1921
The Treaty

We were driven to Dun Laoghaire in Oliver St. John Gogarty's bright yellow Rolls Royce by his chauffeur, a quiet man from the West of Ireland. This really was hiding in plain view as Collins advised. Under the lamplight, the car turned every head it passed and excited gurriers ran alongside us. We raced, a yellow streak, to Kingstown to catch the night mail-boat and then the train to London.

Molly boarded as a first class passenger. But Dilly led me into the sidings where postal workers were upending mail sacks into large wicker baskets. These were placed in a hand-truck to be pulled onto the mail-boat.

I was dressed in a sorter's uniform, over my clothes, with a cap pulled low over my eyes. The mail-boat was called the *S.S. Anglia* and was a new steamer that ploughed through the waves at a rate of thirty miles an hour. Dilly explained to me that the owners got fined if the boat was late so they didn't hang about.

"They sort the mail for Britain on the boat," she instructed me. "When you get to the mailroom, jump out and act as a sorter. Every man jack of them is on our side. Once you're off the boat you can transform back into a schoolboy and join Molly in first class on the train."

"Will I not get thrown out?"

"I've done this hundreds of times!" she laughed. "I go through the letters and you wouldn't believe the top-secret information I've got hold of for Mick. It's one of our best methods for intercepting the mail."

I climbed into the basket, which was like a big version of a picnic hamper with a hinged lid. I was a big sandwich, crouching against the rough sacking lining. Dilly covered me in another layer of sacking in case anyone peeked inside.

It was a strange sensation, being pushed on a trolley onto the boat among all the mail. The briny airless smell of the inside of the boat made my stomach heave and we hadn't even left the dock. Luckily a friendly sorter helped me out of the basket as soon as I was on board.

The mailroom, a compact space in the lower deck with a low ceiling, was a hive of activity. There were about fifteen Post Office sorters on board. They sifted the mail into several piles according to district and post code – like cardsharps at a gaming table I'd seen at a fairground. There were pigeon-holes for each county.

The writing on the envelopes swam before my eyes. The

heave and lurch of the ship made my stomach flip. A kind woman sorter led me outside to a spot by a guard-rail. "Don't lean too far over," she warned me.

The voyage lasted several hours, most of which I spent outside, retching over the guard-rail. It was hard to believe I was my father's son. The sea roiled beneath me and I thought of the many who had drowned. The wind whipped me and I shivered as I imagined it was the cold hand of the corpses. But the mailboat forged on at great speed. I was almost glad of the nausea as it meant I didn't have to think about what I was going to do to hunt down Lees.

As we approached dry land, I was popped back into an empty mail basket and covered in some empty sacking. It was still dead of night and I was desperate for some sleep. The only glimpse I caught of Holyhead was lights flickering through the basket weave. I felt cold and delicate from the lurching sea and the wicker prickled my skin.

I must have fallen asleep as a post office worker had to rouse me once the basket was taken into the reloading shed. It was a relief to hand him back the sorter's uniform and transform once more into a schoolboy. Just before the train left, he led me onto the bustling platform. I was still befuddled from sleep and I boarded the first-class section in a daze to be re-united with Molly.

I did a double take when I was led into the carriage. It was occupied by a fashionable young blonde lady with coiled hair. She was deep in conversation with a striking brown-skinned young man with jet-black hair.

"Mol – Rosa!" I'd nearly betrayed her by the first words out of my mouth. I'd forgotten about her transformation.

"Dan, you look green around the gills! Meet Sanjay. He has been visiting Dublin to find out about the Irish struggle." Molly, in her guise of Rosa, smiled at Sanjay like she was in a film. "He is also a medical student."

"Delighted to make your acquaintance," Sanjay drawled. He had a pleasant rich English accent and smiled broadly with very white teeth. "I have had a fascinating time in your country. Ireland and India both share a desire to throw off the yoke of British tyranny. Though we in India are embracing a path of non-violence."

Neither of them was the slightest bit interested in me. I snuggled into the side of the seat, so grateful to be somewhere soft and cosy that didn't prickle me. I was interested in this pleasant, handsome fellow but my eyelids kept falling down. I wanted to ask him if he wore a turban, though Sanjay looked every inch a British gent.

As if in answer to my thoughts, he said, "My mother is Indian but my father was, like your grandfather, an English army doctor. So I am Anglo-Indian. I was educated in England and my family aren't too happy that I am throwing my lot in with the anti-Imperialists."

"He has been telling me about their leader, Mr. Gandhi," said Molly. "I like the sound of him. He believes in non-violence and non-cooperation with the British in India as the way to achieve independence."

I nodded. Mr. Sanjay immediately started talking and

didn't stop to draw breath until we pulled into Kings Cross Station. I was quite content as his voice was soothing and lulled me into a deep sleep. Occasionally, I awoke with a start as we pulled into some station. Crewe was one.

I heard the odd stray line.

"Yes, Gandhi has dismissed Sinn Féin as a model because they embraced violence," drawled Sanjay.

"Now that Collins is at the negotiating table, I am hoping he has turned his back on the gun and is going to become a statesman," said Molly.

Later I heard Molly asking, "And what about women in India?"

Sanjay said, "India is a country of great extremes of wealth and poverty. Poor women are at the very bottom."

I awoke somewhere nearer London and Molly was writing a letter. I wasn't sure if I was dreaming.

Then in the pitch black of night Sanjay was rabbiting on about stamps of all things. "Did you know that the King is a most keen stamp collector?" he said. "My father shares his hobby and helps with the royal collection of Indian stamps. He said the King is most interested in what will happen to the stamps with his head on it if Ireland becomes a republic."

I thought of my stamp with the upside-down King's head on it. It had vanished with Lees. I longed to ask Sanjay if the King would like such a thing but I couldn't risk it.

Near Kings Cross Station Molly roused me by shaking my shoulder and I rubbed my eyes, confused about where I was. Sanjay had gone to the breakfast compartment and

Molly spoke quickly.

"I haven't told him our mission, but Sanjay has agreed to drop us at Cadogan Square where the Irish delegation are staying. It's our only chance of seeing them. MacBride is their messenger and I will give him a letter for Collins, warning him of the threat from Lees."

"Can we trust Sanjay?" I asked. "How do we know he's not a spy?"

Molly flashed me a stern look. "He's a friend of the Stopford Greens. He's about to be cut off by his family. Of course he's not a spy."

"You're very pally . . ."

Molly cut me with her eyes. Her hair might have changed colour but her temper hadn't. She showed me a few rough maps.

"Sanjay did these for me for London sightseeing. He knows London well."

I looked closer at the maps. Buckingham Palace, The Tower of London, The Royal Mint. All quite detailed with clear lines and markings. "Might be useful."

Sanjay returned with a tray of newly baked breakfast buns and a pot of hot tea with cups, milk and sugar. He also had a copy of the morning's *The Times*. Molly scanned the court circular but there was no mention of any planned Royal visits.

She riffled through the paper, eager to see if there was anything about the jailbreak.

The station clock struck nine o'clock as we pulled in. Lees' letter had mentioned the afternoon. We had little time to lose.

Chapter 24

London Chase
1st November 1921

I feared getting trampled as we made our way to the taxi rank outside Kings Cross Station. I had not seen such crowds since Croke Park. My breath came shallow in my chest. Sanjay ushered me by the elbow and the multitudes parted before us as if Moses was crossing the Red Sea. I gulped the air outside the station but had a choking fit it was so smoky. Luckily Sanjay had a water bottle.

"For comfort and speed, it's all you need," said the beaming cabbie as he led us to his taxi motor car.

I was too excited now to be sick. It was gleaming black with a fold-down leather roof and room enough for four with pull-down seats in the covered back. There was an outer luggage compartment on the front passenger side. The driver wasn't so lucky and was exposed to the elements. But I chose to sit beside him in the "bucket seat" up front, while the other two sat inside.

London was still wreathed in fog in the early morning gloom, but it was grander than I could have imagined. Every street seemed to be filled with fine buildings bigger than all of Dublin's put together. The railway station of St Pancras looked like a fairytale palace. Regent Street was thronged with fashionably dressed people. Billy the cabbie explained they were shop girls and early morning shoppers. Shop girls! They looked like fine ladies to me.

We passed many motorcars and shoals of delivery boys on bicycles. We scythed through the traffic, whizzing past the odd horse-drawn cart. I felt like I was in a chariot race!

Piccadilly was wide enough for a football pitch. But how splendid were the large golden gates of Buckingham Palace between the wide-open spaces of Green Park and Hyde Park! I was open-mouthed. Even Molly and Sanjay stopped their chattering in the back seat.

I saw the guards in their tall hats and red jackets, still as tin soldiers in their boxes. The railings were high, the building closed like a fortress. It didn't seem likely that Lees would be able to get to the King inside. I banished any thoughts of warning the guards directly. They would lock me straight away in the Tower of London and clamp me in irons!

The parks looked like a great place for football. But I felt that I was in a different ballgame now in London. It was as if someone had increased the size of the pitch a thousand times. I could kick a ball and it might go on into space forever and ever. There were no back markers, no wingers. Just Molly and me.

Our cabbie brought us to Cadogan Square, a la-di-dah place full of the "quality". The tall redbrick terraced houses all had balconies and shiny front doors. Maids in uniforms washed down front steps. And nannies dressed in black pushed perambulators into the little park in the centre of the square. We drew up outside the address where the Irish delegation was staying.

"I have arranged for Billy the cabbie to attend to you," said Sanjay. He waved away Molly's protests and bowed low. "I insist." He bade us good day, saying he was looking forward to the walk back to his lodgings.

It took ages for the door to be opened by a man in a black suit. I took him to be a butler. When we enquired after MacBride, the pompous fellow shook his head. He informed us he'd left London just last night to catch the 9.40 p.m. mailboat to Dublin.

Curses! We must have crossed him somewhere en route between Dublin and London. All the delegation including Collins and Griffith had already gone to Downing Street to talk to the Prime Minister. Before I could protest the butler took the letter out of my hand and banged the door in my face. We stood there, stunned at this development. Molly still had Lees' original document for safe keeping. But how were we to get to Collins? Then a maid ran out and told us that other members of the Irish delegation were staying at 22 Hans Place, which was also in Knightsbridge. We got back in the cab and instructed Billy to take us there.

It was another fine-looking square surrounded by redbrick terraces on all sides.

I sat with Molly in the back seat as she dashed off another letter.

"What if there's nobody here?" she said.

"I could take it to the police," I offered.

"They'd put you in the loony bin," she said. "You better go to the door. I'll stay here in case the police are watching us."

I knocked on the imposing door. This time it was opened promptly by a familiar smart woman with neat bobbed hair. Addy, Collins' secretary! I'd last seen her in Harcourt Street when Collins escaped out the skylight. I was so happy I could have cried.

"Dan! My goodness, what brings you here?" She beckoned me into the front room, which had large comfortable sofas and bookshelves all the way up to the ceiling.

I told her we had an urgent message for Michael Collins. She promised to give it to him first thing when he returned in the evening. She explained he moved between both houses, catching up with different members of his team.

"That might be too late! I'll take it to Downing Street," I said.

She laughed. "And get past all the security! Not even de Valera himself could interrupt those meetings. The freedom of the country hangs in the balance. They've diverted so much security to Downing Street they're joking you could walk into the Royal Mint!"

"Oh," I said, like a gom.

"Mick says he's confronted with a real nest of vipers. The Prime Minister Lloyd George is a wily old codger. They won't budge on Ulster having a separate parliament. So there's little chance of a United Ireland. Mick thinks the best we can do is get some temporary settlement, 'the freedom to achieve freedom', he calls it. Otherwise Lloyd George is threatening all-out war."

"What if someone was to kill King George and blame it on the Irish?" I said.

She looked startled and shook her head. "That would finish everything. They'd clamp the whole lot of us in the Tower and Ireland would be the disgrace of the world." I was about to open my mouth to confide in her when she continued, "But that's a far-fetched notion. You've been reading too many comic books!" She glanced out the window and spied Molly in the taxi.

"The lady in the taxi is beckoning you."

"That lady is Molly! It's a long story."

Addy beamed. "I won't ask any questions or draw attention to her. Give her a hug from me. And I hope she's still keeping her diary! As I told you, I made her first one!"

I got back in the taxi with a heavy heart and told Molly what Addy had said. Molly was downcast, but she was pleased to know Addy was in town.

To take my mind off things, I took my football out of the

bag and began to blow it up. Not knowing what else to do, Molly told Billy to drive us to the Parliament anyway so at least we could say we'd seen "Big Ben" the famous clock.

"Let's review what we know," Molly said thoughtfully as we rattled along. "We believe Lees is alive and looking for an opportunity to assassinate King George and blame the Irish. He wants to stamp us all out."

"He was obsessed with getting my upside-down stamp. He must still have it."

"Maybe the stamp was just a way of getting to see the King," Molly mused.

She took out the notepaper with Lees' mad plan on it.

A thought struck me. "See that diagram? It looks a bit like one of the maps Sanjay drew for us."

We compared the two drawings.

Molly's face lit up. "The Royal Mint! Sanjay's uncle told him the King sometimes makes unofficial visits there. He likes to inspect the plates for stamps with his profile on them. He takes a great interest in stamp design, more than in any other subject – and he's secretive about it! So he might be making a secret visit today!"

"Especially if he was being shown a rare stamp with his head upside down by someone who was in the same philately club! Addy said there's so much security at Downing Street you could nearly walk into the Royal Mint!"

Molly sat bolt upright and pulled back the hatch to talk to Billy. "Take us to the Royal Mint, as quick as you can!"

Chapter 25

The Royal Mint Showdown
1st November 1921

London's wide avenues and grand buildings gave way to crooked narrow streets as we raced alongside the mighty Thames. I glimpsed the rounded dome of Saint Paul's Cathedral and then the Tower of London.

"Do you know if we can drive into the Royal Mint?" I asked Billy as we stopped at a corner to let a cart pass.

"You can't drive into it, but you can look through the gates. The front building is really just offices."

"Get as near as you can," instructed Molly.

It was still a long shot. But we reckoned we had to at least try to warn someone official at the Mint that there might be an attempt on the King's life.

I was brewing another idea. If I chipped the ball over the gates, it would attract the attention of the guards. Maybe that would put Lees off whatever he was planning. Or I could be a decoy and Molly could gain access. I finished blowing up my ball under the stern eye of Molly.

"Don't mess with it. It gets on my nerves," she warned me.

"If I cause a diversion, maybe you could sneak in," I said.

"That really is a long shot, Dan," she said.

"It's all a long shot, Molly."

She gave me a sad smile.

We pulled up opposite the Mint. The large imposing building was flanked by two gatehouses. But only the left-hand one had a sentry – still as a statue facing onto the street. This made me feel a bit hopeful.

"It doesn't look very guarded," I said to Billy as we got out.

Billy laughed. "They don't worry too much about the front bit. The serious money is round the back. Behind that building and separated by an open quadrangle there's more buildings. That's where they mint the coins. There's a boundary wall as big as old glory on three sides. All along the inside of that runs a narrow alley patrolled by crack troops from the military guard."

My heart sank.

Billy drove on and waited for us around the corner so as not to block the road. We walked straight up to the railings. The guard couldn't even see us as the gatehouse extended quite far into the path.

It was a big classical building with columns and a

triangular façade over the entrance. A fancy wall called a balustrade ran across the top. There was a quadrangle in front and some trees. It looked solid and secure.

But if Lees was in the same philately club as the King he'd have visited the Royal Mint. He would know its weak spots.

My heart stopped when, inside the railings, I saw a long sleek car parked up outside the main entrance. There was some kind of insignia on the side. What if the King was already here?

But in the cold November light of London, our fears about Lees seemed childish. No one would take us seriously. They would just think it was the ravings of kids. We had no chance of getting through the large iron gates and railings. Even with a bored sentry looking the other way.

We were almost about to give up when everything happened all at once.

As we approached the gates to gawp like tourists, there was a flicker on the edge of my field of vision. Something caught the sun at the top left-hand corner of the building. I told Molly and she took out her field glasses.

"Someone's up there," she pointed. "Crouching behind the balustrade."

In front of the building, the chauffeur got out of the sleek car to open the right-hand passenger door.

"That crest on the side of the car!" I cried. "It's a royal crest!"

"Don't move!" roared Molly. But her cry was drowned out by a speeding car that passed by with a roar.

Each second lasted an hour. I made my calculations. The man on the roof rose to a standing position. I knew by the shape of him it was Lees. His arm was outstretched in front of him as he took aim with a gun. Both of us had one shot. Out of sight of the guard, I placed the ball at a right angle to clear the railings and trees. I gathered my energy for the run and sliced it with my left foot, curving under to give it some topspin. It rose in a perfect parabola as if shot from a cannon.

Time stood still as the ball reached its target, knocking the man back. A shot rang out. Something fell out of his hands and clattered to the ground. The ball dropped down below, its force spent. The chauffeur looked up. The passenger ducked back into the car.

The guard by the left gatehouse came to life and ran towards me, gun cocked.

I held my hands in the air.

"Don't shoot!" I called out. "Up on the roof!"

The guard spun round and looked up at the building, his rifle cocked. Lees teetered on the corner, a stark black silhouette against the pale afternoon sunset. Another guard ran out of the main entrance and raised his rifle. A couple of other guards were now on the roof, clambering to grab hold of him. The guards closed in.

Just as they reached him, Lees took a perfect dive off the parapet and landed at the side of the building. Another group of guards rushed to where he'd fallen. Simultaneously the gates opened and the black car dashed out. The gates closed in a flash as the car sped off. I couldn't see the passenger but the royal crest was unmistakable.

"I'm a medic!" shouted Molly. "Let me in." She handed me her field glasses and stood by the gate.

A guard approached, shaking his head. "No need for medical attention. He's a goner," he said.

A few other people had gathered to see what all the commotion was.

"Move along," a guard said to the onlookers.

I raised the field glasses and watched intently as another guard turned the man's wrist over to check his pulse. The snake writhed. The guard shook his head. I handed the field glasses to Molly.

"He gone. Definitely this time," she said. "It looks to me like he broke his neck."

"They've taken him inside. Let's go."

As we turned to leave, the guard who'd pointed his gun at me shouted out, "Not so fast, you two!"

My heart plummeted in my chest. I gave Molly a rueful look. We were done for and would have to face the music.

"Say nothing," Molly hissed to me.

He led us into the gatehouse and into a guardroom with greatcoats and helmets hanging on hooks from the wall. There was a small bare desk.

A young policeman arrived to take our statement.

I was in a daze and the next bit was a bit of a blur. Molly

stuck to our story. We were tourists visiting London. We were too far away to see much. No, we hadn't seen what happened. We didn't notice any car. The policeman wrote down a few lines. He seemed quite satisfied with our answers. Almost as if he was pleased we didn't know anything. The guard certainly looked relieved.

We were back outside the Royal Mint in no time. I took one last glance. Lees was dead. I'd beaten him at last. But I didn't feel like a winner. Winning and losing. Two sides of the same coin. Like life and death. I didn't suppose there was any chance I'd get my ball back.

Molly gave me a big hug when we were out of earshot.

"You really are a sharpshooter," she said. "Best damn shot in the whole world."

A gust of wind shook leaves from the trees. Something floated through the air and landed in the gutter. I followed it. It was a faded torn envelope, addressed to my grandfather. On it the stamp with the King's head upside down.

I put it in my pocket. Funny that a little scrap of paper not much bigger than your thumbnail could cause so much trouble.

We went around the corner to the taxi.

"Cor, did you see all that action!" said Billy. "I heard someone say some fellow threw himself off the Mint!"

We shook our heads.

"God rest his soul," said Molly.

"Any more sights you'd like to see? Though I imagine

you've had enough excitement for one day."

Addy had told us to call back at seven to Hans Place if we wanted to see Collins. We had a couple of hours.

"There is one place," I said.

Chapter 26

Danball
2nd November 1921

A caretaker led me into a backroom when I turned up at the Officers' Mess of the London Irish Rifles at Camberwell. Molly had decided to wait in the taxi.

I had no idea why they called it a mess. It seemed quite tidy to me even if it was a dingy backroom with a large table and chairs. But the caretaker explained that was the army name for their informal clubroom. The walls were lined with glass cabinets containing flags, trophies and uniforms. Some of them had nametags that I couldn't read in the pale light. There were also several paintings of battle scenes.

There was only one person there, a fit-looking young man drinking a cup of tea. He turned round and we both recoiled in surprise. We both started talking at once and he smiled and told me to go first.

"The man dribbling the ball in Lady Butler's painting!" I

exclaimed. It was Sergeant Edwards in the flesh. But how did he know who I was?

"The boy with the ball! I just saw your shot at the Mint!" he said, equally astonished. "I never saw anything like it since we dribbled towards the Germans at Loos."

He shook my hand warmly and explained that he was a military policeman now. Normally he patrolled the Royal Hospital in Hounslow but because of staff shortages had been sent to the Royal Mint for a week. So Addy had been right. "Security has been a bit sloppy," he admitted. "Most available police and guards are at Downing Street and the Houses of Parliament while the Irish rebels are in town. There's been gaps in the changeover of the guards, like today. And we weren't expecting the King. Luckily you were there."

Sergeant Edwards had been looking out the window at the arrival of the Royal car and wasn't sure if he'd really seen me kick the ball. Thought he might be dreaming it.

"Since the nerve gas on the front I get these flashbacks," he explained. "Thought it was my imagination. So when no one else said they saw you I kept quiet."

I knew all about those kind of flashbacks.

"But how did you know who I was?" he asked.

I told him about meeting Lady Butler in Tipperary and how she'd showed me sketches.

He led me with pride to a painting in the corner of the room. There it was. The original – showing Frank cradling the ball in his right foot before chipping it to another soldier.

I don't know anything about art but it brought tears to my eyes.

"It was a big push," he said. "We were under heavy machine-gun and mortar fire. They used nerve gas. That was the worst thing. There were fifty thousand casualties. Mud and muck everywhere. I got a bullet in my thigh."

"What made you play a game?" I asked. "It was very brave."

He scratched his head. "I don't know. Some people say we were showing defiance in the face of death. Keeping up our spirits. That we wanted to take the game to the Germans. It just felt right, somehow. I wanted to go out with my football, I suppose. You know what I mean."

I did know what he meant. I told him about Lees. About the war. He shook my hand.

"We're just the little guys, Dan. But sometimes, just sometimes we are on the ball. And all you can hope is that you give it your best shot." He rummaged round and in the bottom of a drawer fished out the beaten-up old scuffed ball. The leather was torn in lots of places, where the ball had landed on barbed wire. He started blowing up the rubber bladder inside to see if it still worked. It wasn't bad and he headed the ball to me.

I hardly dared ask. "Do you think you could meet me at half seven in the morning in Hyde Park?" I asked.

He tossed the ball in the air and headed it into his hands.

"I'll bring my ball," he said with a wink.

At seven o'clock that evening in Hans Place, the delegation was deep in session in an upstairs room. Molly and I could hear raised voices and hard arguments. We waited in silence in the downstairs room, too stunned for much discussion. I was starting to fall asleep by the fire when Michael Collins strode in.

"Molly, I told you I'd take the first chance for peace. Though they're driving a hard bargain. The British want us to swear the oath of allegiance to the King. But the Long Fellow back in Dublin won't go for that."

He was distracted and tired-looking.

"The people are happy the fighting is over," Molly said.

"There'll be fighting between us back in Ireland if we don't strike a good deal. I don't care what you call it, a republic, a free state. The Treaty will be just a stepping stone." He raked his hands through his thick hair. "If only some of the hardliners like de Valera could see that too."

"Lees is dead," I blurted out.

"I know," he said.

I was amazed. Of course Collins would have eyes and ears everywhere.

"That policeman took my false name. If –" Molly began.

Collins cut her off. "That policeman's mother is from Cork."

"I thought he went very easy on us," Molly smiled.

He came and slapped me on the back.

"It was a brave thing you did, Dan. But you'll have to be

content with my praise. You have prevented the resumption of war in Ireland. We've agreed to hush it up. The Treaty negotiations are at too delicate a phase for a story like this to make headlines."

I nodded. I didn't mind one little bit about it being hushed up. I just wanted to get back to playing football. We heard raised voices, then someone tapped on the door and said Mick was wanted urgently.

"Lad, if there's ever anything I can do for you," he said, shaking my hand.

I thought about it quickly. "There's three things, Mick."

He whistled. "You little pup!"

First I wanted him to make sure Molly wouldn't go back to prison. Then to find out where my father was. He nodded his assent.

"I feel like the Christmas fairy. Don't tell me you want gold bars now for your last wish," he said.

"Will you meet me at Hyde Park tomorrow at half past seven? And bring as many others as you can? All the people you're negotiating with too."

"Nothing strange, I hope?" he said.

"Just a kickabout," I shrugged.

"I might have more luck with that than the Treaty." He gave me a broad smile as he dashed out the door.

As we were leaving Molly asked Addy to recommend a small hotel. She told us Michael Collins had arranged for us to stay with his sister in Shepherd's Bush.

Hannie Collins lived in a wide spacious apartment on an

upper floor. She was a kind, quiet woman who, of all the jobs in all the world, worked as a clerical officer in the British Post Office! She fed us a tasty supper of Irish stew, the meat so tender it melted in our mouths. She and Molly talked for a while but I was content to read the comic Hannie had bought me. I wanted to relax. It was match day ahead!

As dawn broke an early morning mist wreathed Hyde Park. But it soon cleared in the pale sunshine. I marked out the four corners of the pitch with sticks. Then I blew up the bladders in my three balls: the GAA ball from Croke Park, de Valera's old rugby ball and the battered old football from Loos.

Sanjay arrived first. Then Frank Edwards trim and fit, with a friend who he said was a football coach. A few minutes later Mick Collins turned up with quite a few of the Irish delegation. I recognised Dolan from the Squad. He was one of the hard men who'd been on the botched job at Ranelagh Road on Bloody Sunday. Erskine Childers and Robert Barton, whose faces were often in the newspapers, were there. Arthur Griffith also came and offered to be referee.

"We don't need a referee," I said. "It's an honour game. Anyone who fouls has to take time out and his or her team loses a point. We must all play in a respectful manner. You can be timekeeper."

He nodded his assent and took out his large fob watch.

Molly and Addy also lined up to play. Just as I was about to explain the rules a sleek car drew up. Out came a man chomping on a cigar with another gentleman.

"That's Winston Churchill and Lord Rothermere!" said Molly in a hushed voice. "They are Unionist hardliners. Hard set against an independent Ireland."

"I don't care who they are once they can kick a ball," I grinned.

I explained the rules. Everyone gave me their full attention. "All three balls will be put in play. You have to play the ball according to the rules of its original game. Your team has to work with you. You can only win if you score with all three balls."

I separated the teams at random and called them the Griffins and the Dragons. Churchill, Sanjay and Collins were on my team, the Griffins. Molly, Dolan, and Frank Edwards on the other. Arthur Griffith blew the whistle.

The game was fast and furious. Everyone caught on to the rules and put their heart into it. At first, people stuck to the games they knew. But most soon showed a willingness to have a go at the unfamiliar ones. There was much falling about and laughing also.

I played my heart out. My aim was to score with each of the different balls, which I did with some difficulty. Collins swore when he had to go offside at one stage for fouling. But losing a point soon put manners on him.

Griffiths blew the final whistle. It was a draw. At the end, we all shook each other's hands warmly.

As I was deflating the balls, Frank Edwards' friend, a talent scout, approached me.

"You've a gifted left foot, son. But you're a thinker, I can see, planning moves while you're off the ball. I'm a scout for several soccer teams. Everton in the north and Arsenal in London. I could set up a few trials for you."

I shook my head. "I just want to go home."

"Lots of money in it now. Football's going to be huge. They're even going to build a big stadium in Wembley. You've got what it takes, lad." He handed me a card. "Think it over. Maybe when you're older."

I took the card. *"Archie Cornfield – talent scout"*, it said and there was a number and a P.O. box. I put it in my pocket and got into the taxi with a spring in my step.

Chapter 27

The Balance Sheet of War 1922

Molly didn't have to go back to prison. As the charges were all initiated by Lees, they were quietly dropped.

The Irish delegation came home with the Treaty that was signed on the 6th of December. Lloyd George told them there would be war in Ireland in three days if they didn't sign. So reluctantly they all did. The southern twenty-six counties of Ireland were to become a Free State. The North could opt out but a boundary commission would redraw the borders. Ireland was to stay in the Commonwealth and swear allegiance to the King.

The Dáil, that's the name for the Irish parliament, were to vote for it after Christmas. Already the debates were raging. You couldn't go into a shop without walking in on an argument. De Valera was mad against it and didn't want to swear an oath of loyalty to the King. But Mick Collins

was telling everyone it was "freedom to achieve freedom".
Most of the Volunteers were angry – they wanted to keep
fighting for a republic. But lots of the ordinary people just
didn't want any more fighting.

Mother O'Brien said an interesting thing. "All this
malarkey. It's makin' up a fairytale Ireland where we'll all
be free. But I'll still be out selling fish, whether it's a Free
State or a Republic. And you, Dan, and our Bridie won't be
living in the lap of luxury."

"But our children and our children's children will be
free," I said.

"I hope they'll appreciate the sacrifice," said Mother
O'Brien. "We won't be here to find out."

On Christmas Day we had the best present ever, when
my father walked through the door. He was covered in a
scrum of hugs.

"Wait until you hear my adventures. Arrested in New
York, deported to Bermuda, re-arrested and thrown in jail."

The stories had just begun and we in turn had tales to tell
of our own.

But some people's stories had come to an end. At least two
thousand people from both sides lost their lives between
1917 and 1921 in the struggle for independence.

On the first day of 1922 I paid my own tribute to them.
In the deadly quiet dawn of the New Year, with most of
Dublin asleep, I played keepy-uppy across the city from
Ringsend Park to Croke Park. With every bounce of the ball

I tried to remember a slain person, especially the children. Like ten-year-old Jeremiah O'Leary shot on Bloody Sunday. And fourteen-year-old John Scott. Like the six people killed on O'Connell Bridge. The executed at Mountjoy Jail – including Tommy Whelan and Traynor the bootmaker. Those unfortunates who passed away in the Mater Hospital. The RIC men and even the soldiers out picking blackberries, shot in the back.

My hand would be too tired writing all the names and my head wouldn't remember them. But I could count them and as the ball rose and dropped, I prayed for their souls.

Even Lees, for, who knows, he may have once been a good person before he got mangled by war. Two thousand bounces for two thousand souls, gone from this life to the next.

The End

Author's Note

The War of Independence 1920-22 – Dan's Diary is a follow-up novel to *The Easter Rising 1916 – Molly's Diary*. While the character of Molly is imaginary, Dan is based on my real grandfather, Daniel O'Donovan. My grandfather was a wonderful man who was in the Fianna, buried guns and ran messages for Volunteers. But he also was a talented soccer player and was capped as a junior for Ireland. He later turned down contracts for several top English teams. He was also a massive fan of rugby and GAA – anything with a ball, in fact. In later life he was very anti-violence so I always wondered what he must have experienced during the War of Independence. This is of course is a dramatic re-imagining. The plot is a work of fiction played out against real historical events. While real characters and events have been rendered as accurately as possible minor details have been changed here and there to serve the plot. The mistakes are all my own.

The character of the young girl Bridie is based on my adored grandmother. Her Aunt Nanny really did tell fortunes in her huckster shop in Whiskey Row.

The central character of Jameson/Lees is imaginary but is an amalgam of some of the spies who haunted Ireland in that period. Details such as the tattoos and the mastery of disguise are based on real characters.

The War of Independence was a traumatic time for all the citizens of Ireland, particularly the children. Yet both women and children often played a vital role in carrying messages, guns, supplies and ammunition. Their role as victims and participants is often overlooked. I hope I have remained true to the memory of their experiences.

Real historical characters

Michael Collins – Irish guerilla war leader. He effectively invented modern urban guerilla warfare. He led an elite group of assassins known as "The Squad" and the "Twelve Apostles". He was one of the main negotiators of the Anglo-Irish Treaty 1922. He was known for his pragmatism and his ruthlessness. He was ambushed and killed during the Civil War 1923.

Éamon de Valera – the Irish President during the War of Independence. He spent much of the war in the United States raising funds. Also on diplomatic missions trying to gain recognition for the fledgling Irish state. He opposed the Treaty and supported the anti-Treaty side during the Civil War. He later became head of Fianna Fáil and Taoiseach and President of the Irish Republic.

Arthur Griffith – founder of Sinn Féin (Ourselves) that emerged as the leading party for an independent Ireland after the 1916 Rising. He was a moderate who negotiated the Treaty.

Charles Dalton – an Intelligence Officer with the Squad who was only seventeen when he joined. He wrote an acclaimed memoir.

Vinnie Byrne – member of the Squad.

Dorothy Stopford – a doctor of English ancestry who gave medical aid to the Republicans during the War of Independence. She was later to become a major force in the eradication of T.B.

Alice Stopford Green – historian who supported Irish independence and made many efforts to bring about a peaceful solution. She recruited General Smuts, the former Boer leader in South Africa, to act as a peace-broker. He influenced the British government and King George V to push for peace. He also acted as a go-between with Irish nationalists in the preparations for the treaty.

Dr. Oliver St. John Gogarty – noted Dublin poet and wit, he was a founder member of Sinn Féin with Arthur Griffith. He was originally opposed to violence but became a supporter of Collins after his daughter was terrorised by the Black and Tans in Stephen's Green. He helped organise a prison breakout for several women from Mountjoy Jail who had been detained after the Truce.

Seán MacBride – son of John MacBride, executed for his part in 1916, and Maud Gonne, the Republican activist and noted beauty. He was a volunteer in the War of Independence from the age of fifteen. He was a messenger during the Treaty negotiations but supported the Republican side in the Civil War. He later became a founder of Amnesty International and won the Nobel Prize for Peace.

Dan Breen – a notorious gunman volunteer in the Irish War of Independence. In later years he was a Fianna Fáil politician.

Michael Noyk – a Jewish solicitor and Republican politican who defended many volunteers during the War of Independence.

Thomas Whelan – a young railway worker falsely executed for a murder on Bloody Sunday 1920. His case became a cause célèbre.

Acknowledgements

Many thanks to publisher Paula Campbell for her vision and all the team at Poolbeg, including David Prendergast for his diligent typesetting. I am grateful for the keen eyes of my editor Gaye Shortland, her intuitive understanding of the story and her deft editing. Her detailed knowledge of Cork (and other things) has saved me from many a blind alley.

Thanks to illustrator/designer Derry Dillon for his lively cover design.

To my first readers, Neil, Karen, Audrey, Ken, Patrick and Stephen. But especially to my nephews Daniel and William whose enthusiasm for the story and love of history is an inspiration. Thanks also to Joanne and Luke for their support. Much love to my mother Betty for her anecdotes and memories of Ringsend, Irishtown and Sandymount. I hope she forgives me for pillaging family history!

To my husband Marc and daughter Rosa for their patience with a mother living in the 1920's.

I would also like to acknowledge the memory of all those who died or lived through those turbulent times. Many of the testimonies of participants are in the Irish Bureau of Military History.

I also thank the talented historians and authors whose brilliant research provided background and context. These include:

The Republic – The Fight for Irish Independence by Charles Townsend (Penguin)

The Transformation of Ireland 1900-2000 by Diarmaid Ferriter (Profile Books)

Michael Collins – the Man Who Made Ireland by Tim Pat Coogan (Palgrave Macmillan)

The Squad and the Intelligence Operations of Michael Collins by T. Ryle Dwyer (Mercier History)

Michael Collins and the Women Who Spied for Ireland by Meda Ryan (Mercier)

Seán MacBride – A Republican Life 1904-1946 by Caoimhe Nic Dháibhéid (Liverpool University Press)

Dorothy Stopford Price – Rebel Doctor by Anne Mac Lellan (Irish Academic Press)

British Voices: From the Irish War of Independence 1918-1921 by William Sheehan (Collins Press)

The Footballer of Loos by Ed Harris (The History Press)

There were also several biographies that provided a vivid picture of life on the frontline. Some of these are classics in their genre, including:

On Another Man's Wound by Ernie O'Malley (Mercier Press)

With the Dublin Brigade by Charles Dalton (Mercier Press)

Other colourful accounts include:

Dublin Made Me by C.S. Andrews (The Lilliput Press)
My Fight for Irish Freedom by Dan Breen (Anvil Books)

I am grateful to The Society of Authors as the Literary Representative of the Estate of John Masefield for permission to quote from "Sea Fever".

Thanks also to Walton's Irish Music for permission, on behalf of the estate of Patrick Hogan, to quote the lyrics from "A Shawl of Galway Grey".

For a more detailed list of sources, teacher's notes, resources and further links, please go to my website www.patriciamurphyonline.com. Or check out Facebook page https://www.facebook.com/pages/Deadly-Shot-Dans-War-of-Independence-1920-22/852536338133795

As seen on the RTÉ *Toy Show*

Also available

The number one bestseller
30,000 copies sold

The Easter Rising 1916

Molly's Diary

Her own family is plunged into danger on both sides of the conflict. Her father, a technical officer with the Post Office dodges the crossfire as he tries to restore the telegraph lines while her wayward brother runs messages for the rebels. Molly, a trained First Aider, risks her own safety to help the wounded on both sides.

As violence and looting erupts in the streets of Dublin alongside heroism and high ideals, Molly records it all. The Proclamation at the GPO, the battle of Mount Street, the arrival of the British Troops. But will Molly's own family survive and will she be able to save her brother?
This is her diary.

ISBN 978-1-78199-9745

'Brilliantly imagined and gripping story from the heart of the 1916 Rising, based on meticulous research'
Joe Duffy, broadcaster and author of *Children of the Rising*

Patricia Murphy

Coming in 2017

The Irish Civil War 1922-23

Ava's Diary

Life sucks for twelve-year-old Irish-American Ava when she is dragged back to Dublin by her mother after her parents' messy divorce. She is bullied at her new school and her only friend is moody teenage neighbour Mal, who has secrets of his own.

But when Ava finds a sliver of an emerald and a bundle of old letters in the attic, she is plunged into a historical mystery linking the missing crown jewels of Tsarist Russia to the heart of Ireland's bloody civil war in 1922.

As a newly independent Ireland split over supporting the new Free State or fighting on for a Republic, danger lurked around every corner and friends became foes. Who was the author of the letters, young medical student Molly O'Donovan? Why did her brother Jack the Cat smuggle the jewels from the United States and end up on the run from both sides? And did her football mad cousin Dan survive running messages through the crossfire?

Through the eyes of Molly, Ava encounters the death of Michael Collins, deadly ambushes in Kerry and the tragic fate of former comrades.

As Ava learns about the bitter civil war, she is forced to confront the conflict in her own life. Can the journey into the past help her to learn the importance of reconciliation and new beginnings?

ISBN 978-1-78199-8823

Patricia Murphy